The Norfolk Theatre Murders

ALSO BY JUDI DAYKIN

DETECTIVE SARA HIRST SERIES
Book 1: Under Violent Skies
Book 2: Into Deadly Storms
Book 3: A Brutal Season
Book 4: An Artful Murder
Book 5: The Norfolk Beach Murders
Book 6: The Wild Thyme Farm Murder
Book 7: The Norfolk Theatre Murders

THE NORFOLK THEATRE MURDERS

JUDI DAYKIN

DS Sara Hirst Book 7

JOFFE BOOKS

Joffe Books, London
www.joffebooks.com

First published in Great Britain in 2025

© Judi Daykin

This book is a work of fiction. Names, characters, businesses, organisations, places and events are either the product of the author's imagination or are used fictitiously. Any resemblance to actual persons, living or dead, events or locales is entirely coincidental. The spelling used is British English except where fidelity to the author's rendering of accent or dialect supersedes this. The right of Judi Daykin to be identified as author of this work has been asserted in accordance with the Copyright, Designs and Patents Act 1988.

No part of this book may be used or reproduced in any manner for the purpose of training artificial intelligence technologies or systems. In accordance with Article 4(3) of the Digital Single Market Directive 2019/790, Joffe Books expressly reserves this work from the text and data mining exception.

Cover art by Dee Dee Book Covers

ISBN: 978-1-80573-054-5

We two alone will sing like birds i' th' cage:
When thou dost ask me blessing, I'll kneel down,
And ask of thee forgiveness: so we'll live,
And pray, and sing, and tell old tales, and laugh
At gilded butterflies . . .
(Act 5, Scene 3)

Now, gods, stand up for bastards!
(Act 1, Scene 2)

William Shakespeare, *King Lear*

This book is dedicated to my amazing husband, Rhett, who appears twice in this story. Once as he was and once as he is now.

AUTHOR'S NOTE

I have been delighted to call Norfolk my home for the last forty years. As with all regions, we have our own way of doing and saying things here. The accent is lyrical and open, just like the countryside and skies. If you would like to pronounce some of the real place names in this book like a local, the following may help:

Happisburgh = Haze-bruh
Wymondham = Wind-am
Norwich hides its 'w'.

PROLOGUE

It always feels strange to be the last one in the building, turning off the lights and checking the doors are locked. Theatres are meant to be alive, full of people and atmosphere, laughter and gasps, songs and projected voices. Although Carole often agrees to lock up when she's rehearsing, for some reason, tonight she feels uncomfortable. There seems to be a chill on the back of her neck, the sensation that someone is watching her.

They — whoever 'they' are — claim that the theatre is haunted by the ghost of a monk, the hood of his dark robe pulled up to hide his cadaverous face as he wanders the backstage and performance areas. A monk who takes exception to religious artefacts of any kind on stage, which vanish without a trace from the props table or set. Sometimes, in the middle of a show. Just a practical joker perpetuating a myth, she's always presumed. Carole is a pragmatist. There are no such things as ghosts. Except for the one she spotted hiding in a dark corner of the front courtyard half an hour ago. She knows about him.

There's a set circuit to follow to ensure that the place is locked down tightly. First, the bar, with its outdoor yard. Gates to the yard locked? Check. Rear double doors to the bar locked? Check. She walks around the corner of the bar, rattling the roller shutters to ensure they were locked down after everyone was served their rehearsal coffees. Done. Along the corridor to the rehearsal room. Fire doors firmly shut? Check. She flicks off the humming strip lights, and they plink into silence. Gents' toilet lights are off. Ladies' toilet lights are off. She's already checked backstage, and it's dark and empty.

As she passes the auditorium door, there's an unexpected faint line of light. Then, a sudden heavy crash inside, which makes her jitter with shock. Some fool has left something on stage and it's fallen over, she reasons to herself. With an exaggerated sigh, she opens the door with a swish. Does she have to deal with it now, or could it be left for the morning staff?

The auditorium should be dark and empty. Even the working lights are turned off. But it isn't. A dozen or more stubby candles stand along the front edge of the stage, their lighted wicks flickering, creating a shadowy, pulsating glow. Who's using real candles, for God's sake? They're never used in theatres these days, when battery-powered ones are realistic enough.

The stage is raised above the seats on the auditorium floor, and her eyes narrow as she looks more closely beyond the candles. Is that a figure? Her imagination, surely? Or is it moving?

'Who's there?' Her voice loud from decades of acting and authoritative from her years in charge at work. 'I shall call the police if you don't identify yourself.'

Her hand reaches for the wall switch to turn on the working lights. It fails to find it. Her fingers urgently search along the plastered wall as her eyes adjust to the gloom. She's not alone. Her brain screams, *Run! Get away!*

Standing behind the candles on the shadowy stage is a monk. She can tell by the old-fashioned habit he's wearing. The hood is pulled over his head to hide his face. His arms are bent at the elbow and folded over his stomach as if in prayer. It must be a costume. Someone is playing a horrid practical joke on her. The fabric is black, and the figure is difficult to make out. Her gaze flickers over the stage in panic. It looks as if the wooden lid of the grave trap has been left folded back against the stage floor, and she knows there's a dangerously deep hole underneath. It's almost always closed; few shows use it.

The figure takes a step forward. Carole realises she must be outlined by the light from the corridor behind her. Her fingers flicker more anxiously, rubbing up and down the wall randomly. Breath rasping, heart pounding, she understands real fear for the first time in her life.

The monk raises his head. The face is still in shadow, apart from a tiny glimpse of white where a neck might be.

'I'm throwing you out.' She tries bravado but her voice croaks with fear. 'You shouldn't be here.'

In response, the figure races three paces across the stage and jumps into the aisle. She turns to run, but he's too fast for her. All-too-real hands grab her upper arms and pull her back into the auditorium. The door slams, cancelling the corridor light. Her feet stutter as the floor's rake drags her downwards. Her heels catch in the carpet, and she falls, her head striking the floor with a crunch that makes her senses spin. Now, the man is on top of her, pinning her arms to the floor with his knees.

I'm too old to be raped, she thinks as the man slowly draws back his hood and brings his skeletal face close to hers. Carole opens her mouth to scream.

'Surprised to see me?' he asks in a whisper.

CHAPTER 1

Detective Sergeant Sara Hirst hung her coat on one of the pegs behind the Serious Crimes Unit office door. Her journey into work at Norfolk Constabulary's Police HQ in Wymondham had been a pleasure. It was one of those autumn days when the sun shone through the leaves with almost as much strength as it had six weeks ago. Leaves that were turning all shades of brown, gold and yellow. She noticed them most when she drove around the Norwich Southern Bypass, where forward-thinking planners had planted trees along the banks years before. Mature now, sometimes it was so spectacular that she wondered why anyone would bother to go all the way to Canada or America to see 'the fall'.

'Not sure I'm going to need my coat,' she said to the administrator, Aggie Bowen, née Hewett. Sara filled a mug with coffee from the pot that Aggie kept refreshed all day. One of the tallest on the team, Sara towered over the homely woman, who sat sedately typing at the keyboard, checking emails.

'I love these autumn days, don't you?' replied Aggie with a smile at her husband, DC Mike Bowen. He grunted in reply, keeping his focus on the computer screen in front of him.

'How's the course going?' Sara asked, pointing to the heavy art book on Caravaggio which sat underneath a promising cake tin. As anyone who became a police officer knew, appearances were deceptive. With her motherly clothing and home-baking addiction, it would be hard to guess that Aggie had embarked on an art history degree with the Open University.

'Great, thanks.' Aggie pointed to the picture on the cover. 'He's quite the character. Hard drinker, mad gambler and murderer. And some fabulous paintings thrown in for good measure.'

'Sounds like we should be arresting him,' muttered Bowen. Aggie smiled indulgently at him. Their workplace romance firmly put Sara's rubbish love life in its place. The only cuddles she got these days were from her cat, Tilly, the opinionated Siamese.

'Where's the rest of the team?' she asked, settling at her desk.

'Ian's at a meeting with the Drugs Team.' Aggie knew everything about them all, work or home. 'He thought you might prefer it if he went.'

Sara nodded gratefully. Since her relationship with DC Dante Adebayo had broken down, he had made life at work as difficult for Sara as possible. He glared at her in meetings, blanked her in the corridor if they happened to pass and even made rude comments about their team, the Serious Crimes Unit, loudly in the canteen for all to hear. It had been nearly three months, but he still didn't seem to have forgiven her.

'He'll get over it,' said Aggie in a low voice.

'Or get told to be more professional at work,' added Bowen sagely. He slurped his coffee noisily.

'Hudson's in a meeting with the higher-ups,' Aggie continued. Their DCI seemed to be bogged down in ever more administration these days. 'The boss is getting a search warrant signed off in Norwich.'

They all still called DI Will Edwards 'the boss' from the days when he had led the team without the aid of a DCI.

'For the new scammers' case?' Sara asked. Aggie nodded. 'I'd better get on with the paperwork for the court appearances on our summer one.'

Sara checked her emails before pulling out her notepad with her list of jobs on it. You never knew what a jury would think of the evidence. Settling in for a morning of dullness, she was glad of the distraction when her phone rang.

'Morning, DS Hirst,' said the cheerful voice of Trevor Jones, the desk sergeant. 'Not sure if this is one for your department, just thought I'd ask your opinion.'

'Anything that you think should come our way almost certainly will,' she replied.

'I've just had a call from Bethel Street.' This was the city centre police station. 'There was an oddball burglary last night at one of those city centre townhouses. Belongs to an elderly couple, and the wife seems to be missing.'

'Missing?'

'All night, possibly.' Jones sounded worried. 'Social care worker called the police. Two officers went down to scope it out and rang in, requesting detective assistance. Something very odd about it, they said. I can give you a direct line.'

Sara scribbled down the number with a promise to call immediately. The officer's name was Fraser Shepherd. The line must have been on divert, as he answered on his mobile.

After explaining who she was, Sara asked, 'You think there's something odd about this?'

'Definitely. The house belongs to an older couple,' said Fraser. Sara could hear him going down a set of stairs. 'I'm just going out into the courtyard; I don't want to cause any more upset.'

'Upset?'

'The couple are Carole and James Morgan,' Fraser said quietly. 'She's in her late sixties; he's eighty-two. He has dementia, and she needs help to look after him. A care worker comes in first thing to help get James up, then again at teatime to settle him for the evening. When she arrived, the door was open, and no one was in the house.'

'The door was unlocked or open?'

'Wide open,' confirmed Fraser. 'When she went inside, the house had been turned upside down, and there was no sign of either resident. Meryl, the care worker, was so worried she rang us.'

'Have you found either of the missing couple?'

'Meryl guessed that James might have wandered down towards the Rosegarden Theatre. Apparently, the couple have been involved there for years. I went down there with her, and we found James huddled in the back door of the old church at St John Pottergate.'

'I know it,' said Sara. When she'd first moved to Norwich, she lived on a nearby street. She'd visited the theatre when her first boyfriend in Norwich, Chris Webster, had been in a production there. You reached it by going under an archway belonging to the church and along a narrow alley. The back door of the church and its steps were also in frequent use by local drug dealers, close to the main shopping area but well out of sight.

'Meryl managed to persuade James to come home.'

Sara took the address on Pottergate from Shepherd. She knew the location well. A medieval cobbled street lined with Georgian terraced houses split into flats or townhouses, alongside the occasional newly developed buildings in the gaps caused by air raids during the Second World War.

'He got very agitated when we brought him home. Meryl says he keeps calling his wife's name when he gets anxious. He's distressed and having memory difficulties.'

'Poor thing.' Sara thought how confused and frightened the elderly gent must have been to wander off.

'He's also got a nasty bump on his head. Meryl says he sometimes has falls, so it could be as straightforward as that. It's not helping his recall. I've sent for a paramedic.'

'Did you find out how long his wife had been missing?'

'That's when it got really weird,' said Fraser. 'Meryl thinks she should have been at home last night. Instead, James claims that he was visited by a monk, who told him that she had been called to heaven.'

'A monk!'

'Yes, a monk. Complete with black habit and a skull for a face.'

'I'm on my way,' said Sara.

CHAPTER 2

Pottergate was one of those ancient streets that had once led to St Benedicts Gate in the medieval city walls. It ran parallel to St Benedicts Street, up the slight hill that rose around the marketplace and castle. It was narrow and tortuous to drive along in the modern era. Fortunately, Sara knew the twisting one-way system well. She dumped her car in a private space at the back of Chris Webster's independent coffee shop, hoping he wouldn't recognise it. No doubt there would be a snotty note from him stuck on her windscreen when she returned, but she knew Chris didn't own a car, and the space was for privileged customers.

The Morgans' townhouse stood on one side of a small courtyard, which Sara reached through a brick arch. It looked Georgian in style, like many of the ones which fronted Pottergate. Five houses were spaced regularly around the courtyard, each with a parking spot. The residents' cars were currently boxed in by two police cars and an ambulance. A paramedic's mountain bike was propped against the house wall, its panniers left open to display a variety of emergency equipment.

She assumed Shepherd must have been watching for her as the officer clattered down the stairs to meet her at the front door.

'I'm pleased to see you,' he said. 'We could do with a woman's touch.'

Sara bit back the obvious answer that she was a police officer and her gender was irrelevant. 'Why?'

'This way,' urged Shepherd. The front door led to a tiny hallway. Sara could see into a large room to her right, which appeared to be an office. It looked distinctly untidy. Another door stood ajar to reveal a downstairs toilet. Apart from a long rack of coats by the door, there was little else but a wooden staircase rising in front of them. 'Too many men. Mr Morgan seems frightened of us.'

'What happened to Meryl, the care worker?' Sara asked. She climbed briskly after Shepherd.

'Had to go off to her next appointment,' he replied. 'Promised to return about eleven, when she's finished her morning calls. If we haven't found Mrs Morgan by then.'

The stairs emerged into an open-plan room which occupied the whole width and depth of the building. Sara's first thought was that it would otherwise have been enchanting. The walls had been pulled back to the original brick, giving the place the feel of a fashionable loft in a factory conversion. Bookcases lined the walls and stood between the tall sash windows, jammed with books, files and ornaments. At least some of them were. The floor was covered in scattered papers and broken ceramics.

From one corner of the room, a large antique desk dominated darkly, papers and books piled on and around it. Some seemed to have been ripped up and thrown into the air to fall in confusion. Another set of stairs behind the desk headed elegantly up to the next floor. The central space had been divided up by furniture into a dining area with a table and chairs and a lounge area with large, pale-coloured sofas facing a coffee table and television. Dining chairs lay on their backs, and some of the sofa cushions were covered in what might have been balsamic vinegar, if the smell was anything to go by. It would be hell to get out of the fabric.

A kitchen occupied the far wall, protected by a modern breakfast bar. It seemed to have been the focus of the attack. Cupboard doors stood open, overlooking the gooey, smelly mess below. Tins and cartons had been opened, their contents spread randomly. Bottles or jars had been thrown against the walls, leaving dirty splatters of sauces or oils and a blanket of broken glass on the floor.

Another male police officer stood near the kettle, watching the proceedings on the nearest sofa.

An older man with greying hair and a worried face sat reluctantly gazing at a paramedic who knelt in front of him. Sara assumed this to be Mr Morgan. A second paramedic was attempting to take the man's blood pressure, but Mr Morgan kept loosening the black cuff before it could be pumped up. A third paramedic was leaning over the back of the sofa, gently but firmly holding Mr Morgan's shoulders. Everyone in the room was male. They were all talking at once, trying to get the confused man to cooperate.

'I'm not surprised he's wary of you all,' said Sara as she took in the scene.

'Where's Carole?' asked Mr Morgan. His voice was weak and tremulous. He looked in confusion at the medical men surrounding him. 'I want my wife.'

'All right, you lot,' said Sara, trying to keep her voice calm and authoritative. 'Let's give Mr Morgan a bit of space.'

'He's banged his head,' objected one of the paramedics. He pointed to Mr Morgan's hands, which were scuffed and bloody. 'Looks like he had a fall and grazed himself trying to stop it.'

Sara sat next to the distressed man. 'He still needs to breathe. Tell you what, Mr Morgan. How about if I stay with you and just one of these gentlemen?' She indicated to the paramedics.

Morgan turned his confused face to her. 'Who?'

Sara patted his arm and pointed to the blood pressure cuff. 'Let's get rid of that. A couple of you pop downstairs for a few minutes, eh? And Shepherd?'

'Yes, ma'am?'

'You stay. Sit over there, perhaps? Your colleague can also wait downstairs.'

It took a moment or two for the various men to gather their kit and clatter down the wooden stairs. Shepherd retreated to perch on the top step of the stairs. The remaining paramedic hovered on the edge of the adjoining sofa. The room became more peaceful, and the tension in Mr Morgan's shoulders relaxed. Sara produced her warrant card.

'I'm here to help find Carole,' she said. Mr Morgan took her card in trembly fingers. He squinted at the photo, then looked at Sara.

'Oh, you're one of those,' he said. 'I had one of you in my class a few years before I retired. Did ever so well. Got into Cambridge, actually. Hard worker. Proud of him.'

Sara glanced at Shepherd, who shrugged his shoulders. 'One of what?'

'Jamaicans,' said Morgan. He held out the card for her to take. There was no malice in his tone. 'British now, of course. Windrush was it?'

'My grandparents were of that generation,' she said slowly, touching her braided hair a little self-consciously. People living with dementia weren't always in control of how they said things. 'I'm half Jamaican. My dad was an East Ender.'

'Hard workers, all of you.' He nodded in approval.

'What did you do before you retired, Mr Morgan?'

'I was a teacher,' he said proudly. 'Science and maths. At the Cathedral School.'

'And your wife?'

'She was head of children's social services for years. Tough job.'

'Why?'

'They wore her out in the end.' Morgan gazed dreamily at the stairs. 'Where is she? When is she coming home?'

'That's what I'm here to find out,' said Sara. She patted his arm, resting her hand there, hoping it would be a comfort. 'Do you know where she was last night?'

12

'Thingy,' said Morgan. He frowned in concentration as he tried to find the right words. His face was turning pale with the effort. 'Reading thing. Acting practice. Damn it, I can't . . .'

'That's okay, Mr Morgan.' Sara thought for a moment. 'Do you mean a rehearsal?'

The lined face suddenly relaxed into a smile. 'Yes. A rehearsal.'

'At the Rosegarden Theatre?'

Morgan nodded sadly. 'Still able to do it. I can't.'

He reminded Sara of a toddler; his emotions were like sunshine and showers. They flitted across his face unfiltered.

'So, Carole went to the theatre for a rehearsal?' The place was only a few minutes' walk away. 'Can you remember what time?'

It was a question too far. Mr Morgan shuddered, his face twisting between anger and tears. He looked at Sara, then hurriedly around the room. With a grunt, he began to shuffle forward on the sofa. 'I don't know. I can't remember. Everyone knows I can't remember anymore. Why is everybody going on at me? Leave me alone.'

He pushed Sara's hand away and tried to stand. For a moment, he wobbled, trying to regain his balance. The coffee table impeded his legs as he tried to step forward. Frightened he was going to fall, Sara shot up to hold him as the paramedic moved swiftly to his other side. With a muffled cry, the older man shook off their helping hands and slumped back onto the sofa. He put his trembling hands in front of his face and cried loudly.

'Ask the monk. He frightened me. He threatened me. Ruined everything.'

CHAPTER 3

Nafisa Ahmed tugged at her hijab to prevent it from slipping backwards from her forehead. It was annoying her this morning, which wasn't usually the case. With her free hand, she searched in her desk drawer for an extra hair grip to secure it. It was her favourite scarf in a bright peacock blue and was the only flash of colour in her outfit, the rest being black trousers and a long-sleeved shirt. Contrary to popular belief, she chose to wear a scarf for herself and not because she was required to do so. It helped keep her mind on the teachings that had brought her into social work in the first place.

Her caseload was so large she could almost see it as a mountain of paperwork, threatening to topple off her desk. Some days, it felt taller than her slight, 5' 3" figure. Part of the social services team for five years, Nafisa had life experience way beyond her age of thirty-two.

This morning, she had a team meeting, followed by a stint at the needle exchange in the help hub near the railway station and a dozen or more home visits to arrange. She was also due to check up on the temporary tent city that was growing in the graveyard of St John Pottergate church in the city centre.

Of all the jobs, this one presented the biggest and most urgent problem. Full of long-term homeless people, the encampment was already causing issues. It wasn't the first time this had happened. The land was private, and the churchwardens had wasted no time approaching the local authority to get the campers evicted. Part of the medieval city, the graveyard stood behind the church between the small street of Lower St Johns and the narrow Church Alley, which ran under the church via an archway and past the entrances for the Rosegarden Theatre. For ancient reasons, the graveyard was taller than either of these thoroughfares, enabling the tent's occupants to look down on anyone walking there or across into an office building's windows. It wasn't a comfortable situation, and if Nafisa couldn't persuade any of the campers to seek help through them or one of the city charities, it was only a matter of days before the police would move them on.

Gathering her laptop and notebook, Nafisa stopped to grab a coffee from the staff kitchen as she headed for the meeting room. She had five colleagues in the outreach team. They were one of three drug- and alcohol-related teams, which, in theory, meant eighteen workers to cover the entire city. If only all the vacancies were ever filled.

Their boss, Samantha, sat at one end of the table, tapping at her mobile. Nafisa was pleased to see she wasn't the last to arrive. That honour went to Russell Goddard. The tall and untidy thirty-something man staggered into the room, unsuccessfully juggling the same set of items Nafisa had capably organised in front of her. He looked even more harassed than usual, and she felt a pang of sympathy. Russell's heart was in the right place. He was just incapable of coping with the workload. They all knew this, especially poor Russell, who was in fear of being sacked every day. His desire to help people remained undiminished.

Nafisa went to rescue him, taking the coffee mug before the contents shot all over the place and guiding him to the seat next to her.

'Thanks,' he murmured. 'Again.'

She nodded slightly in acknowledgement. Although he managed less than half the cases that the rest of the team coped with, they all took turns to ensure Russell kept going because, if they didn't, they knew he would never be replaced once he left. Better half a colleague than none at all.

Samantha glanced up at the team before laying her mobile face down on the table. With a sigh, she clicked on her laptop. 'Okay. Everyone got a copy of the agenda?'

They agreed they had. The meeting began with case reviews. Always time-consuming, it did at least ensure that each team member got suggestions for actions where needed. In theory, it also meant that Samantha knew about all their cases, although Nafisa had never understood how she was expected to remember the details of so many people in need. After an hour, they reached the tent city.

'You picked this up, Nafisa?' asked Samantha.

'I have.' Nafisa clicked on the file on her screen.

'How many now?'

'Seven tents, some with more than one occupant.' Nafisa checked an email from a police officer at Bethel Street. 'Of course, it's possible that it will get resolved without our intervention. I suspect the police will move them on soon enough. However, I think one of my former clients may have pitched up there.'

'Which one?'

'Zach Wilson.'

'Ah, our veteran friend.' Nafisa was impressed. Zach hadn't been around for three months, so hadn't been mentioned in their weekly catch-ups. 'What makes you think that?'

'I walked past last night,' said Nafisa carefully. 'I'd been out for dinner with a friend. It was dark, so not so easy to see, but I think I recognised his tent.'

'You nearly got him into the Luke Project last time, didn't you?'

'Had a place booked,' replied Nafisa. 'Then he just vanished. Walked off into the night back in July.'

'Some people like to be in the countryside during the summer,' suggested Russell.

Nafisa glanced at him. 'Very true.'

'You want to see if you can reconnect with him.' Samantha nodded.

'If I can. I was so close to getting him off the streets last time.'

There wasn't a person on the team who didn't understand her frustration. All of them knew that addiction wasn't like that. Not everyone wanted their help. Not everyone wanted to be 'cured'.

Zach might be different, Nafisa hoped. He deserved to be. His army service record was extensive and admirable. The man was lucid and intelligent, when he wasn't drinking. Unfortunately, his PTSD made him unpredictable. Nafisa thought Zach could return to the everyday world with the right support. Or at least a life where every day wasn't full of so many difficulties. If he wanted to.

'You can't go in there alone,' said Samantha firmly.

'I'll go with you,' said Russell hurriedly before anyone else could offer. 'Least I can do.'

With a sinking feeling in her stomach, Nafisa accepted.

CHAPTER 4

It took Sara some time to calm Mr Morgan down. Shepherd tiptoed across the debris to make a cup of tea for him, which Mr Morgan grabbed and sipped. In between sips, Sara found a chance to encourage details from him about the previous evening. At some point after Carole Morgan had gone along Pottergate to the theatre, someone dressed as a monk and with a skeleton's skull where his face should be had let themselves into the Morgans' townhouse, physically threatened the bewildered older man and then trashed the place.

'Kept yelling, "You deserve this!"' Mr Morgan said. He looked round him in confusion.

'Mr Morgan, was the front door locked?'

He considered this, then shrugged. 'Our daughter was here for a while.'

'Can you remember when your daughter left?' This was the first mention of a relative. Sara could only assume she was an adult. 'What's her name?'

'Helen.' Mr Morgan seemed pleased to have remembered something easily.

'Helen came to spend the evening with you, and your wife went to the theatre to rehearse?'

'If you say so.'

Sara sighed quietly, wondering what it must be like to be caught in this twilight world in your mind. 'Helen left you before Carole came back?'

Mr Morgan nodded, although Sara wasn't sure he understood what he was agreeing to. 'Can you remember what time that was?'

'It was dark.' He shrugged and looked at her anxiously. 'Carole doesn't like me being locked in, you know.'

The fact that it was dark meant little. It was 29 October already, and the clocks had gone back last weekend. It was dark from teatime onwards, leaving a long window of darkness for someone to get in. Sara needed to get in touch with their daughter, Helen. She went out into the courtyard and rang the office.

'I need a search for Mr Morgan's next of kin,' she told Aggie, giving her the address. 'They have a carer coming in to help, so the local council should be able to give you the daughter's details.'

'Shall I call her and ask her to come over?'

'Yes, please. ASAP. Mr Morgan needs a familiar face, and I need to clear the scene.'

'How is the poor chap?'

'Very confused. Whoever came in here made a real mess of the place. Is Mike still in the office?' Aggie said he was. 'Ask him to organise a visit from Forensics. Then get him to meet me at the Rosegarden Theatre. Tell the DCI, will you?'

'Of course.'

When she got back upstairs, Mr Morgan had slipped into a doze on the sofa. Sara spoke quietly to the paramedic and encouraged him to leave. 'I don't think you can do much for him until we track down the daughter.'

'Do you need to go somewhere?' asked Officer Shepherd. 'I'm due off shift, but I can stay for a while.'

'If you don't mind,' agreed Sara. She checked the time. It was after half past ten. 'Let him rest. Wait until either we get hold of the daughter or Meryl gets back. Don't let them tidy anything up. I want Forensics to go over this first. I'd like to see if anyone is at the theatre this morning.'

'I'll update you as soon as I have news,' said Shepherd. He double-checked Sara's mobile number, then settled back on the step at the top of the stairs and opened a game on his mobile to pass the time. Mr Morgan slept on.

It was only a few minutes' walk along the cobbles of Pottergate to reach the theatre, past some of the independent shops in the Lanes area of the city centre. Halloween decorations and fake cobwebs festooned the shop windows. There was no shortage of skeletons here. Turning down the alley next to the Belgian Brewhouse restaurant, Sara walked under the arch of the church. The back gate entrance to the theatre stood open. As she approached, the double doors into the bar swished apart, and she wove around the tables and chairs to reach the box office window.

'Good morning!' A middle-aged woman smiled encouragingly at her through the open portal. 'How can I help you?'

The woman's smile fell when Sara produced her warrant card. 'Can I speak to someone about the rehearsal last night?'

'Lindie,' she called over a screen behind her, 'this one's for you.'

A chair creaked, footsteps crossed the office and a thirty-something woman opened the office door.

'Lindie Howes,' the woman introduced herself after inspecting Sara's card. 'What can I do for you?'

Lindie was tall and slim. She was dressed in what Sara thought of as goth style. Her skirt was a black handkerchief affair trimmed in black lace. Her blouse was a floaty purple fabric covered with a tight dark grey waistcoat. Black Doc Marten boots were laced to halfway up her calves. She had several piercings in her ears or about her face. Black kohl lined her eyes. She had a silver ring on every finger and thumb.

'We've received reports that Carole Morgan may have gone missing,' said Sara.

Lindie's eyes widened, and she turned white under her already pale make-up. 'Our Carole?'

'Lives on Pottergate. Should have been here last night for a rehearsal?'

'Oh my God! We'd better go and sit down.' Lindie led Sara to the bar, sitting heavily at a table. Sara sat opposite. 'How long has she been missing?'

'We're not sure.'

'Poor James,' breathed Lindie. 'How is he coping? He has dementia, you know.'

'So I understand,' said Sara. 'We're trying to contact their daughter.'

'Helen?'

'Yes. Do you know her?'

'Oh yes, she used to act here regularly before she had her family. Too busy now, as you'd expect with toddlers in the house.'

'Would you have her contact details?'

'I think so. Hang on a minute.'

Lindie left Sara at the table and darted back into the office. A minute later, she reappeared with a large grey file. Sara was surprised to see it said 'Members' on the outside. Surely information like that would be computerised these days. After flicking through a selection of forms, Lindie found the one she was looking for and pulled it out.

'These are the current details I have.' She pushed the paper towards Sara. 'I think she still lives here. That's her mobile.'

Sara punched the number into her phone. 'Can I have a copy of this?'

'Don't see why not.' Lindie nodded anxiously. 'This is an emergency, after all.'

She headed back to the office with the form. Sara rang the number.

'Yes? Who is it?' The woman who answered sounded harassed. Sara could hear a child having a screaming tantrum in the background.

'I'm DS Sara Hirst,' she began.

'Is this about Mum?' asked the woman. 'Be quiet, Tarquin.'

'Yes. Have you heard from our office?'

'Some woman called me a few minutes ago. I'm Helen Morgan-Harris, and I'm on my way if I can get these two into the car. I'll be fifteen minutes. Where are you?'

'At the theatre.'

'Why?' snapped Helen. 'How dare you leave Dad on his own!'

Before Sara could explain, Helen ended the call.

CHAPTER 5

Lindie Howes had thrown up one of the roller shutters into the theatre bar and put on a pot of coffee. As if lured by the aroma, DC Mike Bowen joined them, climbing the stairs at the front of the building.

'Aggie managed to get hold of the daughter,' he told Sara as he accepted a drink and handful of biscuits from Lindie. 'Lovely stuff, thank you.'

'I gathered that,' said Sara. 'So did I. Sounded a bit harassed, but she's on her way.' Despite his daughter's accusation, Sara knew James Morgan was in good hands with Officer Shepherd, and if Meryl, the carer, had returned as promised, she would be at the townhouse by now.

Although she remembered some details of her former boyfriend's involvement at the Rosegarden, Sara wanted a fresh perspective. It had been a bone of contention between them when they had been going out. Being involved here took up a lot of their volunteers' time. 'Tell me about how your rehearsals work.'

Lindie drew a deep breath. 'What do you know about us?'

'You put on plays,' said Bowen with a grin.

'Indeed, we do.' Lindie smiled at him. 'Twelve a year. One a month, every month. They run for ten nights, apart from Christmas, which is longer.'

'That seems a lot for an amateur company,' Bowen sounded suitably impressed.

'It is,' agreed Lindie. 'We usually have two shows in rehearsal at any time, one getting ready to perform and the other just starting out. It's a big commitment, as they have to be consistently available in the evenings.' She produced a thick A5 brochure and put it on the bar for them to look at. 'Then we have other stuff in between. Bands, visiting musical theatre companies, guest lecturers. We're very busy.'

'How on earth do you manage?' Sara had not really grasped how big an operation the place was. She flicked through the colourful pages with interest until she reached the entries for the current week.

'The company is amateur,' explained Lindie. 'The staff are full- or part-time paid professionals. There are seven of us.'

'Nothing on this week?'

'Our next show opens in a week. That part of the company has moved their rehearsals onto the stage. They were the only ones here last night. The Christmas show was rehearsing off-site.'

Sara looked in surprise at the full-page entry for the first show in November. It was Shakespeare's *King Lear*, an ambitious choice by anyone's standards. 'You do a lot of Shakespeare?'

'One a year. Or an equivalent. Like a Christopher Marlow or a Thomas Kyd. We're proud of our heritage in that regard.'

This was unfamiliar territory for Sara, and she hurried on. 'Carole Morgan is in this production?'

'She is,' nodded Lindie. 'We do gender-blind casting for Shakespeare these days. There are never enough men to go around. Besides, we have plenty of talented women who are capable of doing these big roles. Our Lear is a woman. Carole is playing Goneril, even though she is technically a little old for it.'

'She would have been here last night, then?' asked Sara. 'Would the whole cast have been in the building?'

'You'd have to ask the director. They decide on the rehearsal schedule. I'll get his details.'

'And a copy of the cast list with their contacts as well,' suggested Bowen. Lindie nodded. 'Who locks up the building afterwards? Do you?'

'Not if I've been in all day,' said Lindie. She sounded weary at the thought. 'Ben Marsden, our full-time stage manager, would have been here. He should have locked up.'

'Is he here?' asked Sara.

'Not yet. He's due in at two because he has to work until the rehearsal is finished. Lear is a long one. They were probably done about half past ten.'

They were interrupted by the sound of hammering. Sara looked round in surprise. 'You have builders in?'

'No, that will be the carpenter. He's building the set in the auditorium. If you like, I'll show you both round in a minute.'

'That would be helpful.'

'I'll get you Ben's details and that cast list.'

Sara waited until Lindie went back into the office. 'I had no idea it was such a big enterprise.'

'Aggie and I come here sometimes,' said Bowen. Sara knew that Aggie had been expanding her husband's cultural horizons. He blushed slightly. 'To be honest, I can't tell the difference between the shows here and the ones at the bigger places. Except the big ones clearly have more money for costumes and stuff.'

'Do you enjoy them?' Sara had once sat through a performance of *Romeo and Juliet* here to support Chris and found it incomprehensible. She didn't have a natural ear for Shakespeare.

'Not sure about the highbrow jobs.' He pointed to the advert for *King Lear*. 'This would give me a numb bum. I like the comedies best.'

In a large poster holder next to the bar, someone had pinned up a selection of photos. Sara turned to inspect it. Some were black-and-white headshots with the actors' names and parts in the play written underneath. Others were colour photos of what Sara assumed to be rehearsals. Carole Morgan looked boldly out from her picture. It was the first time Sara had seen what the missing woman looked like.

Her eyes travelled along the ranks of leading actors until she came to a face she recognised all too well. Her former boyfriend, Chris, smiled down at her, and the note underneath told her he was playing Edmund. Sara groaned.

CHAPTER 6

Ben Marsden was finishing his second cup of tea as he packed up his food for the day. He needed to leave for work shortly, as it was already lunchtime, and he was due in at two. When his toast popped out of the machine, he spread a thick layer of cheap pâté on it to wolf down as he selected a ready meal from the freezer. The constant diet of ready meals, snacks and snatched sandwiches was beginning to play havoc with his middle-aged figure. Go into showbusiness, everyone said. It's such a glamorous life. Ha!

Crunching on the last mouthful, he gazed out of the window of the half-glazed backdoor at the rear of his house. The garden was long and wider than the house, much to the envy of his neighbours. Unfortunately, he never had time to look after it, so it was also overgrown and full of brambles, which the neighbours didn't like so much. When you worked the weird hours he did, there was little time for things like mowing the lawn. A machete would be more appropriate after the long summer. Somewhere down there were two large, rickety sheds full of stage props and old furniture. His own personal world from which he often selected items for the shows at the Rosegarden Theatre, where he was the full-time stage manager.

Ben hadn't always worked in theatre. Years ago, it had been only a hobby, until he'd been made redundant from the print works and used the money to set himself up making sets and props for small theatre companies. After a couple of nail-biting years living on a subsistence economy, this job had come up at the Rosegarden. The day they rang him to say he'd got it was one of the happiest in his life. He'd been there for over ten years now, expanding his knowledge of sound and lights until he looked after all the technical aspects of the venue for both in-house and visiting shows. He had the help of a wonderful team of volunteers, of course. But it took its toll. He rarely used his holiday allowance in any given year. He had long since given up the idea of having a girlfriend and was now a confirmed bachelor. His skin was pasty white from spending most of his time in darkened spaces. Sometimes, his heart beat painfully hard when he got out of breath lifting or carrying. Almost his entire wardrobe of clothes was black for work. He smiled fondly. Ben loved his job despite everything.

'Oh, now what?' he mumbled when his mobile rang. He could see that it was the theatre office. 'Hello, Lindie. What's up?'

'Hi, Ben. I know you're not due in for a while, but I thought you ought to know. We had a visit from the police this morning.'

'Really? Why?'

'It's Carole. She's gone missing.'

For a moment, Ben looked blankly at his chaotic garden. 'Carole Morgan? Missing?'

'I think it might be serious,' said Lindie. She sounded upset. 'They wouldn't tell me exactly. It would seem she hasn't been home since rehearsal last night. They want to talk to you.'

'She was at rehearsal, all right,' said Ben.

'Did she leave before you?'

'No, she said she'd lock up for me. You know she has a set of keys. I left her to it.'

'That's what the police are asking about.'

'Should I come in early, then?'

'It might be best. Oh, and by the way, I bunged the candles in the wheelie bin.'

'What candles?' asked Ben in confusion.

'The ones around the front of the stage,' said Lindie. 'I know it looks more authentic, but you should know better than to allow Glyn to persuade you to have naked flames near the costumes.'

'What are you going on about? We haven't got any candles on the stage. I'd put the flickering battery-powered ones out if he wanted them.'

'That's weird, then. There were thirteen of them. The wax had melted too, so they must have been lit at some point.'

'Nothing to do with me,' said Ben firmly. 'Maybe it's the ghost.'

'Ha-ha,' said Lindie sarcastically. 'Obviously, I'll have to read the riot act to the cast at some point. See you soon.'

Ben's van was parked on the small gravel drive at the front of the house. He hurriedly threw his food carrier onto the passenger seat and climbed in. He lived on one side of Wroxham Road in Sprowston. Although, in theory, he could get buses into work, there were few left running by the time he finished in the evening, so he commuted the four miles each day there and back, leaving his van in the multi-storey car park across the road from the theatre.

Weaving impatiently across the city streets and complex one-way system, he reached the rooftop level of the car park before he found a space. Lindie was watching for him from the office window when he got to the theatre, and she hurried out to greet him.

'They've gone back to the Morgans' house,' she said, sounding out of breath. 'Helen is coming over to look after James. They said they'd be back later to talk to you.'

Ben felt put out. He could have stayed home long enough to clear up after himself in the kitchen. Not that he was a tidy person. In fact, he was notoriously untidy.

He gripped his food carrier. 'Okay. I'll put this in the green room, and you can tell me what's been going on.'

Lindie had a cup of tea waiting for him when he returned to the office. 'It's pretty shocking. Sounds like you may have been the last person to see her at the end of rehearsals.'

'Great!' Ben groaned.

'I showed them round and explained how we did things. Who was in rehearsal last night?'

'Principals. We were working on a selection of big scenes for Simone, not doing a full run-through.' Simone was playing King Lear.

Lindie pushed a copy of the cast list across the desk to him. 'They have a copy of this. Can you mark who was here?'

'Sure.' He began to put a tick against a selection of names. 'Most of them went straight home. It's a bit early in the week to go to the pub afterwards.'

'You and Carole were the last here?'

'Yep. Apart from the monk, of course. He was in the courtyard as I left.'

CHAPTER 7

Helen Morgan-Harris was struggling to take two toddlers out of the back of her car when Sara and DC Bowen arrived back at the townhouse. Tall, slender and blonde, she looked flushed and angry as she glanced at their warrant cards.

'I'll let you off the hook this time,' she snapped, unbuckling the car seat of a wriggling, screaming, red-faced boy of about two. A girl of four was watching the performance with a world-weary boredom that was entirely adult. 'I've been upstairs, and Meryl is there. You shouldn't have left Father alone. Tarquin, please wait for Mummy.'

'We didn't,' said Sara as calmly as she could, almost being drowned out by the screaming toddler. 'He was asleep on the sofa. Officer Shepherd volunteered to stay with him until you or the carer arrived.'

'Volunteered?'

'Yes. He should have finished work some time ago, but as he was the first to respond to the call, he wanted to ensure that your father was safe.'

This should have made the woman pause, except that the boy, now free of restraints, was pushing past his mother's legs and heading towards the townhouse at a rapid toddle. Helen scooped up the girl, hitched her handbag on her shoulder and raced after him, calling over her shoulder. 'You'd better come in. Shut the door, will you?'

Bowen closed the car door, which locked itself without a key. Sara hoped it was in the woman's handbag. They also closed the front door, climbing the stairs to the first-floor living area into noise and chaos.

Mr Morgan sat on the sofa looking bewildered. Officer Shepherd was trying to prevent a short, middle-aged woman in a care worker's tabard from tidying the kitchen. Sara assumed this to be Meryl.

The boy reached a large pine box and heaved open the lid, which clattered against the wall. He began to pull out toys and scatter them around the place, adding to the chaos of the burglary. Bowen stood at the top of the stairs, unwilling to go any further or get involved. Sara watched with a sinking feeling as any chance of preserving forensic evidence at the crime scene was being effectively ruined.

Helen looked round in dismay. 'Who could have done this?'

'That's what we're hoping to find out,' said Sara quietly.

'I've put the kettle on,' said Meryl defiantly after she'd confirmed her identity. 'Tea for everyone?'

'Yes, please,' said Helen. She approached Mr Morgan and sat softly beside him on the sofa, putting the young girl on her lap. The child reached out her arms to her grandfather. 'Hey, Dad. How are you doing?'

Mr Morgan briefly looked at the pair of small, graceful arms, then pulled the girl onto his knee and hugged her. She snuggled against him as he placed his head gently on top of hers. 'Ophelia, my baby.'

A crash from the toy box distracted Helen. Meryl caught the boy by the hand as a wooden hoop game headed towards the wall. 'How about some *Hey Duggee*?'

With the practised hand of parenthood, Meryl soon had the toddler settled in front of the television with a biscuit and plastic beaker of juice.

'Will you allow me to tidy up after I've made everyone a drink?' Meryl asked as she passed Sara.

'Not yet. I've asked for a forensic team to come and look over the place. In fact, I'd like to get everyone out of here as soon as possible.'

Meryl nodded as she went back to determinedly making drinks for everyone else.

Helen looked at Sara, tears welling in her eyes. 'What's been going on?'

'I need to ask you some questions first, then I can explain,' said Sara. Helen nodded. 'Your mother, Carole, was due at rehearsal at the Rosegarden last night?'

'That's right. I came to sit with my father. I have two brothers. We're all married, and all six of us take turns being with him so Mum can go and do things for herself. It's hard being a full-time carer.'

'I imagine it is,' agreed Sara. 'It was your turn last night?'

'It was.' Helen looked around her in distress. 'I got here about half past six. We watched some television. Had a bit of supper. To be honest, I enjoy the quiet time myself.'

Sara glanced at the currently pacified Tarquin and understood. 'When did you leave?'

'Mum called me about quarter past ten.' Helen pulled her mobile out of her handbag and checked her calls. 'Ten seventeen to be precise. She said they'd finished, and she had offered to lock the building up.'

'Does she often do that?'

'Sometimes. Mum is an official keyholder for the place. Has been for years. Usually, one of the staff would do it.'

'Not last night?'

'She said she'd told Ben . . .' Helen paused.

'Ben Marsden, the stage manager?' Sara consulted her notebook.

'Yes. Mum had offered to lock up so Ben could get off. He works such long hours. Told me she would only be ten minutes and that I could get off if I wanted.'

'And you did?' Helen nodded. Sara continued. 'Leaving your father alone and the front door unlocked?'

'Yes.' Helen's voice was little more than a whisper. That explained the woman's fury at her father being left alone this morning. It was simple guilt. 'He can manage for a few minutes. And I'd been here later than usual. What happened?'

'It would seem that your mother never made it back,' said Sara as carefully as she could.

'Dad was alone all night?'

'We suspect so. When Meryl arrived this morning, she found he was missing and called us.'

'Why didn't you call me?' asked Helen.

Meryl's face darkened. 'I rang the office and told them where I'd be,' she snapped. 'They said they would call you or one of the other emergency contacts.'

Helen turned her anger on Sara. 'Surely someone else was here? Someone must have done this.'

'Do you think it could have been your father if he had been left alone all night?'

'I very much doubt it. His condition makes him clumsy, but he isn't an angry or violent man.' Helen held up a hand to indicate the chaos. 'This is spiteful and vicious.'

'Your father says it was a monk. Or at least, someone dressed up as a monk. As far as I'm aware, there are no functioning religious communities in the city, so not a real one.'

'A monk came in here?'

'Apparently. Whoever it was, they threatened your father, then trashed the place as he sat here on the sofa.'

Sara winced as she said this. The image of the frightened, confused older man cowering there while someone vandalised his home around him was powerfully disturbing. Helen reached out to take her father's hand in hers.

'Obviously someone real did this,' she said. 'But I think it must be a youth in a hoodie or something like that. The monk thing is just Dad getting confused.'

'Why's that?'

'Because of the theatre. It's supposed to be haunted by the figure of a monk. Everyone there knows the old story; sometimes, they even claim to see him. Dad told us he'd seen him walking across the stage once during a show.'

CHAPTER 8

Nafisa had been busy at the help hub during the morning. Even in a picturesque ancient city like Norwich, so cultured on the outside, plenty of people still needed help with all sorts of issues and addictions. Sometimes, the stream of burdened humanity left Nafisa feeling drained. She was grateful when the next team member came to relieve her. Russell was waiting in the staff room, holding two packs of sandwiches.

'I got hungry, so I brought us some lunch,' he said shyly, proffering one of the packets. It was cheese and tomato. 'That's all right for you to eat, right?'

Nafisa sighed. Russell kept giving her these little gifts. She suspected he was building up to asking her out, and she wished he wasn't. She liked him as a colleague, nothing more. 'It's fine. I'm not vegetarian, you know.'

He dropped his head to hide a blush. 'I know about pork, I think.'

'Shall we have a cup of tea with it?' she asked brightly. There was no point in explaining her food choices to him. He would only forget again. They decided against the drink, ripped open the packets and ate the contents in an awkward silence.

Outside, it seemed the day was offering one of those warm, sunny autumn afternoons that, despite being enjoyable, hinted at colder days to come. The pair walked along the riverside path and up through the cathedral grounds. Nafisa kept the chat impersonal, hoping to leave no gap for Russell to invite her for coffee after their visit to the tent city. She lived with her parents on a side street along the Unthank Road and fully intended to catch a bus home from Castle Meadow as soon as they had finished. Cutting through the medieval cobbled streets, they reached St John Pottergate church.

The flint-and-stone church stood on a small rise at the end of Pottergate. The old street turned at one end of the building and descended to some traffic lights. At the other end, part of the bell tower arched above a narrow alley. The alley and ancient street met at a point below the church, forming a triangle of land at the rear. This was the graveyard. The retaining walls, built centuries before to hold back the earth, were now crumbling with age. In places, old gravestones leaned perilously against the dilapidated bricks and out over the alley. Centuries of travellers had worn down the land around. At the top of the rise, the graveyard stood at least eight feet higher than the road. At the bottom, it was even taller.

Turning under the archway, Nafisa and Russell reached the old wooden gate that guarded a narrow set of steps into the mini plateaux of ancient tombstones. She could see some of the tents from here. They might have looked jolly and colourful if this had been a music festival. These homes of necessity looked drab and worn out though.

'If you think about it,' said Russell, patting the old brick wall, 'there must be coffins and bodies sitting behind this that are higher than we are.'

'Did you have to say that?' asked Nafisa. 'What a grizzly thought.'

Russell blushed again. 'Sorry. I just like that sort of story or film. Bit of a horror geek.'

Why wasn't Nafisa surprised?

She had been expecting to have to climb over the gate, which could have been a challenge. Instead, it was open and pushed back on rusty hinges against the retaining wall, the lock and chain that usually held it shut missing entirely. Someone must have cut them off.

'I'll go first,' volunteered Russell with faux bravery. Nafisa let him, though she didn't think it would help. Checking her ID card was clearly visible on its lanyard, she followed him up the steps.

There were seven tents and one makeshift cardboard shelter, propped up on one side by an old chest tomb. Without any attempt at regularity, they had managed to place the tents so that a circle of sorts had formed. The front flap openings all looked towards each other while they turned their backs to the outside world. The remnants of a small bonfire lay smouldering on the grass in the centre. Around the edges were a couple of those cheap single-use barbeque trays in silver foil. The area was littered with empty booze bottles and food packaging, and it wasn't hard to spot evidence of hard drug use.

It seemed that not all the occupants were 'at home'. One man lay under the cardboard shelter, watching them without moving. Two people stood up when Nafisa reached Russell. A grubby-looking man of indeterminate age in worn clothes stood with his arms folded, legs wide apart, ready for battle. A woman with dark matted hair hovered behind him, watching them with wide eyes.

'What the fuck do you want?' demanded the man. His hard Scottish accent made him sound more threatening to Nafisa. She took a deep breath.

'It's all right,' said Nafisa before Russell could open his mouth. She held up her ID badge. 'We're not the police. We're from social services.'

'So?'

'We came to see if there was anything we could do to help.'

'Leave us alone,' called the woman in a shrill voice. 'We're not doing any harm.'

Nafisa was sure that lots of other people wouldn't feel the same. She looked swiftly around the collection of tents until she found the one she'd hoped for.

'Is Zach with you?'

'How do you know him?' The man sounded even more suspicious. 'You don't know any of us.'

'I've met him before. Thought it would be good to catch up with him, see how he was getting on.'

'We don't need your sort. Bugger off and leave us alone.'

'You should know that the church has applied for you to be moved on,' said Russell. Nafisa flinched. She wouldn't have used that information at all if she could have helped it. Russell's weaselly tone made it sound like a lame threat.

'Oh, have they? What a surprise.' The belligerent man stepped up to Russell, his face so close that it must have been out of focus. 'Is that what you came to tell us? Well, fuck off then.'

He shoved Russell hard on the shoulders, making him stagger backwards. Nafisa grabbed his flailing arm before he tottered onto the tent behind him and crushed it. As she helped her uncoordinated colleague regain his balance, she held up a hand to the other man.

'That isn't what we came to say,' she said. She hoped her tone was calming. 'We came to see if we could help you with any services before that happens. A night in the hostel, perhaps? A little counselling? Clothes? Self-care products? Anything really.'

'A bottle of vodka would be nice,' laughed the shrill woman. The man joined in.

Nafisa smiled. 'Don't seem to have one on me. Do you know if Zach will be around later on? I could come back.'

'No need,' said a new voice. A tall, well-muscled man in dirt-stained army fatigues squeezed out of the tent set up furthest away from the others. 'I wondered if you would be along. Nice to see you again, Nafisa.'

CHAPTER 9

Ben was in his office rummaging through the large box of prop swords when the two police detectives returned. The term 'office' was euphemistic at best. It was a pair of old storerooms, one leading off the other, at the back of the green room. The walls were lined with shelving piled high with everything from glassware to pewter tankards, leather-bound books to quill pens and Art Deco coffee sets to jewelled caskets. Much of the random stuff had been collected or made as props over the century the company had occupied the theatre. No one ever seemed to throw anything away. Ben added to the jumble by creating specific new props whenever the need arose. He heard Lindie talking to the pair as she led them into the green room and called his name.

'I'm in here,' he replied. He locked the box and carried out the three swords he had chosen. A stifled gasp from one of the detectives belatedly warned him that it might not be the best way to approach two police officers. He grinned apologetically. 'For the play. Don't worry, they don't work.'

'Well, perhaps as a cosh,' joked the male detective. He was middle-aged and running to a beer belly, like Ben himself. With a cheeky grin and casual ease, he hefted one of the swords as Ben laid them on the kitchen work surface for later use. 'Heavy, aren't they?'

'Old ones often are,' agreed Ben, deciding he liked this apparently down-to-earth copper. 'We're going with the traditional Shakespeare period for this production. Some of these go back to Nugent Monck. Never been anything but props.'

The woman held out her warrant card for inspection as she gave her name. Ben eyed her more warily. She was tall and smartly dressed, her hair braided in multiple thin plaits and held tidily by a matching scrunchie. An air of absolute efficiency about her made Ben cautious. He'd been fooled by that sort of appearance in a detective before. 'I'm DS Sara Hirst. Who's Nugent Monck?'

'Our founder,' Lindie interrupted with enthusiasm. 'Set up the company back in 1911.'

'I hadn't realised this place had been here so long,' said the man. He also produced his warrant card. 'I'm DC Bowen.'

'In this building? Since 1921,' said Ben. It was the same old story. 'We always seem to be the best-kept secret in Norwich.'

DS Hirst looked surprised. 'I knew it had been around for some time, but not over a century.'

'So, what can I do for you?' asked Ben. 'You didn't come to see me for a history lesson, I assume.'

Lindie gave Ben a quick smile and exited through the green room door.

'We wanted to ask you about last night,' said the DS.

'Lindie said you might.' Ben pulled a tea-stained piece of paper from under his mug on the side table. 'Do you have a copy of the cast list?' The woman nodded. 'Last night wasn't a full company call, so I marked everyone who was here.'

'What time did you finish?' Hirst asked.

'About quarter past ten,' said Ben.

'Did everyone leave together?'

'No, people left as they were finished.' Ben tapped at the list. 'In the end, there were only a few of us still here.'

'Chris Webster was at rehearsal last night?'

It was Ben's turn to be surprised. 'For a while.'

'He left earlier than you?'

Ben pointed to the ceiling. 'Actually, he was upstairs in the gents' dressing room when we did the clear-down. I always check each room before we leave. People have personal stuff in them, so they get locked each evening and opened again before a rehearsal or a show.'

'He left at the same time as you?'

'With Simone, they left together.' Ben's curiosity was roused when he saw Hirst wince. 'Why are you interested in him?'

DC Bowen cleared his throat. 'DS Hirst knows Mr Webster personally.'

'Oh. Right.' Ben shrugged. It didn't seem wise to pursue the comment. She didn't look happy about it. 'Carole offered to lock up for me. After we'd made sure the place was empty, I went over to the car park.'

'Leaving her alone?' asked the woman. There was a clear tone of disapproval, which made Ben feel hot.

'It's not unusual,' he said defensively. 'Carole is a trustee and a keyholder. Has been for years. She only had a few more doors to check and then the alarm to set. I doubt I would have got as far as the bottom of the alley before she did that.'

'She's also nearly seventy and a lone female. Should she have been left on her own like that? Did you actually see her leave?'

'Well, no,' admitted Ben.

'Or hear the alarm activate?'

Ben shook his head. He hadn't thought twice about Carole's offer to finish up, just been grateful for the chance to get away. She'd done it often enough for him before. Now he felt guilty that he hadn't taken more care of her. Should he have offered to walk her home? He could imagine the sarcastic answer he would have got to that.

'Was there anyone else in the alley or outside the theatre when you left?' DS Hirst continued relentlessly.

'In the alley, no,' replied Ben hurriedly. 'The people in the tents were having a high old time.'

'How so?'

'You must have seen them.' Ben waved towards the church graveyard beyond the wall. 'High as kites and pissed to boot by that time of night.'

DC Bowen nodded. 'We know about them.'

'You moving them on soon?' asked Ben. Despite himself, Ben felt sorry for the homeless crew and often made them cups of tea when he thought no one was looking. He hurried on to justify himself. 'It really puts off the punters. They get pestered for money sometimes. Last night, they'd got a bonfire going as well. Could end up hurting themselves, if you ask me.'

'And no one else?' DS Hirst was clearly not going to be drawn into an argument about the people in the graveyard.

'Just the monk in the courtyard.'

'The monk?' asked DC Bowen. 'Are we talking ghosts here?'

'In a manner of speaking.'

'Are you telling us that you passed a ghost on the way out?' demanded DS Hirst incredulously.

'Sort of. It happens a lot at this time of year. It's a man dressed up. They wait behind the corner and jump out to shock people when the tour arrives.'

'Tour? What tour?'

'The Norwich Ghost Walk,' explained Ben. He heard DC Bowen start to laugh, then stop himself. 'It's Halloween soon. They go out twice a night at this time of year. We're one of the stop-off points because of our own ghost. I was surprised, though, as he was a bit early. The late-night tour wouldn't be due here until after eleven o'clock.'

CHAPTER 10

After speaking to the stage manager, Sara and Bowen returned to the office. It felt like it had already been a very long day as she handed the accumulated paperwork to Aggie. The team was waiting for them, eager to get involved if there was anything to be done.

Aggie pinned up the picture of Carole Morgan that Sara had brought from the theatre before returning to her desk. 'I've scanned the photo you sent me, and Ian has put it on social media.'

'I put it across all our platforms,' said DC Ian Noble. The youngest member of their team was acknowledged by them all as the best at anything to do with computers, CCTV and photographs. Anything that needed manipulation or data that needed assessing went directly to his desk. He was the only team member taller than Sara and curled his long legs under his chair to make it easier to lean towards his computer. 'We've already had some shares. It's our best bet.'

DCI Hudson nodded. 'Good work. Let's see if that brings any information in. What about the family?'

'It took a while to get them out of the place,' sighed Sara. 'They didn't seem to understand that they were sitting in a crime scene and we needed to get on.'

'Mr Morgan got very upset,' added Bowen. 'Which didn't help matters.'

Sara thought of the scene with Helen Morgan-Harris strapping the two children into the back of her car while she and Bowen tried to encourage Mr Morgan into the passenger seat. Two Forensics vans with their crime scene operatives sat in the courtyard, waiting for the scene to be available. It had been loud and chaotic. Sara thought it was enough to put you off having children for life. DI Edwards sat at a spare desk rather than in his office for the catch-up. He watched Sara as she spoke.

'We managed to get them off,' she sighed. 'Mr Morgan will stay with his daughter for now. I just hope he won't wander off again like he did in the early hours of this morning. Forensics are going over the place for trace evidence.'

'At the moment, all we have is a missing person and vandalism at the Morgans' house,' said DI Edwards. 'How are we treating this?'

'I think it looks bad, boss,' said Sara. Edwards nodded in agreement.

'Well, let's be clear,' said Hudson. She began to scrawl a timeline on the incident whiteboard. 'Carole Morgan goes to rehearsal at half past six while the daughter sits with Dad. All is well until later, when she rings to relieve Helen as she's about to leave the theatre.'

'Daughter leaves Dad alone,' continued Sara. 'The front door is left unlocked.'

'But Carole never makes it home,' added Bowen. 'Probably.'

'Ben Marsden accepts Carole's offer to lock up the theatre and leaves at ten fifteen,' said Sara. She pointed to Aggie's desk. 'Aggie has a list of all the people there last night. Marsden passes someone dressed as a monk in the courtyard, who he assumes to be with the ghost walk.'

'What's that?' asked Hudson.

'Lots of places have them,' said Aggie. 'I've looked at the Norwich one online and got the contact details.'

Hudson started a jobs list. 'Let's check with them to see who was on last night, then arrange an interview. They could well have seen something helpful.'

'The next thing we know for sure is Meryl arriving at the Morgans' house this morning,' said Sara. 'She finds the door open and the place empty and vandalised. Unsurprisingly, she calls the police. With the help of Officer Shepherd, they find Mr Morgan behind the church near the theatre.'

'We'll need DNA from the family, Meryl and any regular visitors,' sighed Hudson. She scribbled it on her list.

'Was he dressed or undressed?' asked DI Edwards. 'Was he wearing day clothes or his pyjamas when they found him?'

'I didn't think to ask,' admitted Sara. 'Why?'

'There's a wide window here for Mrs Morgan to have gone missing,' said the DI. He was leaning on the desk, his hand supporting his chin as he thought it through. 'We know that she was at the theatre at ten fifteen. Did she leave immediately, go home and put her husband to bed? Did she never make it home? Did she go home and then back to the theatre later on?'

'Why would she do that?' asked Bowen.

'Maybe she forgot something,' shrugged Edwards. 'I'm just trying to fill this big gap.'

'Mr Morgan was wearing day clothes when we arrived,' said Sara. 'I wouldn't know if he'd had them on all night or if someone had dressed him. Mrs Morgan could even have done that and then gone back to the theatre early this morning.'

'Let's not get ahead of ourselves,' interrupted Hudson. She turned to the jobs list. 'We can ask the care worker what she knows. Let's also get a statement from Shepherd. If Mrs Morgan doesn't turn up soon, we will need to speak to all the cast who were there last night.'

'You going to be okay with that?' DI Edwards looked at Sara. 'Given that your ex-boyfriend is on the list?'

Sara couldn't admit that a frisson of something had run down her back when she'd seen Chris's face on the wall. She dismissed the thought with a shrug. 'Haven't spoken to him in a couple of years. Someone else can do that interview if you think it might hurt any evidence.'

'Not a problem either way,' said the DCI. 'Don't worry about it.'

'Would anyone else have seen Mrs Morgan going home?'

Noble looked up from his computer screen. 'The City Council have CCTV on Pottergate. It's the shortest route home for her, so I should be able to spot her. I'll put in a call for last night's footage.'

Hudson added this to the jobs list.

'What about those homeless people camping in the church graveyard?' asked Sara. 'They might have seen something.'

'Not very reliable witnesses,' said the DCI with a sigh. She added them to the bottom of the list. 'We'll only go there if we have to. There's not much more we can do tonight. After all, she might just have decided she couldn't cope and gone off on her own. Let's wait to see if we get anything through the missing person call-out.'

'I don't understand why Mrs Morgan would just vanish and leave her husband on his own,' said Noble suddenly. 'She was obviously caring for him and had help from her family and social services.'

'Caring is hard work,' said Aggie quietly. Bowen turned to look sympathetically at his wife, who was looking down at her desk to hide her face. He reached out and squeezed her hand. 'Back when I was nursing my first husband at home, there were times when I felt that it was all too much. I'd have given anything to just get away for a few days.'

CHAPTER 11

Zach Wilson was a tall, well-built, muscular man. His army record indicated that he was forty-three, but it was difficult to tell in his current condition. His hair fell in natural dreadlocks as low as his shoulders. He had once told Nafisa that he had refused to have it cut since leaving the army as a protest against the army's standard look. The same applied to his beard, bushy around his face but bedraggled the longer it grew. His skin was wrinkled. The folds looked engrained with dirt, although Nafisa knew Zach went into the hostels occasionally to shower and wash his clothes. Now, his trousers were dirty and torn, and his padded jacket, which he'd need to sleep at night, had been patched with stained denim.

'Nice to see you too, Zach,' said Nafisa. She offered him a smile, and he nodded in return. 'Been a while.'

'I was away,' said Zach, stating the obvious. His voice was gruff and deep, his accent betraying his Yorkshire upbringing. 'Before you ask, I got a few weeks' work for a farmer up near Binham. Fruit picking. Let me camp in his field.'

'That's good to hear.' Nafisa could feel Russell shuffle closer as though he was trying to protect her. She was sure there was nothing to fear from Zach. The rest might be a different matter. 'Can I treat you to a coffee and sandwich or something?'

'If you like.' Zach zipped up his coat and stepped through the debris on the grass and gravestones. Nafisa followed him, sparing a smile for the man under the cardboard shelter. She dropped her card into the woman's hand as she passed.

'In case you think of anything you might need,' she said quietly. 'Come on, Russell. We should leave these folks in peace.' They went down the steps into the alley before she turned to look at her colleague. 'Best you get off home.'

'You sure?' Russell looked dubiously at Zach, who was already walking away from them under the church arch.

'Yes, I'm sure. See you in the morning at the office.'

Leaving no room for argument, Nafisa turned to follow Zach. He glanced down at her when she caught him up. 'Got rid of your puppy dog?'

With a wry smile, she pointed along Pottergate. 'That obvious, huh? The café up there has outdoor tables. Shall we?'

The town hall clock boomed its message over the rooftops. The day was moving on, and the sky was darkening. It was already four o'clock. The Wizard's Lounge independent coffee shop stood in a parade of shops along the side of St Gregorys Alley and opposite a small green. Several sets of metal tables and chairs were left out there all day for the use of its customers. Despite the chill in the air, Nafisa knew they wouldn't welcome Zach inside the shop. She could smell that he was ripe with old sweat as she walked next to him. Not only that, but many people weren't happy to see a homeless person sitting outside their business, even when they were paying for their food. Zach automatically took the table furthest away from the door, looking carefully around to assess if anyone would move him on.

It was almost closing time, so there wasn't much left in the way of food inside. Nafisa quickly pointed to a couple of cakes and ordered two coffees.

'Could you bring those outside when they're ready? Thanks.'

The bored-looking girl behind the counter nodded and Nafisa slipped back outside with the cakes, relieved that Zach was still there.

She put the two plates on the table. 'Help yourself. There wasn't much choice.'

'Carrot cake?' Zach pointed to the nearest plate. Nafisa confirmed it was. 'That'll do.'

'Did you enjoy being out in the countryside?' she asked, sitting opposite the man. Zach extracted a tin from his jacket and deftly rolled himself a cigarette. He focused on it until it was ready before replying. Then he looked up at the old church behind Nafisa. It was an antiques centre these days.

'It was good, actually,' he said, lighting his roll-up and drawing a heavy pull. 'No one bothering me. Lots to do.'

'Did you think I was bothering you?' Nafisa watched his face. He considered his reply carefully before dropping his gaze to her own.

'Not as such,' he admitted. 'There were some others. Thought it was better to get out for a bit.'

'How did you know about the work? What made you go up there?'

'Been before. He's all right, that old boy. It was the right time of year, so I tried my luck.'

'You back in Norwich for a while now?'

Nafisa was interrupted by the bored girl bringing their drinks. When she saw Zach, she dumped the cups on the table with a clatter before backing away, curling her lips in disgust. Turning sharply away, the girl strode inside as if she couldn't escape fast enough. Nafisa knew it wouldn't be long before the manager would appear to move them both on.

'Don't know,' said Zach. He loaded several packets of sugar into the cup, stirring it with one of those useless little wooden sticks.

'I'm pleased to see that you're all right,' said Nafisa. She took a dainty sip from her hot coffee and eyed the rather tired-looking jam doughnut on the other plate before deciding against it. 'Would you like to try again with the Luke Project? I'd be happy to do that.'

Zach picked up the carrot cake in his grimy fingers and took a large bite of it. 'Not sure.'

Behind them, Nafisa heard the door to the coffee shop open hurriedly. Without looking up, Zach took a large gulp of the coffee to wash down his cake.

'Would you like some takeaway cups for those?' a man asked in a passive-aggressive way. Nafisa looked at the manager in his fashionable wine waiter's apron, bristling with indignation. 'I don't mean to be rude . . .'

'But you'd rather we weren't here,' she said with a sigh. Suddenly, Zach looked at the man intensely.

'Fuckin' hell. Ross, man. Is that really you?'

CHAPTER 12

The microwave pinged to announce that Ben's teatime ready meal was supposedly cooked. He didn't even bother to tip it out onto a plate. With a quick stir of a fork, he balanced the plastic tray on a tea towel and began to eat the macaroni cheese with little enthusiasm. It tasted of wallpaper paste, or at least how it smelled. Ben had never eaten wallpaper paste, not even by accident. All the same, the ready meal tasted like it might be the stuff. He had barely sat on the green room sofa before Lindie bustled through the door.

'Oh, sorry,' she said. 'I just came to say that I'm off. I've locked up in the back courtyard.'

'Is it just our rehearsal tonight?' Ben shovelled more pasta into his mouth.

'The Christmas show people are rehearsing off-site until next week,' she replied.

'Gives us a breather. How are they doing?'

'You know what it's like with a big cast. People take these things on and then tell you they can't do half the rehearsals. Early days, though.'

Ben nodded glumly as he scraped up the last of his food. 'Mark's looking after that one. He's keen and reliable. We've got a full run-through this evening.'

Lindie glanced round the green room, then pulled open the fridge door. 'It's going to be busy; you'll need some milk. Would you like me to pop up to the supermarket before I go?'

'Yes, please.' Ben was grateful. It was one less thing to do. 'I need to clean under the stage before we start. Glyn wants Poor Tom to come up out of the grave trap.'

'Hardly original,' murmured Lindie. 'Has it been used recently?'

'Not for a while. I just wanted to check for rat bodies and clear any rubbish.'

'Has there been a smell?' Although the theatre wasn't particularly known for having rats, the little buggers sometimes expanded their runs or nests into the building from the gardens of Strangers' Hall, the adjacent museum. The two neighbours kept a watchful eye out and let each other know if they suspected a problem. Ben also kept a series of rat poison points topped up, just in case. The smell of putrefaction was usually the first indicator of a victim.

'No, but you know it can be missed if they get into the grave pits.'

Lindie nodded. 'Won't be long. I'll dump the milk and run, if you don't mind. The front door is on the latch.'

Ben heard the main door bang shut as he threw the plastic tray into the bin and dumped his fork into the dishwasher. He better get on with the job, much as he disliked it. Strapping a head torch on, Ben collected a dustpan and brush, then went to the stage-left wings.

The theatre had been designed by its founder to be one of the first modern recreations of an Elizabethan theatre, the sort of space that Shakespeare himself could have recognised. The building had originally been a Roman Catholic chapel, which had been deconsecrated. Nugent Monck had bought it as a home for the Norwich Players in 1921, and the performing area had been built in the same place where the altar had originally stood. Just as the Globe would have had, the stage was built on wooden pillars, raising the acting area above the auditorium to give a better view for the audience and leaving a dusty void underneath. Cut into the stage floor about a third of the way back from the front edge was an oblong wooden lid traditionally opened for the grave digger's scene in Hamlet. It was, therefore, commonly known as the grave trap.

The space beneath the stage was cramped and low. Not even their smallest actors could stand upright in it. Although some could move along at a crouch, most crawled on their hands and knees. The only access was via a wooden panel in the wing backstage. Ben set the board to one side and flicked on his head torch. The extra pounds he seemed to gain so easily these days made this job harder each time. He squeezed his food-baby belly through the gap with a grunt. A couple of lights were wired up under there, which he flicked on. Moving his head, he swept the torch around.

There were some bits of old wood, probably thrown through the grave trap by a previous set designer who couldn't be bothered to empty it into the skip provided. Ben sighed. It would have to wait until after this show was over, as the new set was already nearly finished, and he didn't want to cause any damage by lifting out the old timber. There was also a small amount of general rubbish, like crisp packets, chocolate bar wrappers and crumpled-up programmes. Ben often wondered where all this came from as he cleaned it out periodically. In theory, none of the audience could reach inside the void from the auditorium, and backstage, there was only one entrance. With a snort, he decided it was a toss-up between the theatre ghost and the rats.

It was easier for his 5' 10" frame if he crawled. Sweeping with the brush as he inched along, Ben made a path through the dust and rubbish towards the grave trap. It wasn't a direct route.

The one thing very few people knew about the theatre was that there really was an actual grave down here below the stage. Back in the days when the chapel was still consecrated, it was a priest's right and honour to be buried under the altar he had served. Over the decades, just one had chosen to do so before the chapel had been closed. When the Roman Catholic cathedral opened at the top of Grapes Hill in 1910, his coffin had been exhumed with all honours and transferred there. His brick-lined grave remained, gaping wide under the wooden stage.

When Ben took over as stage manager, the empty grave pit and sub-stage area had been used as a dumping ground. It was full of rubbish like rotting old carpets and piles of ancient newspapers. He'd organised a working party of strong-stomached volunteers to clear it out. Subsequently, he'd got the set carpenter to make a wooden panel, which they placed in the gap to prevent the rubbish from piling up again and, more importantly, to stop any actors from falling into the hole.

It was dark under here despite the working lights on the stage above, but Ben could make out the grave trap in the light from his head torch. He slid back the retaining bolts and threw it open on the stage with a crash. The dust made him sneeze as he stood up through the hole. Pulling a tissue from his pocket, he blew his nose and looked at the empty auditorium. He should be alone until Lindie returned with the milk, as none of the team for tonight's rehearsal had arrived yet. It was rare for him to be entirely on his own, which was perhaps why a sensation of being watched crept across his back.

The working lights left shadowy areas among the seats, especially on the balcony. With a start, Ben suddenly thought he could see a dark figure up there. He began to pull himself onto the stage, squinting at the three tiers of seats that looked down at him. Was that a flicker of movement?

'Hey there,' he called loudly. 'You shouldn't be up there, we're shut tonight.'

His knee made a thudding noise as he hooked it onto the wooden stage and levered himself up. With a huff of effort, he clambered out, legs and feet scrambling in an ungainly way. It took a moment to straighten himself up and inspect the balcony again. The beam from his head torch couldn't reach that far, but there was a little ambient light and Ben half expected to see a grinning actor or techie sitting there to frighten the life out of him. There was no one. Holding his breath for a moment, he listened for sounds, any noises that might be footsteps or even someone breathing. There was nothing. He gasped a new breath. He really ought to do something about his lack of fitness.

'Getting jumpy in my old age,' he mumbled with a frown and returned to the grave trap. Vague light seeped into the sub-stage space.

'I'll get a couple more lights put down there,' he promised himself. Crouching down, he scanned the access he had created.

'Who's moved that?' he grumbled when he saw that the protective panel had been removed from the grave void. He'd missed it in the dark as he'd swept his way forward. It lay on the ground beside the hole. Ben pushed himself back under the stage and crawled towards the panel. 'Damn thing's heavy too. Bet it was the same arsehole who put that timber down here, lazy sod. Bet there's more old set been shoved down there.'

He leaned over the hole to check. It wasn't old scenery. Laid out as neatly as one of the old priests might have been, her hands folded across her chest, was Carole Morgan.

CHAPTER 13

When her phone rang, Sara had reached the Wroxham Road roundabout on the northern bypass. A glance told her it was the office. Just when she had been looking forward to a quiet evening. She was supposed to be having a Zoom call with Adie Dickinson, her friend and landscape gardener.

They had met just as her relationship with Dante Adebayo had been breaking down. Her neighbour, Gilly, recommended Adie to help Sara with her out-of-control back garden. Adie was several years younger than Sara, making her cautious of considering him more than a friend. The truth was that she longed for him to be much more. His body was toned and tanned by his work outside. There was a hippy vibe to him, his hemp clothing and long blonde dreads out of keeping with his cultured, upper-class accent. He was intelligent and kind, his voice soft, his manner considerate.

After he'd finished clearing her garden, they'd seen each other several times. She'd agreed that he could create a new one for her as part of the final year of his horticultural training course. They'd visited two show gardens, shared afternoon tea and walked at the beach near her home. She'd been taken to his home, Richmond Hall, and introduced to his mother, a more friendly and welcoming visit than she'd anticipated. So far, all he'd done was hold her hand or peck her on the cheek when they'd parted, apart from the hug he'd given her when he'd returned to college in late September. That had been strong. He'd called her several times a week ever since, never complaining if she was too busy at work to spend much time with him. Despite a kind of desperate physical attraction, Sara remained unsure of her feelings. In her own opinion, her track record with boyfriends was poor, and she didn't know if Adie considered her his girlfriend or 'just good friends' as the saying went. She was willing to find out.

Slickly negotiating the traffic, Sara clicked on the pad on her steering wheel.

'Hirst? Where are you?' It was DCI Hudson. This couldn't be good news.

'About halfway home.'

'Choice is yours,' said Hudson succinctly. 'They've found the missing woman. You can come back, or I can send Bowen with Edwards.'

Sara admired her original boss, DI Edwards. She thought the whole team worked together well these days, but she especially enjoyed the rapport she had built up with the DI in her early days in Norfolk.

'I'll go.' Sara indicated to turn into a small side road so she could turn around. 'Where?'

'I'm not sure how to explain it,' admitted Hudson. 'Let me just say at the Rosegarden Theatre. Something about a grave trap, which means nothing to me.'

'I'll soon find out.'

'I've notified Dr Taylor,' said Hudson, efficient as ever. 'He's also on his way.'

Sara swung her SUV in as tight a circle as it would go, scraping up the damp grass verge and bumping back down. Turning towards Norwich, she put her foot down as best she could through the rush-hour traffic.

It was a squeeze to get her vehicle into the multi-storey car park across the road from the theatre, more due to the height of the roof than the lack of parking spaces. There was a drift of rain in the air as she crossed the road and past the cafés with their spooky seasonal decorations. As she strode up the alley between the wall of the theatre and the wall of the graveyard opposite, she saw someone had lit a small bonfire in the middle of the tent city among the graves. Weird red-and-black shadows danced among the trees, lending an oddly appropriate atmosphere to her short journey.

There were lights on inside the theatre, although all the doors looked closed. Ben Marsden, the stage manager she'd met earlier in the day, was engaged in what sounded like a heated argument with a tall man at the top of the stairs which led into the front foyer.

'You can't have any rehearsals tonight,' Ben was insisting.

The tall man looked red in the face. 'We can't stop now. We should be having a full run-through tonight. You know this.'

Sara stopped by the men. She pulled out her ID card and brandished it. 'And you are?'

The man turned to inspect her card, then turned even more red. 'Glyn Hollis. I'm directing the next play.'

'That would be *King Lear*, I understand,' said Sara. She folded her card. 'I'm sorry, but no rehearsals tonight. Perhaps you could help us both?'

Glyn looked bemused and shrugged. 'I just want to get inside.'

'The theatre is out of bounds for everyone except officially authorised personnel,' said Sara. 'You could wait here and turn away anyone who arrives with our apologies.'

'Lindie's in the office, trying to call everyone to let them know.' Marsden waved at the office window. Sara could see the woman speaking rapidly with a phone against her ear.

'Excellent.' Sara nodded at Marsden. Turning back to Glyn, she asked, 'Can you do that? There should be a police officer along soon to help you.'

Glyn now turned as pale as he had been red. 'Yes, of course.'

When Sara and Marsden got inside, the theatre was ablaze with lights. All the doors she could see were propped open. There was activity in the auditorium, and a pair of forensic investigators were suiting up in the bar area. Marsden hovered at her side. He looked overwhelmed by the fuss. Unsure where to start, she was relieved to see Edwards appear from the auditorium. He was already wearing coveralls over his clothes.

'Ah, good, you made it,' said Edwards. 'I thought you'd want to come given the circumstances. She's under the stage.'

'Under the stage?' Sara was confused.

'Come and see.' Edwards gestured to Sara and the stage manager. 'Mr Marsden here can tell you all about that area.'

The auditorium was well-lit. The stage lights blazed down on two forensic officers staring at the floor. One held a camera with a light ring attached to the lens. The other was trying to direct a pair of lights on a stand to illuminate the crime scene. Sara could see Dr Stephen Taylor, in a blue coverall, somehow standing halfway into the stage, only his upper chest, arms and head visible. Someone had pulled back a square of flooring in the corner to reveal a set of steps leading up to the performance level. She heard Marsden mutter something behind her. When she turned, Sara saw him slump into an auditorium seat.

'I can't,' he murmured, looking distinctly ill. 'Not again.'

'That's okay, Mr Marsden,' said Sara. 'You can stay there.'

Edwards glanced at the man as they climbed the stairs.

'He found our lady,' he muttered. 'Must have been quite a shock.'

Their footsteps on the wooden stage attracted Dr Taylor's attention. He smiled when he saw Sara approach. 'My favourite detective team. Come and have a look, DS Hirst.'

Taylor pulled himself out of the hole in the stage. Sara could see it was a large rectangular space with what appeared to be a door hinged on the far side, which had been thrown back and lay on the stage, leaving access underneath it.

'It's called a "grave trap",' said Taylor as Sara bent down to look underneath. 'Traditional in Elizabethan theatres, Mr Marsden tells me. You'll see better if you actually get down into it.'

One of the forensic officers offered Sara a coverall and some nitrile gloves. Pulling them on, she let herself drop gently into the hole until her feet hit solid ground. When she glanced at Taylor, he squatted down on the stage next to her and handed her a torch.

'If you crouch down, what can you see?'

Sara did as he suggested, then shone the torch in an arc. There was a space beneath the entire stage, which appeared to reach all the way to the venue's back wall. It was dimly lit by several LED lights on the structural posts. She'd seen shows here but, not knowing much about theatres, had never really bothered to consider what might be under the raised stage.

'It's dusty,' she began. 'There's some rubbish.' She trained the beam along the back wall. 'There seems to be a gap at the back. I can see lights that way.'

'Only access to this space from backstage,' confirmed Taylor. 'What else?'

Sara looked at the floor. 'There's a door-like panel on the floor near me. It looks like a void to one side.'

'Look in there, and you'll find our lady.'

Sara was tall. If she tried to walk under here, she would bang her head. Dropping to her knees, she crawled the few feet to the hole.

It was about seven feet long and three feet wide, just about the right shape and size to hold a coffin, and the inside was lined with bricks. The faint light from the LEDs didn't reach here. Nor did the additional light on the stage help much. The darkness inside the hole seemed to reach long fingers towards her, drawing her downwards. The people above seemed to have stopped moving. The bustle from the auditorium had faded away. An oppressive silence enfolded her. All she could hear now was her own breathing, loud and quick inside her. Sara's hand shook as she pointed the torch beam into the darkness.

The light skittered downwards, past the crumbling bricks until it hit the bottom of the pit. With a shudder, Sara saw a pair of feet wearing smart navy-coloured shoes. Their victim was lying on her back. Sara slowly moved the light further up. A pair of well-cut slacks encased legs that had been straightened out. A rainproof jacket had been zipped up to cover the upper body. The deceased's arms had been folded across her chest as if she were lying in a coffin.

The beam flickered onto the face. In her revulsion, Sara almost knocked herself out as she shot backwards. In that brief moment, she didn't doubt that she saw Carole Morgan's face, and Sara couldn't bear it. The poor woman's eyes were wide open in fear, and her mouth locked in a silent scream.

CHAPTER 14

The coffee shop manager stared at Zach for a conspicuous amount of time before his face suddenly changed with recognition. Nafisa watched his reaction carefully, as she had been trained to do. Unfortunately, not much training was needed as it was obvious that the man knew Zach, but he was unsure if he wanted to acknowledge him in his current state.

'Zach Wilson?' he'd asked cautiously.

Zach must have read the conflict in his old friend's face. His head dropped in embarrassment. 'Yeah. Still me, I'm afraid, Ross.'

Ross squared his shoulders, which were almost as broad as Zach's muscular pair. Now that she was paying more attention, Nafisa saw that the man was tall and powerful, like his old friend. His blonde hair was cut unfashionably short, and his boots looked freshly polished. His work top was a dark blue polo shirt with the shop's logo. It was immaculate and had a sharp ironed crease in the sleeves.

'What the hell's happened?' demanded Ross. 'How did you get in this state?'

'I take it that you two are old friends?' Nafisa smiled at Zach.

'Yeah, well, we used to be.' Zach looked at Ross uncertainly. 'Served together in Afghanistan. Two tours.'

'We still are,' said Ross with determination. He reached his hand out to Zach. After a moment's hesitation, the homeless man took it. Ross hauled him out of his seat and hugged him in that masculine way that men sometimes do when overwhelmed with emotion for another man but unable to quite articulate it. He slapped Zach on the back, a gesture Nafisa admired him for, given Zach's personal smell and his filthy clothing. After another moment both men suddenly burst out laughing. 'You need a shower and a shave, Lieutenant!'

'Tell me about it, Corporal,' returned Zach. 'Only you would dare say something like that to me when we served.'

'I know you well enough for that. Picked you up off the roadside more than once.'

'Sometimes on the way back to the barracks from the pub!'

'Who's your lady?' Ross peered at Nafisa speculatively. His look was unfriendly.

She bristled and returned his stare. No doubt he'd had some poor experiences with Muslim women if they'd been in Afghanistan, where some people had regarded them as occupiers rather than protectors. But this was Norwich, and she was nobody's 'lady'. She tugged at her headscarf defensively.

'Nafisa Ahmed,' she snapped. 'Social worker.'

'She's all right, man,' Zach urged his friend. 'Been trying to help me.'

'I still am, if you'll let me,' she said.

Zach shrugged. 'I don't like being obliged.'

'Well, I don't mind paying back an obligation,' said Ross. 'Where are you staying?'

Zach explained about the tent city in the graveyard. Nafisa half expected his friend to offer Zach a night at his home. It seemed Ross wasn't quite ready to go that far.

'I've got a bunch of food going out of date,' he said. 'Sandwiches, cake and all that. I'll get you some stuff together.'

He vanished inside the shop, dragging the young waitress behind him, her mouth still flapping open at the scene.

'Thought you might have got a bed for the night,' said Nafisa carefully. She didn't want to put a damper on Zach's reunion. Was out-of-date food the best this old friend could offer?

'Wouldn't have gone.' Zach wolfed down another mouthful of cake. 'He's right. I'm disgusting. Or didn't you notice?'

'I noticed.'

'You didn't mind?'

'Perhaps a little. I've seen and smelled worse with less excuse. You wouldn't believe some of the so-called homes I've been into.'

Zach considered this as he slurped his coffee. 'You like your job?'

'Yes, I do. Very much. Especially if I can help someone who actually wants to be helped.'

Zach didn't reply. They sat in silence until Ross returned with a cardboard tray box that claimed to contain apples. It was full of sandwiches, croissants, flapjacks, sausage rolls and something Nafisa couldn't identify wrapped in flaky pastry. The tent city residents would have a decent picnic out of it if Zach chose to share it with them.

'You going to be here for a few days?' asked Ross. Zach nodded. 'If you come back at the same time tomorrow, I might be able to do more.'

'Thank you.'

Nafisa walked back down the cobbles of Pottergate next to Zach. A glance over her shoulder told her that Ross watched them until they passed the fish and chip shop on the corner of Lower Goat Lane, after which they would be out of sight. Making sure they were gone, she assumed.

'I'll share this with the others,' said Zach. 'For some reason, they seem to have allotted me the post of camp captain.'

She wasn't surprised. 'You look out for them.'

'If I can. They don't always want my advice.'

'I didn't think it would be this busy,' she said as two teenage girls walked by, openly giggling at Zach's appearance. 'Half-term, I suppose.'

'Halloween,' replied Zach. He nodded towards the shop windows, wreathed in cobwebs and skeletons, black cats in pointy hats and witches on brooms, ghosts dressed in bedsheets. Orange and black dominated it all, even at the specialist wool shop, which displayed an autumn crocheted blanket on a bed of brown leaves surrounded by pumpkins and toadstools.

'Christmas next,' nodded Nafisa. 'With barely a break for Bonfire Night.'

She'd spoken without thinking. When Zach stopped dead, his eyes glazing, she inwardly cursed herself. The noise of the explosions must be difficult for him to deal with. At least the big city display had moved out of the city centre.

'Not my favourite night of the year,' she admitted. 'Our cat hates it. Sits under the sofa crying.'

Zach looked at her slowly. 'Had a dog once. He hated it too.'

They reached the end of the church, where the alley turned downhill.

'I'll get off for my bus,' she said. 'Here, take my card. I'd really like to try and get you back together with the Luke Project.'

'I haven't got a phone.' Zach still took the card. He tucked it into a grubby pocket.

'Can I pop by tomorrow? Same sort of time?'

'Yeah, why not?' Zach turned to go down the alley. 'What the hell's going on?'

Nafisa had to lean to one side to see around Zach's bulk. Two uniformed police officers stood behind a length of blue-and-white tape stretched across the arch. One held a clipboard. The other eyed Zach with barely concealed disgust. Nafisa's heart began to beat quickly. Her brain raced to think of possible refuges for Zach if the action to move the tent city people had already started.

It was dark behind the two men. The alley had poor street lighting, and it was well past nightfall. Nafisa could see that the theatre had lights on inside, although the ones outside were off. There were several people in the alley, none of them wearing uniforms. She couldn't see any of the homeless people.

'Come on,' hissed Zach. 'We can get in round the other side.'

Nafisa followed him along the church and down the narrow road beyond. There was a second set of steps up onto the graveyard here. Overgrown with old buddleia bushes, weeds and brambles, it seemed impassable. Zach plonked the food box on the top of the wall before pulling aside a mass of twisted branches.

'Secret entrance,' he said as Nafisa followed him.

The steps were broken, crumbling and in darkness. A vague light filtered down from the graveyard. Nafisa saw that the tents were untouched when they pushed up to the higher level. More of the inhabitants seemed to be there now. Zach collected the food box, but his arrival was met with indifference. The small tribe of homeless people stood on the opposite side, looking down into the narrow alley by the theatre.

'What's happening?' asked Zach.

The sassy woman from earlier in the afternoon spoke with relish. 'Not sure. They've locked down that place, and the Forensics guys are here. You can see their vans down there. Look. We reckon there's been a murder.'

CHAPTER 15

From where he sat in the auditorium, Ben heard a gasp and a muted squeal from the female detective under the stage. A thump followed, which he assumed was her banging her head, trying to escape from the sight of Carole Morgan lying in the old grave. It had shocked him too when he'd shone his head torch on the poor woman. DS Hirst struggled out of the grave trap with the help of the chap in the bow tie. Doctor something or other. They'd all been introduced when they'd arrived, but Ben hadn't been able to remember their names.

He ruefully rubbed the swelling on the back of his head. He'd done the same thing himself, scrabbling backwards, bumping into the stage floor above him and shooting up from the trap, calling for Lindie. Luckily, she had just returned from the supermarket with the milk and heard him. Despite his reputation for being unflappable, it had been Lindie who'd taken control of the situation, who'd called the police and thought to start ringing the people due in for rehearsal. His main contribution had been to prevent her from looking down there. For all her gothic pretensions, he didn't think she'd really want to see Carole like that.

'Thanks, Dr Taylor,' said DS Hirst.

'It is rather shocking, isn't it?' the man asked as he brushed cobwebs from the woman's back. 'I can't tell at this juncture if the way she looks is because of how she died or if it's just post-mortem muscle contraction. Don't invest too much in it.'

Hirst nodded. The second detective, DI Edwards, turned down Taylor's offer to go and see for himself, although he did kneel down to peer under the stage to be sure where the body would be.

'We'll get cracking,' said the doctor, waving forward the forensic officer with the camera. 'Placement photos first. Then we'll have a good look around before we work out how to get the poor woman out of there.'

Ben felt nervous as the two detectives approached him. The man sat on the row in front of him and the woman across the aisle. She was still shaking a little.

'You know this place best, I think,' said Edwards. Ben agreed that he probably did. 'And you found Carole Morgan? Were you looking for her? Is that why you went under the stage?'

'I'm afraid not,' replied Ben. 'We knew you were searching for her, of course. Spoke to your lady over there this afternoon. Lindie reposted your social media call-out on our feeds.'

Hirst seemed to gather herself. 'You did. And DC Bowen. You may have been the last person to see her.'

Ben was too smart to be caught out like that. He knew the police could be tricky. Sitting up a bit straighter, he looked her in the eye. 'You mean, apart from her killer?'

The detectives shared a discreet glance. 'Indeed,' Hirst said.

'Why were you under the stage?' asked Edwards.

'The director wants Tom to come out from there during the "Poor Tom's a-cold" scene. I needed to make sure it was clear enough for him to get through. Otherwise, it's a bit of a nightmare for the poor sod doing it.'

'Bit cramped for anyone,' muttered Hirst.

'It is,' agreed Ben. 'Which is why we don't use it very often. In fact, we skin the stage floor regularly with big sheets of marine plywood, and it's often covered up entirely.'

'What's that hole in the ground? With the door affair.'

'A real grave, no longer occupied.' Ben briefly explained the history of the place and its previous use. 'I had the stage carpenter make a panel to fit. It was filling with rubbish, which didn't feel right. Besides, when we use the trap, an actor could fall in and hurt themselves.'

'Why didn't you just fill it with concrete or something?' asked Edwards. He sounded genuinely curious.

'That didn't feel right either. It was a priest's last resting place back in the day. I felt it was more respectful to cover it up.'

'And now it's Carole Morgan's last resting place,' said Hirst. 'Who would know about this old grave pit?'

Ben thought about this for a moment. 'Almost anyone who might have volunteered here at some point could know they were there. We don't broadcast it, as it freaks some people out. But it's not a secret either. More likely to be known among the acting or backstage crews than the front of house people.'

'Would people in the audience or the city, in general, be aware?' asked Hirst.

'Not so much, I imagine. We sometimes have open days when we give backstage tours. Some of the guides might mention it, but others wouldn't. I suspect they would be more likely to have heard about the ghost.'

'What made you look in there?' Edwards picked up.

'The lid panel was lying to the side. I was checking to see if there was any rubbish before I put it back.'

Ben was beginning to feel tired from the shock. He shuffled uncomfortably in his chair, aware that it was starting to look bad for him. He'd been the last person to see Carole alive, and now he'd been the unfortunate one to find her body. The image of her face was tapping insistently at his mind. He wasn't going to make a fool of himself by mentioning that he might or might not have seen a stranger up on the balcony. Who knew what they would make of all this. He didn't trust coppers, not after last time.

'Was the grave trap open when you came in today?' asked DI Edwards.

'No,' said Ben. He frowned in concentration. 'Actually, the grave trap door was bolted underneath when I went to clean up. I had to undo it so we could use it tonight. And the backstage panel was in place too.'

'If you were putting our poor victim down there yourself—'

'Which I wasn't,' interrupted Ben hastily.

'Hypothetically,' said Edwards, not very smoothly. 'If you were, what would be the quickest way to do it?'

'Down the trap itself.'

'Not from under the stage at the back?'

'Wouldn't think so, boss,' said Hirst, unexpectedly coming to Ben's rescue. 'It's a long way to drag the victim in a narrow space.'

Edwards looked at his fellow detective. 'So, in through the grave trap, lift the panel to the grave pit, dump the body, shut the grave trap behind you and lock it. Then crawl out backstage and shut that behind you as well. But leave the grave pit panel off. Why? Why not shut her in so she wouldn't be found for ages? And how would a stranger know to do all these things?'

Hirst shrugged. Ben shuffled in discomfort again. It was the very same set of questions that had been plaguing him.

'Because they wanted one of us to find her,' he suggested. 'Because they knew the place and how it worked. Because they knew us personally.'

CHAPTER 16

Sara had missed her Zoom call with Adie. She'd sent him a text explaining she was at a crime scene, but there'd been no reply. Double-checking her emails on the laptop on the desk in her cottage, there was no message there either. With a sigh of resignation, she'd rolled up Adie's plans for the garden and stuffed them in the desk drawer. He hadn't called her for several evenings. Perhaps he was moving on or fed up. Maybe he didn't consider it a relationship at all.

Sara's work often caused problems in her private life. Few boyfriends understood that she couldn't predict her hours or discuss what she was investigating, and Adie wasn't actually her boyfriend. He didn't owe her an explanation.

She had lit her open fire, more to drive out the darkness of the night than for the heat. Her cat, Tilly, had settled beside her on the sofa to enjoy the warmth. Both of them were grateful to have no visitors.

The next morning, her car was covered in the first frost of the autumn. Sara sprayed the windows to clear them and drove cautiously until she got to the main road. Even though the road she lived on eventually passed the village school, it wasn't always gritted.

Aggie and Bowen were, as usual these days, the first in. Slowly, the team assembled as Aggie bustled about efficiently making coffee and pinning information on the whiteboard. Bowen and Edwards scrutinised a computer screen while DC Noble was on the phone, his printer chugging next to him. Sara topped up her caffeine levels and checked her emails while she waited for DCI Hudson to call them to order.

'What do we know so far?' asked Hudson. She stood in front of the board with a marker pen poised in her hand. She looked at the picture of Carole Morgan. 'Timeline?'

'Carole went to rehearsals on the evening of Wednesday the twenty-eighth,' said Sara. 'The last two people in the building were the stage manager, Ben Marsden, and Carole. She offered to lock up for him, something she often did.'

'So, this stage manager was the last to see her alive?'

'So far, yes,' agreed Sara. 'Carole rang her daughter to relieve her of dad-sitting duties at about ten fifteen. Daughter Helen left Dad alone, confident that Mum was only five minutes away.'

'Did she ever make it home?' asked Noble. He'd just put down the phone.

'We can't be sure,' said Sara. 'James Morgan has dementia, which makes his memory unreliable. Claims a monk got into the house, threatened him, then trashed the place.'

'Forensics?'

'They've been through the house,' offered Bowen. 'Report on its way. Unfortunately, the place is well lived in. No disputing the fact that someone had done a lot of deliberate damage.'

'Not likely to be James? Given his dementia?' asked Hudson.

Aggie pursed her lips in frustration. 'Not all dementia makes you violent. It depends on the individual and also how aware they are.'

'Let's see if we can discreetly ask the daughter about her dad's condition, then,' said Hudson. She scribbled the action on the board under the heading *Morgan House*. 'And this supposed monk?'

'Helen seemed fairly certain that was one of Dad's dementia symptoms, seeing things differently,' said Sara. 'Personally, I think it might have some credence. Ben Marsden told us about the ghost walks for one thing. It's Halloween for another. Easy to get costumes like that at this time of year.'

'Good cover, you mean?' Hudson started a new column headed *Monk*. 'Have we set up an interview with the ghost walk people?'

'Just waiting for them to call me back,' said Aggie.

'Where are we with Carole?'

Sara nodded towards her computer screen. 'Dr Taylor has brought her into the mortuary. Says he'll do the post-mortem this morning.'

'Did he give anything away at all?' Hudson looked at Edwards with one sarcastic eyebrow raised.

'Said she must have died sometime in the night, as rigor mortis was already beginning to dissipate. Possible bruising around the neck.'

'Well done, Edwards!' Hudson sounded genuinely surprised. 'More than he'll usually gives away. What about the crime scene?'

'Working assumption is that she was murdered in the theatre somewhere,' said Sara. 'The place is closed until further notice while they search for evidence.'

'I bet they're thrilled by that,' said Aggie quietly.

'Can't be helped,' snapped Hudson. 'So, not killed under the stage?'

'I took some pictures under there,' said Edwards. 'Ian is sorting them out for you.' Noble waved a couple of sheets of photo paper. 'It's very restricted. It would be more likely that she was murdered and then placed in the grave pit, especially as she was laid out as if in a coffin.'

Sara shivered at the memory of the woman's face. 'It would need someone strong enough to carry her onto the stage, wouldn't it? Then arrange her carefully. That might narrow the field for us.'

'Agreed,' replied Edwards.

'Empty graves under a stage,' said Hudson to herself. 'Who would have thought it? Deeply macabre, if you ask me.'

None of them disagreed with her.

'Hence the ghostly monk stories,' added Bowen helpfully.

'Come on, then. What theories do we have about the murder?'

'Two possibilities, I'd say,' said Edwards. 'Someone got into the building after Ben Marsden left. Or Ben Marsden did it. So, did he have it in for Carole for some reason?'

'Either way, it seems unlikely that anyone who didn't know the place would know this grave space existed,' Noble pointed out. 'It has to be an inside job, surely?'

'Let's get a list of all staff for a start,' said Hudson. 'What about other actors Carole may have worked with? One of them could have a dodgy background. And how might someone get in?'

'I can talk to the theatre manager,' offered Aggie. 'She'll have lists, I'd imagine.'

'What about internal CCTV?'

'I'll check with the venue,' offered Noble. 'I've just spoken to the City Council about external cameras. Unfortunately, there are none at all in Church Alley. If the theatre doesn't have anything, it's a blank canvas.'

'No CCTV in the alley?' Hudson sounded outraged. 'I know it's not our team, but aren't there lots of issues with drug dealing behind that church? Do Drugs have any spyware down there?'

'I'll check that,' said Bowen quickly, glancing at Sara. She nodded gratefully.

'What about Pottergate?' asked Hudson.

'That's on the way,' said Noble. 'We'd already requested it.'

'The first job for you, Noble, is to analyse it.' Hudson scratched more notes on the board. She stood back to look at the lists. 'The murder and the vandalism have to be connected, don't they? See if we can find out what time James thinks this monk turned up. Perhaps whoever did this went to the theatre first and then to the house.'

'Dressed as a monk?' Edwards sounded unconvinced.

'They might not have been dressed that way at the theatre,' Sara pointed out. 'They could have dressed in the street or outside the house. I couldn't see any security cameras in the courtyard outside, more's the pity.'

'I guess it'd be easy enough to slip on a costume. Frighten the old chap even more,' said Aggie. 'Poor thing.'

'Or to disguise themselves,' said Hudson. 'And what about the family? Have they been informed?' In the silence that followed, Hudson looked around her team. 'I take it that's a no.'

She turned to the board and wrote *family visit*, and next to it, added Sara's name.

CHAPTER 17

As doorsteps went, considered Sara, this was a pleasant one. Belonging to a smart, semi-detached build from the 1980s. In a row of equally smart homes in the quiet, suburban cul-de-sac in Drayton.

Helen Morgan-Harris wrenched open her front door in answer to Sara's ring on the doorbell. Behind her, Sara could hear toys crashing and a small boy's petulant shouting. When she held up her warrant card, Helen waved it away and looked at the woman standing slightly behind Sara.

'This is Tracey Mills,' Sara explained. 'She's a family liaison officer.'

'Ah, this isn't good news, is it?' Helen said. Her shoulders slumped as she fully opened the door and stood back. 'Come in if you can bear the racket.'

The home was clearly well cared for underneath the chaos caused by Tarquin's tantrum. James Morgan sat on the sofa, his hands over his ears, rocking slightly.

'Ophelia goes to playschool on Friday mornings,' explained Helen, picking a jumble of toys from an armchair. 'He thinks he should be going too. Sit down if you can.'

Given the news she was bringing, it wasn't the best scenario for her to talk to the adults. Sara was grateful to have unperturbable Tracey beside her. 'Is there somewhere we can talk to you and your father?'

'Somewhere quieter, you mean?' Helen sighed. 'Hang on a minute.'

It actually took more than ten minutes to placate the irate toddler. Helen bribed him with his favourite biscuit, a drink of juice and *Hey Duggee*, which was clearly the best method to get him to sit still. She spoke gently to her father as the cartoon chattered from the television.

'Come away, Dad.' She pulled gently at her father's hands. He looked at her, then at Tarquin on his television-watching cushion, and the stress left his face. 'Let's go to the kitchen for a cuppa.'

The four adults trooped into the next room. It took several more minutes to bring James back into the present. When Helen had also placated him with a drink and a biscuit, they sat cramped around a small kitchen table. Sara felt uncomfortable and refused the proffered cup of tea.

'So?' asked Helen. The tension hadn't left her body, even if her father had been distracted.

'I'm so sorry to bring you this news,' Sara began. 'Would you like any of your family with you?'

Helen shook her head. 'They're at work. I said I'd call them when we had any news. Dad's safe enough with me for now. You'd best get it over with.'

Keeping her tone sympathetic, Sara spoke carefully. 'We have found someone we strongly believe to be your mother at the theatre.'

'Dead?' asked Helen. She looked almost resigned. 'Are you sure?'

'I'm sorry to say that the person we found has been deceased for some hours,' explained Sara. She spoke clearly and steadily to explain what she could without going into unnecessary detail. 'We have identified her from the photo held by the theatre of her. Naturally, we will need a family member to do a formal identification.'

There was a long silence. Helen's eyes filled with tears. 'Was it an accident?'

'We're treating it as suspicious, at least for now,' said Sara. She never felt that she should sugar-coat the situation. Family members usually preferred the truth. 'Which means we will be investigating it fully.'

James looked between the three women blankly. Tracey gently placed a hand over his.

'Do you understand, James?' she asked quietly. 'We are so very sorry to tell you that Carole has died.'

James looked at her in horror. 'Died? No, she can't be dead. I only saw her last night.'

Sara glanced at Helen, who shrugged. 'He might think he did. Unfortunately, my father's type of dementia can cause hallucinations. It's called Lewy body dementia. His claim to see the ghost of the monk at the theatre was one of the markers which made us get an assessment for him.'

'How long ago was this?'

'Dad was diagnosed about a year ago,' said Helen. Her hands were trembling with shock as tears began to run down her cheeks. 'Although, I think he'd been drifting for some time before that. He's got steadily worse since then, which is why we don't leave him alone for more than a few minutes if we can help it.'

'I'm so sorry,' said Sara. Helen walked unsteadily to the sink and pulled a length of kitchen roll off its holder. She blew her nose loudly. 'There are one or two questions I need to ask if you feel up to it.'

Helen nodded as she pulled out another length of kitchen roll and crumpled it.

'Can you tell me what your mum was wearing when she went out?'

'Oh, er . . .' Helen looked confused. 'I'm not sure. Trousers, she prefers them for rehearsal. Her navy shoes, the comfortable ones.'

'Coat?'

'It was quite chilly, wasn't it? I think she put on her warm jacket. It's maroon, padded, rainproof.'

'With a zip fastening?'

'Yes.'

It wasn't conclusive, but it sounded like they had found Carole still wearing the same things she'd left the house in at teatime.

'Did she take a bag with her?'

'A brown leather one with a shoulder strap. Big thing, it is. We always teased her that it's bigger than the one Mary Poppins had. She never went anywhere without it.' Helen's face crumpled as she realised she wouldn't be teasing her mother about it again. Sara wondered if the investigators had found the bag at the theatre.

'And when you joined us yesterday morning, was your father still wearing the same clothes as the night before?'

Helen nodded. 'Yes, he was. I've had to put him in some of my husband's things for now. Until I can go and retrieve some stuff from the house.'

'Do you think Mr Morgan would be able to answer a question?' asked Sara. She was really addressing this to Tracey, but Helen shook herself and replied.

'Dad is confused this morning,' she said, slipping back into the chair beside him. 'Tarquin's wobbler was too much for him. He gets so anxious. It's part of the condition. What did you want to ask?'

'You told us you left Pottergate about ten fifteen?' Sara trod carefully; she didn't want to make this sound like an accusation. Helen nodded. 'We are checking street cameras, but we aren't sure if your mother ever left the theatre. Perhaps she went home and returned to the theatre later on for some reason?'

'I'm not sure Dad would remember that. He can get confused about times. Why do you need to know?'

'What was the condition of the house when you left him?'

'Oh, I see. It was as tidy as usual. Not like it was when I got there yesterday.'

'Therefore, someone must have done the damage afterwards. Are you sure it wasn't one of your parents?'

Helen looked confused. 'Mum? Why would she do that? They were both so house-proud. Loved their art and antiques. Dad doesn't break things on purpose, even when his anxiety is strong.'

'So, someone must have got in and done it. Would your father be able to say when?'

'I doubt it.' Helen took her father's other hand. 'Dad, when you were alone the night before last, do you remember what happened?'

'Shouldn't be on my own,' began James. Sara could see him struggling to focus his thoughts. 'You left me. Your mother should have been there. Then the monk came.'

'Any idea what time? Where you on your own very long, Dad?'

James shook his head. 'I heard the door slam and his tread on the stairs. Then I saw who it was. The monk from the theatre. I didn't know why he had come to our house. He doesn't belong there. He lives near the old altar. Had he followed me? Or your mum? First his cowl, then his body, rising up the stairs.'

'He had his cowl up?' asked Sara quickly. 'Could you see his face?'

'No, not his face.' James's eyes widened at the vision he was conjuring in his mind. His speech began to quicken anxiously. 'It was a skull with grinning teeth and real eyes. His hands were folded in front of him. White hands. Young hands. You know, you know.'

Sara felt the hairs on the back of her neck begin to stand up. Clearly, James had been a good actor in his day, and he had lost none of his storytelling capacity despite his anxiety.

Helen squeezed his hand. 'I know, like in the pictures.'

'He walked right up to me and shouted angrily. Then he was running around, throwing things, smashing things. Oh, I can't . . .'

James folded almost in half as he hugged himself.

'I'm sorry to distress your father,' said Sara. She moved to stand up, thinking James wouldn't recover enough to say any more. Helen put her arm across his shoulder and shushed him like a baby. Suddenly, his head snapped up, stopping Sara in her tracks.

'Midnight. Of course, it was midnight. When else would a ghost appear? I heard the town hall clock strike twelve as he came up the stairs. And I knew his voice. I recognised his voice. I just can't remember where from.'

CHAPTER 18

Nafisa watched her boss typing on her computer. The window behind her showed a grey and miserable day. Damp hung in the air, although it wasn't quite raining. At least the forecast was dry for tomorrow, when the children would be out doing their Halloween thing. Last year, Nafisa's mother had bought piles of sweets. This year, she didn't seem to have remembered. Perhaps Nafisa should get some on her way home.

'Yes, here it is,' said Samantha. Her voice snapped Nafisa back from her Halloween ramblings. '*Eastern Daily Press*. "Police investigating an incident at the Rosegarden Theatre." Doesn't give much detail.'

She swung the computer screen around for Nafisa to see the article, which was headed by a dingy photo taken the previous evening. The photographer had been standing at the bottom of the alley. They'd caught the shadows on the wall of the theatre on one side and a couple of police officers behind a token tape barrier in the middle of the alley. If you knew to look for them on the other side above the raised wall of the cemetery, you could just about make out the figures of the tent city troop watching from among the headstones.

'All looks very spooky,' said Samantha with a low giggle. 'You were up there with them? What was going on?'

'I was talking to Zach Wilson.' Nafisa had already told Samantha that she had successfully found the homeless veteran. 'You couldn't really see anything. Then the police officers realised they were watching and shouted at them to go away. I left soon after that. I don't think they spotted me.'

Samantha nodded and turned the screen back to face herself. 'On more important matters, I've had the formal notification that they've obtained an eviction order for the tent encampment after I registered our interest in your client with the authorities. Any chance they'll move them on today?'

'I suspect the investigation at the theatre might get in the way,' said Nafisa thoughtfully. 'Would they want two sets of officers down there for different reasons?'

'It's Friday.' Samantha creased her eyes in calculation. 'I'd say they're unlikely to want a bunch of people watching when they move the tent people on. So, Saturday is probably a non-starter as well. Sunday?'

'The church isn't in use. I doubt there would be a service on Sunday.'

'Sunday or Monday morning, then,' nodded Samantha. 'Let your man know when you see him. Any luck with the Luke Project?'

'I've managed to get hold of the man I worked with last time.' Nafisa thought of her phone call with the sarcastic project worker. He was unhappy to be looking at Zach again after he had walked away from them the previous time. 'I think I talked him round. He's agreed to see me this afternoon to discuss it.'

'With or without your client?'

'Without.'

Samantha sighed. They both knew this lowered the chances of a good result. It was better for the project worker to meet Zach again to hear his reasons for not taking up the placement in the summer. Nafisa had already been on the phone trying to find a short-term solution for Zach. Mercifully, he didn't have a pet, which always complicated matters, but she still hadn't managed to find him a temporary stay. There was one place she could try after her meeting, and then she would have to get to her appointment at the Luke Project.

'Let me know how you get on,' said Samantha. 'I think you should focus on this for a few days. Do you have anything more urgent in your caseload?'

'There is one I'm worried about. Possible abuse of a teenager by a stepfather, but mother not cooperating.'

Samantha's face clouded. 'They never learn, do they? Bring me the file, and I'll look at it on Monday if you're still tied up with Zach Wilson.'

Russell Goddard was hovering by Nafisa's desk when she went to fetch the file.

'Everything all right?' he asked anxiously.

Nafisa wondered briefly if he was concerned about her or whether he was worried they might be discussing him. She smiled brightly. 'Everything's fine,' she assured him. 'You can't think of anyone with temporary accommodation for my homeless veteran, can you? Probably from next week.'

Russell reeled off a list of places they often used. Nafisa had already tried all of them. 'From the first of November? Tent city being disbanded then?'

'Looks like it,' nodded Nafisa.

'What about the Winter Night Shelter project? They opened on the first of November last year. I can ring them, if you like?'

Run by two local church groups, each opened their city centre church halls for three or four nights a week during the winter. It was a floor to sleep on in a warm room, with a meal and a cuppa included, no questions asked.

'That would be great, thank you. Can you give me a call when you know? I've got to go out soon.'

Russell smiled. 'Happy to help.'

Without much hope of success, Nafisa called the last of the charity shelters. She was unsurprised to hear they were also oversubscribed. The weather was already turning cold, and people were heading indoors. If only she could persuade Zach to do the same.

Her meeting at the Luke Project was imminent. As it didn't seem likely that she would return to the office that day, Nafisa gathered a pile of paperwork that she could work on over the weekend and shoved it into a supermarket bag-for-life. She could only hope that it would survive her current visits. At least her laptop carrier and handbag were more robust. She dragged them over her shoulder.

Russell waved her over as she headed for the door. 'They're opening from Monday. Baptist Church Monday through Wednesday, St Anselms Thursday through Sunday. Referrals through the City Council. Do you need a lift into the city?'

'It's not far. I'll manage, thanks,' she said with a smile. 'That's good to know about the churches. See you Monday.'

Offering a silent prayer of gratitude for Christian charity and for a successful outcome to her meeting, Nafisa struggled down the stairs and out into the lunchtime crowds.

CHAPTER 19

Ben Marsden had spent a sleepless night. Every time he'd begun to doze off, he was haunted by the vision of Carole Morgan's terrified face and woke up again. By six in the morning, he had given up, and got up and showered. The bump on the back of his head was about the size of a ping-pong ball and throbbed as he shampooed his hair. He was worried about what the police would make of his situation. Unlike some people he knew, Ben wasn't a great believer in Norfolk Police or any other police force. His previous experience with them had left him with a bad taste in his mouth. It hadn't ended well on that occasion for the only official apprentice he'd ever had. It also created tension between himself and Chris Webster, making him the only actor in the place Ben was wary of.

Knowing that things would be difficult for Lindie, he went to work earlier than usual only to find the alley to the theatre blocked by a police cordon. Turned away by an officious woman in uniform wielding a clipboard, Ben walked round the old graveyard to the opposite road. Several vehicles from the forensic team were lined up close to the graveyard wall, making it obvious that something serious must be happening. Unwilling to stand around in the damp, drizzling morning and unsure what to do, he was relieved when he heard his name called.

Lindie was waving to him from the window seat in the coffee bar across the street. 'Come and join me,' she mouthed.

Ben had never been in the Olive Tree before. There wasn't much time to visit coffee shops or restaurants during his working day. It had one of those Scandi-vibe interiors with grey walls, wooden tables and branches decoratively nailed up displaying small craft items for sale. Ignoring the big bowls of healthy salad, he ordered a sausage sandwich and a coffee.

'Thank you for coming in early,' said Lindie. She was forking mashed avocado on toast into her mouth, a mint tea brewing in a clunky hand-thrown teapot by her plate. 'They wouldn't let me in either. Apparently, we should be allowed back in this afternoon.'

'Carole?' asked Ben.

Lindie shuddered. 'I believe they took her away last night.'

Ben nodded. His tiredness was already making him feel morose. 'Poor woman.'

'You left her to lock up?' asked Lindie. She eyed him speculatively.

'Yes. Why not? She'd done it a hundred times before.'

Lindie nodded before stuffing more green-smeared toast into her mouth. Ben struggled to open a sachet of ketchup to spread on his sandwich. Even that seemed like a challenge he needed to concentrate on.

'May I join you?' A chubby man sidled up to their table. Neither of them had seen the detective come in. 'I'm DC Mike Bowen. You might remember me?'

'I'm sure we do,' muttered Ben through a mouthful of sausage.

'Have a seat,' said Lindie, waving towards one of the uncomfortable stools at an adjoining table. Bowen pulled it over and plonked himself down. 'Any idea how it's going?'

'Thank you. I was hoping to have a quiet word with you both away from the theatre.'

Ben's first impression of the man was that he was genial and friendly. Someone you might go for a pint with. Now, he looked businesslike and serious, and studiously avoided Lindie's question. Ben chewed his sandwich to avoid having to speak.

'As you both work there full-time, I'm afraid we will need to ask you for DNA samples.'

Lindie looked surprised. Ben flinched.

'Obviously, the building is a public space,' Bowen carried on. 'Hundreds of people pass through it in a normal week. DNA will probably not be a major feature in our investigations.'

'We'd be all over the place anyway,' said Lindie. She poured her tea out. 'Access all areas for work, and I act in the shows sometimes as well.'

Except for under the stage, thought Ben. *Dust, rubbish and me. That's about all they'll find under there. And poor Carole.*

'Exactly. It will be helpful to have it, though. We'll need to ask all the staff.'

Lindie nodded and glanced at Ben. 'I don't mind at all.'

'No problem,' he said reluctantly.

'I'll arrange for that to be done today,' said Bowen. 'The other thing was about these ghostly monks.'

'Monk,' said Lindie. 'There's only supposed to be one of them. You know the story?'

'Yes, we're aware of the legend.' He looked directly at Ben, who turned his gaze out the window. 'It's the ghost walks that you mentioned.'

With a tingle of relief, Ben shrugged. 'Oh, those.'

Lindie stretched past Ben to a pile of leaflets on the window ledge. Selecting an A5 flyer, she handed it to Bowen. On the front was a photo of a man in a Victorian evening costume, complete with a top hat, cane and evening cloak. On the back were a series of dates and times.

'It's run by Daryl Stone,' she said, pointing to the leaflet. 'It's his business. He leads the walk, telling stories as they go.'

'And the monk?'

'I think you'll find that he hires a student to dress up and jump out at people at various points in the evening. Give them a thrill.'

Bowen looked less than amused. 'Or a shock.'

'It can cause some screaming,' agreed Lindie. 'Isn't that the point? It's effective in our yard sometimes, as we're not open every night. So, it's dark and easy to hide in.'

'And you saw this student waiting the night of the rehearsals?' Bowen turned to look at Ben, who could feel the back of his neck prickling. Unable to continue feigning nonchalance, he looked back at the DC.

'Yes.'

'You mentioned before that he seemed to be there too early? What time was this?'

'Would have been about ten fifteen,' said Ben.

Bowen turned over the flyer and inspected the dates and times. 'Walks that night were leaving at eight o'clock and ten thirty. Why is ten fifteen too early?'

'We're one of the last stops,' explained Lindie when Ben didn't speak. 'The walk takes over an hour. He wouldn't need to be there in that costume until an hour later.'

Ben dropped the last of his sandwich onto his plate. 'He was in the wrong place as well.'

'He should have been elsewhere?'

'You'd have to ask Daryl about that,' said Ben. 'I've never done the walk. I meant that the fright monk usually waits behind the wall near the alley. They can't be seen as the tour walks down from Pottergate. That night, he was standing in the corner by the entrance stairs. I almost didn't see him myself.'

CHAPTER 20

Sara left Tracey Mills at Helen Morgan-Harris's house with whispered instructions to find out more about James's condition and hallucinations. She was convinced that the monk was a real person who had chosen to dress up that way. It was an effective cover, hiding the attacker's shape and face. Whether James was reliable in terms of remembering the voice which had shouted at him was another matter. That's what Sara wanted Tracey to assess. All the same, it was a cruel trick on someone whose grasp on reality was slipping. It all strongly suggested that Ben Marsden was correct when he said whoever it was knew the theatre and its regulars very well. Checking with Aggie in the office, she headed into the city.

'The ghost walk people don't have an office,' Aggie had explained. 'I suspect it's not a big business. The owner is called Daryl Stone. He said he'd happily meet you in the café near the theatre. It's just across the other side of the graveyard.'

Sara was unsurprised to find Mike Bowen in the Olive Tree café. It was lunchtime, and he was unlikely to be far from a bacon buttie or piece of cake. By way of variety, he seemed to be enjoying a sausage sandwich today.

'Recommended by Ben Marsden,' he explained when Sara joined him. 'Best to stock up while we can, don't you think?'

Sara agreed and ordered a mixed bowl of the delicious looking salads. 'You've seen Marsden this morning?'

'And the office manager.' Bowen nodded. 'They were waiting here until Forensics had finished in the theatre.'

'Where are they, then?' Sara looked at the other tables, all of which were occupied.

'They've gone off shopping or something. Forensics won't be finished before three. Agreed to do DNA swabs, although I sensed he was more reluctant than she was.'

'Something to hide, perhaps?'

'Maybe.' Bowen wiped his fingers with a paper napkin, then patted his stomach. 'I got the impression that he wasn't keen on either of us. Just a gut feeling.'

Sara knew she could trust Mike Bowen's instincts. He might seem long in the tooth and a dinosaur in some areas, but it was always worth paying attention to anything he picked up on. 'Has he had any dealings with us before? Or is he trying to protect the theatre's reputation?'

'I'll get Aggie to check the national database. Give me a minute.' Bowen stepped outside into the drizzle with his mobile pinned to his ear as Sara tucked into her lunch.

It wasn't hard to guess at Daryl Stone's job when he strode past Mike and into the café. The tall man was flamboyantly dressed entirely in black, with a long outer coat, a shirt with frills down the front, a double-breasted waistcoat and heavy boots. His shoulder-length dark hair curled out from under a brimmed hat that had a pair of brass flying goggles fastened on it. The outfit was completed by an old-fashioned watch on a chain draped across the waistcoat, and when he peeled off his black leather gloves, there were skull rings on both hands. Part Cromwellian New Model Army and part Whitby Steampunk Weekend, his smile was genuine when Sara greeted him.

'Thank you for agreeing to speak to us,' she said as he settled opposite her. His dynamic entrance had caused a stir among the lunchtime diners, as he was handsome beneath the razzamatazz. He sported a well-trimmed moustache and beard which was more Laughing Cavalier than Puritan. There was no doubting his magnetism, even if it was dressed up rather eccentrically. Several sets of female eyes watched him curiously as he ordered his drink and lay his hat on the window ledge. With theatre ghosts and steampunk storytellers appearing in the flesh, Sara felt as if she had wandered into a parallel universe.

'No problem.' There was that smile again. 'Your lady said you urgently needed some information about our walks.'

'It's good of you to join me,' said Sara. 'You don't have an office?'

'No, I run the business from home. Customers book tickets through the website or the Tourist Information Centre. I don't need more than that.'

'Indeed. What can you tell me about them?'

'We have two different ones,' he explained. 'Obviously, we go off in the evening and stop at various places that are reputed to be haunted. We tell the story in brief and then move on. Each walk has at least seven stops and takes over an hour.'

'I had no idea Norwich had so many ghosts,' said Sara in surprise.

'A city this old is bound to have lots of material.'

'And you have people jumping out at your customers? To frighten them?'

Daryl grinned. 'Yes. A little added frisson. Works better on dark nights, of course.'

'You include the Rosegarden Theatre in both walks?'

'No. Each walk is unique, with no repeats. We're doing the city centre one twice a night at the moment, because of Halloween. That's the one that calls at the theatre. There are two people on each walk. One tells the stories and the other runs round the back way with a bag of costumes. They change into them and wait, do a fright scare, then run off, collecting the bag when the walk moves on to repeat the process at the next scare point.'

'You were doing the storytelling on Wednesday night?'

'We're sharing at the moment.' Daryl stirred sugar into his cup of tea. 'I have a friend who does a lot of acting. He's good at both. Two full walks in an evening are tiring on your voice because it's outside, and you have to speak loud enough for the whole group to hear. So, I do the first one, then we swap for the second tour.'

'You would have been hiding at the theatre on the second trip?' confirmed Sara.

Daryl nodded.

'No, nothing like your photo,' said Bowen. Sara jumped as Mike appeared suddenly at her side. Obviously, this ghost business was getting on her nerves. He dragged out his warrant card for Daryl to inspect, but the storyteller waved it away. Bowen put an advertising leaflet between them as he sat down.

'That was my dad,' said Daryl. His smile subsided. 'He set up the business twenty years ago.'

'Then handed it on to you?' asked Bowen.

'Not really.' Daryl's eyelids fluttered, and Sara wondered why. He looked at her and sighed. 'I'll explain if I need to.'

'Please,' said Sara.

'He died about ten years ago. I was still a student at the time. I used to do the jumping out, and Dad used to lead the walk. After he died, I came home and took it on. I never saw his problem coming, though my mum had her suspicions. We keep using his photo as a sort of tribute.'

'Was he ill?'

Daryl shook his head. He picked up the leaflet and stared at the photo of his father. 'He had a car accident when I was fourteen. A bad one. His leg was smashed to pieces, and he had loads of surgeries to fix it. I didn't understand at the time. He was in constant pain.'

'He carried on working? Taking walking tours?'

'It became a point of honour with him.'

'How did he manage?' asked Bowen.

Daryl carefully laid the leaflet back on the table before carrying on. He ran his hand over the photo gently.

'At first, it was the doctor's heavy painkillers. Then it was smoking pot as well to get him through. When that wasn't enough, he turned to harder drugs. And more of them. His heart packed up one night as he sat watching television. Mum watched him die.'

There was a shocked silence. Obviously, people at the adjacent tables had been listening in too, drawn in by the power of Daryl's storytelling. When he looked up at Sara, his face twisted with anger.

'And if I ever get hold of that fucking scumbag who sold them to him, I would strangle him with my bare hands.'

CHAPTER 21

The meeting at the Luke Project had left Nafisa feeling exhausted. Her contact had been as difficult as he dared without actually saying he wouldn't cooperate. The truth was, they had a waiting list so long it vanished over the horizon and only one unit of ten rooms available. Although Zach fitted their target help groups in two respects, being both ex-military with PTSD and being long-term homeless, he had walked away from them once without explanation, and the man had no intention of delaying help to another person for the sake of someone who may or may not turn up. Nafisa wasn't sure she had won her side of the debate, although the project worker let slip that one of their clients was moving into a flat at the end of the following week, which would create a vacancy.

With a heartfelt sigh, Nafisa stopped outside the Luke Project office to draw breath and organise her bags. It was situated in a converted medieval house in one of the narrow streets just south of the river in the city centre. Hitching her bags over her shoulder, she began to walk briskly through the tangle of alleys, lugging the large carrier bag of papers. The town hall clock rang out three booming chimes as she headed to the graveyard to talk to Zach. The heavy carrier bag bit into her fingers as she swapped it in her hands every few minutes.

She climbed the little rise past the Playhouse Theatre and cut up Bridewell Alley. There was a definite sense of Halloween being in full swing as she crossed Exchange Street. All the shops were decked out with autumn colours and spooky displays. It might be mid-afternoon, but she passed what appeared to be a hen party dressed as witches (very sexy ones in skimpy skirts and laced red-and-black corsets carrying mini-brooms) near one of the bars. They had clearly been drinking for some time. Their screams and laughter were decidedly loud. Nafisa occasionally wondered what it must be like to be that out of control. Was it as much fun as the hysterical witches seemed to make it appear?

Church Alley was mercifully clear of police and forensic officers. The theatre still looked locked up, although Nafisa could see people moving inside through the glass entrance door. It was easier to access the graveyard through the forced-open gate and stairs than through the secret entrance's overgrown bushes.

The tent city looked worse than it had the day before. More litter was scattered about, and the fire in the middle of the area was being fed by broken pallets. It looked to be burning dangerously high to Nafisa. The remnants of last night's picnic, courtesy of the Wizard's Lounge café, lay trampled in the grass and would soon be attracting rats. No city was immune from packs of rats, not even polite and cheerful Norwich.

The man under the cardboard shelter was lying curled up into a ball, clutching an empty bottle of cheap whisky tightly to his chest. He was snoring, which indicated that he was still alive. The aggressive couple lay close to the bonfire, sharing a joint. The man started to get up when he saw Nafisa appear up the steps but sank back onto his blanket when he recognised her. Raising his hand in a half-hearted salute, he gestured towards Zach's tent, giving Nafisa permission to go through.

With a nod to the couple and giving the fire a wide berth, she picked her way through the rubbish and tent ropes. Zach was sitting outside his tent on a broken tree branch, watching her approach.

'I wasn't sure you'd come back,' he said. 'You managed to get up here all right?'

'I said I would,' Nafisa said quietly. She nodded towards the theatre. 'The cordon has gone, so I could use the alley. The police have finished in there, then?'

'Left about half an hour ago.' Zach glanced towards the street on the other side of the graveyard. 'All apart from one van.'

Nafisa turned to look at the roof of the plain white van. Its back doors were propped open, and she could hear the clatter of equipment being loaded into it. 'I have some news if you want a coffee?'

'I might.'

'We could go to see your friend again.'

Zach snorted. 'I get the impression he wouldn't be thrilled if we did.'

Nafisa shrugged. 'If we're paying, he has to put up with it.'

'You look loaded down.' Zach eyed the couple by the fire, then the bags Nafisa had dumped on the muddy ground. 'Kells? Can you look after this shite for my friend here? I'll leave it in my tent.'

The woman stared myopically at them, struggling to focus on Zach before she scrambled up and walked erratically to join them.

'Yeah, okay,' she grinned as she looked at Nafisa's bags. 'No problem.'

'I shouldn't leave them,' murmured Nafisa. She wasn't sure she could trust Kells not to burn the papers on the bonfire. 'They're private.'

'Whatshh youse need,' slurred Kells, 'ish a better bag n'that.'

She pointed at the supermarket carrier. It was beginning to fall apart, and the handles that had been cutting into Nafisa's fingers were stretched to breaking point.

'Got jusht the thing.' Kells nodded sagely. 'Cost ya' though.'

'Oh, give over, Kells,' said Zach. 'Will you keep an eye out or not?'

Kells frowned in concentration. 'Bag. Proper leather jobss. Twenty quid to you. Fetch it.'

'Sorry,' muttered Zach as the woman lurched away. 'I'll carry that for you if you're buying coffee.'

Nafisa nodded and gratefully handed over the heavy bag. Zach hitched it into his arms. 'Come on.'

They picked their way carefully around the bonfire as Kells noisily rummaged in a pile of what looked like rubbish and old clothes to Nafisa. With a cry of triumph, she suddenly held up a large leather satchel-type bag.

'Told you,' she said, staggering after Zach. 'Here yu'ar. Twenty quid.'

The bag was clearly made of leather and was a matt brown colour. A flap with a buckle clasp and a long shoulder strap swung randomly as Kells shook the thing. She lifted the flap and opened it wide.

'Looksh. Loadsa room for your papers.'

Nafisa frowned.

'Where did you nick that from?' Zach demanded. He leaned the carrier bag against his legs and grabbed the leather bag where it swung in front of him. There was a momentary struggle, Zach intent on pulling the bag away and Kells unwilling to let go. He was much stronger than her; it wasn't an equal match. 'Let me have a look.'

Kells unbalanced and let go with a stagger. 'Okays. Didn't pinchsh it.'

Zach gave her a world-weary look. 'Yeah, right.'

'No, honest,' protested the woman. She waved over the wall towards the café. 'Found it. By the binsh, up the road. Put them out early, didn't they? No onesh about, so had a look.'

Nafisa watched as Zach inspected the bag. Although well used, it was obviously expensive and not broken, so why had it been in the bin? It was amazing the sort of stuff people just threw away these days. Nafisa was tempted. It was big enough to take all her papers.

'Was there anything in it?' she asked Kells, who struggled to move her attention from Zach.

'Nope.' Kells pursed her lips in disgust. 'Jusht a few bits of paper. Left them in the bin.'

'No phone? No purse?' demanded Zach. Kells took a ragged step back.

'No. I told you. What you getting crosh about? You gonna buy it or not?'

Zach looked at Nafisa, who nodded. She pulled her purse from her handbag. No one carried much cash these days, but she'd just drawn some out to buy Halloween treats on her way home. She pulled out a crisp new twenty. 'Here.'

'Acesh!' cried Kells, grabbing the note. She turned away and weaved back to her boyfriend by the fire, making little crowing noises.

'You sure?' asked Zach.

'Why not?' Nafisa took the bag and stuffed her papers into it. The thing was heavy when she swung it onto her shoulder. 'Come on, coffee time.'

CHAPTER 22

Lindie had let the forensic officer swab her mouth for a DNA sample without apparent thought. Ben's heart had hammered in his chest when his turn came. It was nonsense to feel nervous about doing it. He wondered if the officer in her white coverall spotted the sweat popping out on his brow. She thanked him and packed it away without further comment as the final members of her team carried out boxes full of sample bags. As the front door banged shut, Lindie appeared at the office door.

'They say we can open up again,' she said.

'So, we just carry on as if nothing has happened?'

Lindie chewed her lip. 'We can't, can we? I emailed the trust committee last night. I think they intend to have an emergency meeting tonight before we carry on.'

The trust committee was made up of elected company members who oversaw the running of the theatre on behalf of the rest of the company. Ben occasionally felt that they worried too much about day-to-day things. After all, it was what they paid Ben, Lindie and the rest of them to do. This time, he was grateful that it would be their responsibility to decide how to proceed. After all, it was their theatre and their choice. The amateur company were his collective boss.

'I've just emailed them to say they can come in when ready. There's the show to consider, not to mention the publicity we're getting at the moment. Some sort of statement ought to be made.'

'Anything I can do to help?'

'I think we should keep the place locked up, don't you?' Lindie dropped the latch on the front door. 'Can you make sure the rest is secure?'

'Sure.' Ben dug his set of keys out of his work bag and began to check all the entrances and exits.

Normally, when he got to work, the theatre would be alive and full of activity. The workshop would buzz with power tools as sets were constructed. The wardrobe would hum with chattering voices covering the noise of washing and sewing machines as the wardrobe mistress, Rachel, and her volunteer assistants made or maintained their huge stock of vintage or hand-crafted costumes. The bar manager might be checking stock ready to open for the evening show, clinking glasses or making mysterious gassy noises in the cellar. A volunteer would be sitting behind the box office window, watching for customers with a ready smile. Lindie or one of her helpers would be on the phone or computer dealing with the day-to-day business of running the venue. Delivery drivers would appear with printed publicity matter or stock for the departments. Members would drop in as they passed, often just to hang out or blag a coffee.

Today, it was silent, apart from Lindie tapping at her computer keyboard.

The forensic team had left the auditorium lights on. The grave trap stood open. Ben climbed up onto the stage and peered underneath. He could see the brick-lined side of the grave pit in the limpid light. The cover still lay to one side.

Ben felt his skin crawl as he saw Carole Morgan's face in his mind once again. He sat on the stage and swung his legs into the trap. The idea of crawling under there to put the lid back on made him feel nauseous. As he pushed himself off the lip, his legs locked in resistance, almost as if someone was preventing him from going down there. He swung uselessly in space for a second or two, pivoting on his hands, arms locked straight. A hiss of breath seemed to rush past him from under the stage, and his skin was suddenly clammy. With a moan of disgust at his cowardice, Ben hurriedly pushed himself back onto the stage, misreading the distance and falling onto his side on the wooden floor.

He lay there panting for a moment or two until his heart rate calmed. Rolling onto his hands and knees, he shook his head to dislodge the image of Carole's screaming mouth and fear-widened eyes.

'I'll check the rest before I go down there again,' he mumbled as he strode out of the auditorium.

The rehearsal room was secure and clean. The toilets seemed to have been used, but that was hardly surprising as the forensic team would presumably have needed them at some point. He climbed the stairs to the gallery. There were two emergency exits up here. One led to a set of metal stairs outside the building. Ben could hear his footsteps on the wooden floor echoing in the arched roof that gave the theatre such good acoustics. The fire door was securely fastened. He clumped back across the row of gallery seats, trying not to glance down at the stage below and the job that waited for him.

He almost didn't check the wardrobe door as he passed on his way downstairs again. The black door with a small metal plate saying *Wardrobe* was unobtrusive. The workshop and costume store behind it were out of bounds for the audiences except on open days. Rachel was particular in ensuring it was locked when she left. She hadn't been in today because of the forensic teams. They might have left the door unlocked, and Rachel wouldn't like that. He pushed casually on the handle, expecting the usual resistance. It swung under his hand.

The light switch was immediately to his right. He flicked it on. A narrow corridor led into the workroom, formed by row after row of two-story racks jammed with over twenty thousand costumes. It was growing dark outside, and the room was wreathed in shadows.

Ben stepped inside as the heavy black fire door banged shut behind him. He gasped in shock.

'Fucking hell,' he said loudly.

The floor was strewn knee-deep with clothes. In the corridor and the access spaces between the racks, costumes, apparently chosen at random, had been pulled off their hangers and dumped on the ground. Ben climbed carefully over the piles, hanging onto the wall as his feet twisted in the uneven piles of fabric.

When he reached the workspace, the damage was worse. Rachel was a meticulous woman. She always left the place immaculate at the end of her day. Only the costumes she was working on for the current show should be hanging on a rail near the sewing machines.

Costumes had been pulled from the adjacent racks and thrown around. Some had been ripped apart. Hats and bonnets that usually hung on hooks above the window in a curious display had been smashed, crushed and thrown about. Boxes of fake jewellery had been scattered around in multi-coloured anarchy, beads rolling free. Jars of buttons and fancy fastenings lay smashed in the sink. Packets of fabric die had been ripped open, their contents thrown at the wall or on top of the piles. The only things that seemed to have escaped were the machines themselves.

Ben struggled back to the door. Had the forensic team actually been in here? Did they not understand that it shouldn't be like that? Had anyone even asked? Not for one moment did Ben believe that Rachel had left it like that. Someone else had deliberately done this. He wrenched open the black door and stumbled down the stairs.

'Lindie! Lindie! Call the police again. They need to see this. Someone has trashed wardrobe.'

CHAPTER 23

Although she hadn't been back in the office for long, it was almost dark when the phone rang on her desk, and reception put Lindie Howes through to Sara.

'We thought you ought to come and see this,' said the Rosegarden's office manager.

'How was it missed?' Sara asked crossly.

'Our wardrobe mistress always locks it when she goes home,' said Lindie sheepishly. 'It didn't look any different to normal, so we just sort of, well, assumed it was locked up as usual.'

'But it wasn't?'

Sara looked up to find Mike Bowen watching her. She raised her hand in a gesture of aggravation.

'It would appear it wasn't,' agreed Lindie. 'I've rung Rachel, and she's on her way in.'

'All right,' sighed Sara. 'We'll be there soon.'

'The theatre?' asked Bowen, as she put down the phone. He was already pulling on his suit jacket.

Sara nodded. 'Did anyone mention the wardrobe to you?' Sara reached for her bag to stuff her mobile in, extracting her car keys, ready to leave. 'Do you remember when that woman took us on our tour of the place when we were still looking for Carole? Did we see it then? You're free to come with me, I take it.'

Bowen nodded and followed her out of the building. As Sara drove them towards the A11, he suddenly perked up. 'I think I do remember it. Wasn't it at the top of the stairs near the gallery door?'

Sara concentrated on the traffic as she sped towards Norwich. 'Not sure.'

'Black door on the left. I think Lindie said that was the wardrobe. Assured me it was always locked unless the wardrobe mistress was working.'

With a grunt, Sara drove on. They found a parking space in the multi-storey across the road from the theatre. They heard voices raised in the graveyard above them as they walked up the alley. Bowen rolled his eyes.

'Sounds like they're falling out,' he said, nodding at the tent city. 'Sooner they get moved on, the better for the city, I should imagine.'

Sara didn't comment. The courtyard outside the theatre was in darkness. Inside the building, lights shone from the bar and office. As they climbed the entrance steps, Sara saw Lindie Howes watching for them from the office window. She hurried to the front door to let them in.

'It's this way,' she said, locking the door behind them.

Bowen had been right. They reached the wardrobe at the top of the gallery staircase. The black door was hooked open, as was an internal bare wooden one. Bowen checked them as they passed, and neither seemed to have been forced.

The room beyond was unlike anything Sara had ever seen before. Double sets of racks, one at ground level and a second above which reached the ceiling, ran along one side of the room. They were absolutely rammed with costumes, each rack labelled with a historical period or individual type of garment. *Dress Shirts* vied with *Elizabethan*; *Restoration* hung above *WW1 Uniforms*. The floor was littered with piles of random costumes reaching almost as high as Sara's knee. There was a peculiar and unfamiliar smell in the air.

Pushing through the debris, they reached a work area with a large cutting-out table and two industrial sewing machines. The damage here was much worse. A woman stood leaning against a washing machine by the far wall. Her hands covered her cheeks in horror as she surveyed the mess. Her dark green velvet jacket complemented her Titian red hair, which was scooped up into a bun. Ben Marsden stood next to her, resting a hand on her shoulder.

'How could they? It's so spiteful,' she breathed when Sara and Bowen produced their warrant cards. 'Look at this. It will take weeks to sort it out. Look at the fabric dye.' She pointed at a delicate cream-coloured lace blouse dumped on the worktable. A pile of bright-red dye powder lay in the folds of the fabric. 'That was an original. Edwardian.'

'We'll help you sort it out,' Ben assured the shaking woman. 'Even if we can't rescue all the costumes.'

The woman nodded and held out her hand to Sara when she introduced herself and Bowen. 'I'm Rachel Clayton, the wardrobe mistress.'

'I take it you didn't leave the place like this?' asked Sara, just to be clear. 'When were you last in here?'

'Of course I didn't,' said Rachel sharply. She rubbed her face with one hand as if to clear her emotions from it. 'I only work three days a week. My assistant and I were last in here on Wednesday. I stayed to the start of rehearsal to do a fitting for one of the actors.'

'Are you sure you locked it up when you left?'

'Absolutely.' Rachel nodded vehemently. 'I have to be really careful about it. Some of this stuff is valuable. No one comes in here unless Eileen or myself are here.'

'Run us through the evening, will you?' asked Bowen. He was scribbling in his notepad.

Rachel nodded. 'Wednesday is one of my regular days. Eileen is a volunteer, but she's here most days with me. She loves sewing and enjoys being here. We fitted a couple of people in the afternoon, and Eileen went for her bus at about four o'clock. I stayed on to see Chris at half past six.'

'Chris?' asked Sara. She glanced at Bowen.

'Chris Webster,' said Rachel. 'He's playing Edmund. He came in on his way to rehearsal.'

'After that?' asked Bowen.

'I locked up and went home. It would have been just before seven. Everything was in order when I left.' Rachel's voice was tight with emotion.

'You don't work on Thursday?' confirmed Bowen. 'Monday, Wednesday and Friday?' Rachel nodded. 'So, no one should have been in here all day Thursday.'

'That's right,' agreed Ben. He looked embarrassed. 'I assumed the door was locked when I walked around up here after rehearsal.'

'Wednesday evening?' asked Bowen. 'Before you left Carole to lock up?'

Marsden nodded, a glum look on his face. 'We were shut out after that for your people to do their work.'

'Who has keys to the room?' asked Sara. The strange smell was beginning to get to the back of her throat and she coughed. 'And what is that smell?'

Rachel thought momentarily. 'Ah, that would be the pest treatment. We have it done every year, or we lose endless costumes to clothes moths. Little buggers eat holes in everything, especially silk or wool. We had it done a couple of weeks ago. I just get used to it, I suppose.'

'And the keys?'

'There are three sets for wardrobe,' put in Marsden. 'Rachel has one, obviously. There is a complete set for the whole building locked up in my office.'

'The third set is in the key cupboard in the office,' added Rachel. She pulled a set of keys from her jacket pocket. 'These are mine.'

'Have you checked the other sets?' asked Bowen.

'Not yet,' Marsden shook his head.

'Tell me,' said Sara cautiously. 'Would you have monks' habits among your stock?'

'Yes,' replied Rachel. She frowned in confusion. 'Why?'

'Would you know if any were missing?'

The wardrobe mistress nodded and eased herself through the piles of clothes towards the long side wall. The double-height racks of costumes also ran the full length of the wall, divided into sections with more labels. Sara followed her, climbing over the piles until Rachel stopped by a stepladder with a standing platform at the top. She turned to look at Sara.

'This wasn't here when I went home.'

'Are you certain?'

'Yes. I'd left it over in the Elizabethan racks down there.' She waved at some costume rails further along. 'The religious stuff is up there.'

Sara looked up at the top rail. Monks' and nuns' habits were jammed closely together, along with purple bishops' robes and vicars' shirts. Next to the ladder, several brown and black wool monks' habits had been dragged out from the rack.

'Can you tell me if anything is missing from this area?' Sara pointed at the rail of habits.

Rachel gazed for a moment at the chaos. Sara watched her eyes flick along the garments as she counted. When she was sure, Rachel turned to look at Sara. 'Two black wool monks' habits. Definitely.'

'I'm going to need Forensics up here,' Sara called back to Bowen.

CHAPTER 24

Nafisa took Zach back to the Wizard's Lounge coffee shop. When she appeared at the counter to order drinks, Ross was hovering at the door to the kitchen. She suspected that he had been waiting for her.

'You outside again?' he asked defensively. It wasn't a good start. She nodded, and he spoke quickly to the young woman behind the counter. 'Make those drinks to go and take them out for me.'

Nafisa shrugged and returned to where Zach was waiting for her. 'I don't think your army chum is pleased with our custom.'

'I didn't think he would be,' he grimaced. 'It's been too long. Now I'm muscling in, expecting favours.'

'Hardly!' exclaimed Nafisa. 'We didn't know he worked here when I brought you for coffee, did we?'

She barely had time to sit at the outdoor table before the shop door banged open. The young woman barista plonked a brown paper bag on the table.

'Ross says you've got to take these away.' Her nose wrinkled in disgust at the sight and smell of the homeless veteran. Even so, she pointed inside the bag and hissed, 'I put a couple of cakes in there for you. No charge.'

Charitable feelings assuaged, the barista headed back to the shop, holding the door open for her boss as he stalked out carrying a small box. Nafisa watched as Zach went rigid with tension at the old friend's approach. Sweat began to pop on his face, and he ground his teeth. Ross dumped the box on the table.

'You can't stay here,' he said briskly. 'It's bad for business. Here's some more food. Take it and don't come back.'

'You seemed like a kind person yesterday,' said Nafisa. She stood up and began to load her bags onto her shoulders. Ross turned on her angrily.

'Mind your own business. I'm just doing my job.'

'So am I,' she replied. Digging in her purse, she found a £5 note. 'Here. For the coffee. Then you can't say we stole them.'

'Did I say that?' demanded Ross. 'I can't have you bringing clients here begging like this.'

'Or what?' asked Zach. He rose slowly, gathering his bulk, looking ready to spring. 'You offered to help if we came back.'

'I have,' snarled Ross. 'I can't again. You're not welcome here.'

'Some friend you turned out to be.' Zach's voice had dropped an octave, and his face twisted in anger. Ross stepped forward, grabbing Zach's arm.

'Look. Just piss off, why don't you? I can—'

He pulled sharply, and Zach staggered to one side into the path of a passing pedestrian. The woman cried out in alarm. She raised her arms defensively, her hand swinging a laden carrier bag up in surprise. It caught Zach on the back with a thump. Caught between his friend manhandling him and the shocked woman, Zach began to wave his arms in panic, swatting at the people who seemed to be attacking him. Nafisa dropped all her bags. She rushed between Zach and the pedestrian, grabbing the woman's bag before the contents could escape.

'Sorry, so sorry,' she babbled. The woman retreated backwards, unable to take her eyes off Zach. Nafisa tried to guide her away. 'He's not well. Let me help you.'

'Punished!' Zach was talking loudly now. His arms were flailing, his fists starting to bang against his upper arms. His right arm swung out violently, catching Ross under the chin. The coffee shop manager staggered backwards, clutching his jaw. 'Punished. You deserve to be punished. Hurting people like that. You know what you did.'

Now, his fists were connecting with his own head. He battered himself remorselessly until Nafisa thought he must be doing brain damage because his head was rattling so much. With a cry, he fell to his knees and began to bash his forehead onto the pavement.

'Stop him!' screamed Nafisa to Ross. 'I can't.'

As she hustled the pedestrian back along the pavement, Nafisa heard a scuffle and grunting noises behind her. Unable to bear it, she turned to look. Ross had pulled Zach's arms behind his back and was holding him still by force, one arm pinning the flailing arms, the other across Zach's chest just below his throat. Zach's violent rocking suddenly subsided, and his whole body went floppy.

'My God!' breathed the woman. 'What's the matter with him?'

'I can't say.' Nafisa wished she could. The pedestrian deserved an explanation. Nafisa's heart was pounding with shock. The woman looked in her fifties to Nafisa, who worried she might be injured. 'I'm really sorry you got involved in that. Are you all right? Are you hurt?'

The woman watched round-eyed as Ross slowly released his grip on Zach. Panting with the effort, he helped Zach to his feet. The homeless man's coat fell open, revealing his military fatigues underneath. The woman winced.

'Oh, I see. Forces stuff, is it?'

'I'm afraid so.'

The woman straightened her coat, pulled her bobble hat back into place and checked her bags with Nafisa's help. 'Nothing missing.'

'Are you well enough to carry on?'

'Bit shocked, that's all,' replied the woman. She eyed Zach and Ross nervously. 'They shouldn't be allowed out if they're that sick.'

Then, gathering her dignity as best she could, the woman walked away with a nervous glance over her shoulder.

Drawing a deep breath to calm herself, Nafisa hurried back to the panting Zach. Ross was still holding him firmly by one arm. Zach's eyes had a far-away look as he glanced around, not seeming to recognise where he was or who these two people standing by him were.

'Thank you for stopping him,' said Nafisa as she gathered her bags up again.

'Does he often go off like this?' asked Ross quietly.

'I'm afraid I don't know. I've never seen him like it before. Do you know what happened to him back then?'

Ross shook his head. 'I'd already been shipped home when it happened. He was out on patrol.'

'IED, I understand?'

'I believe so. He spent a lot of time in the hospital when he came back. I left soon after that, and we lost touch. I've not seen Zach for years, as you gathered yesterday.'

'But you were good mates once?' Nafisa noticed that Ross had the grace to look ashamed. 'Did you have to be so horrible to him today?'

'My boss,' said Ross. He glanced up at the second floor of the building which housed the café. Nafisa saw a dark shape in a window up there, which moved back as she watched. 'Said he didn't want homeless people hanging around. It was bad for business. Told me to make sure I got rid of him if he returned.'

'He realised you knew Zach?'

'Yup.' Ross dropped Zach's arm as his friend seemed to have stopped swaying. 'Said he'd sack me if I kept giving away food, and I can't afford to lose my job. I'm sorry I was so aggressive. I didn't realise he was so bad.'

'Neither did I,' said Nafisa honestly. 'I'm assuming it was a flashback. I ought to get him into somewhere. Hospital? Maybe I should ring for an ambulance?'

'No!' croaked Zach. 'No hospital.'

He spun around, pushed past Ross and ran down the alley.

CHAPTER 25

DC Bowen accompanied Ben to check on the keys. Lindie was hovering in the office. She explained the system for the building keys before unlocking the key cabinet. Each hook was labelled and colour-coded, as was every key on every hook. The wardrobe set had a small purple plastic label. It was still in place, and the cabinet had not been forced open.

'This is a complete master set for the building,' she explained. 'The key to this is locked in the safe.' She patted a large, old-fashioned dark green lump of steel, which would obviously take machinery to move. Lindie continued. 'Some people have different sets according to where they need to go. Staff all have sets like that.'

'You mentioned that Carole Morgan offered to lock up for you,' said Bowen, turning to Ben. 'How would she do that?'

'We have some other keyholders,' explained Ben. He pointed to a combined burglar and fire alarm panel with winking red lights. 'If we have an emergency during the night, they're the people deemed trustworthy and who live close enough to come and open up the building if necessary. They would know the alarm codes as well.'

'There's a list held by the Police and Fire Services,' added Lindie. 'I live out in Long Stratton, so I'm low on the call-out list because it's a half-hour drive for me.'

'And you?' Bowen was watching Ben closely.

'I'm about fifteen minutes away, in Sprowston. I'm in the middle of the list.'

'And was Mrs Morgan on it?'

Both Lindie and Ben nodded in unison.

'She was at the top of the list,' said Ben hurriedly. 'Because she lives just up the road.'

'A sixty-eight-year-old lady was the emergency services first port of call?' asked Bowen.

'When you put it like that —' Ben stumbled over his words — 'I suppose it's not ideal.'

'I assume Mrs Morgan had her set to lock up that night?'

'Yes,' rushed on Ben. 'She always had them in that big bag of hers. She called it her portable theatre office.'

'You saw it that night?'

'And the keys. I wouldn't have left if I wasn't sure she had some with her.'

'Only, we haven't managed to find the bag,' admitted Bowen. 'Would you recognise it if it was stashed in the place somewhere?'

'Of course,' said Lindie. 'She always had it with her. Brown leather, with a long flap and a buckle fastening. A man's courier bag. Would you like us to search for it?'

'We might,' Bowen sounded cautious. 'Might have to do it ourselves. Didn't you say you had another complete set of keys?'

'In my office,' replied Ben. 'This way.'

The two rooms Ben called his office were actually props stores. He waggled the padlock which usually held the main door shut. 'There are only two keys to this. I have one, the other's in the key cupboard.'

'So, in theory, no can come in here if you aren't in the building? What about when you're on holiday?'

It would be nice to take proper holidays, thought Ben. *There's always too much to do.*

'I leave my keys in the office if I go away.'

He led Bowen through the first props store and into a smaller room beyond, which seemed even more crammed with random objects. It was poorly lit, and Ben flicked on his torch. Ducking down, he pushed aside a wooden rocking chair and dropped slowly to his knees. Behind it was an old Red Cross wooden cabinet that might have graced a World War One set. Or it would have if it had been undamaged. The front of the cabinet was smashed open as if someone had hit it several times with a hammer. Ben froze.

'What's the matter?' asked the detective, hovering in the doorway.

'The other emergency set is kept in here.' Ben pointed to the cabinet. 'But it's been broken into.'

'Don't touch anything,' snapped Bowen. 'Come out of the way.'

Ben heaved himself up as the detective stepped forward, pulling on nitrile gloves. Ben held out his torch, and the man grabbed it.

'This cabinet?' Bowen shone the torch at the broken door.

'There should be a large metal cash box inside,' said Ben quietly. 'Is it there? The cabinet wasn't broken like that last time I looked in here.'

'When was that?'

'About a week ago. I was getting some props out.'

'Did you check that the cash box was there?' asked Bowen.

'I'm afraid not. Is it there now?'

Bowen pulled the broken door aside with one finger and shone the torch inside the cupboard. The metal box was there, its lid standing open. Judging by the fresh damage to the lock area, it had clearly been forced with something like a screwdriver. Ben peered over the detective's shoulder to look.

'Oh my God!' There was a tangle of old keys with labels and strings in the box.

'Are these the ones?'

'No. Those are just old ones. There was a blue tray that fitted in the top. That had the master set of keys in it. It's missing.'

'We'll have to get Forensics to look at all this as well.' Bowen levered himself upright. 'Is anything else missing or damaged?' The pair looked around at the chaos of artefacts piled high on the floor and shelving. 'Though God knows how you would be able to tell.'

'I don't think so,' said Ben quietly. He knew where everything was, even if no one else did, and how could you store all this stuff any other way?

'Who knows you keep a master set in here?' asked Bowen. He had pulled out his mobile and was flipping through his number store.

'A few of the staff, like Lindie. Some of the Trust committee. Maybe ten people in total.'

'What about volunteer helpers or actors or these backstage tour people?' Bowen hustled Ben out of the storerooms. 'We should go back to the green room.'

'They shouldn't know anything about it.'

'Anyone who opened the box and took keys could let themselves in and out of the building at will or into wardrobe to get at the costumes?'

'I'm afraid so.'

'And they could have been doing that for up to seven days?'

Ben nodded glumly. *Naive*, he scolded himself. *You're too trusting. You didn't think it needed to be checked every day.*

Bowen frowned as he selected a number to call. Ben suddenly stopped in his tracks. He'd forgotten all about him. The detective paused.

'What? Have you thought of something?'

Ben hesitated, knowing he ought to tell the man, but didn't want to drop a good volunteer in the drink, even if they didn't get on too well.

'Come on. What is it?' Bowen demanded.

'It was a couple of weeks ago,' said Ben slowly. 'I needed a practise sword out for a stage combat session. They're all locked up in the big wooden box in the first storeroom.'

'Good to know they're locked up securely.' Bowen's voice oozed sarcasm. 'So?'

Ben brandished his bunch of keys. Like some old-fashioned jailer or manorial housekeeper set, at least thirty keys of various sizes hung in groups on secondary metal rings.

'Jesus,' said Bowen. 'You could lock up the Tower of London with that lot.'

'Right.' Ben selected a padlock key on a separate holder. 'This opens the weapons box, but I couldn't find it. Turns out it had dropped off in my work bag. I found it when I got home.'

'So?'

'The only other keys to that padlock are in the master cupboard or my secret stash. Lindie had gone home, and the director was hassling me. So, I went to the secret stash and got the key from there.'

'And the director went with you?'

'No. It wasn't him.' Ben felt himself flush with sweat. Even this genial detective could twist his words like the last one had tried to, but what choice did he have? 'It was the actor who needed the sword who saw what I did. It was Chris Webster.'

CHAPTER 26

'I just want to be clear about all these damn keys,' snapped DCI Hudson with an exasperated look on her face. She was leaning on the spare desk, her hands balled into fists and her arms locked straight. The marker pen in her right hand looked ready to pop out of her grip, it was squashed so tightly. 'There are hundreds of the things. Almost anyone could get access.'

'Not really,' said Bowen. He glanced at Sara for support. 'Each member of staff has a set appropriate to their work areas. There are seven of them.'

'It seems there are four lesser sets, which are held by trusted people in case of an emergency call-out,' added Sara. 'Carole Morgan was one of those. Then, there are two master sets. One in the locked key cupboard in the office and one hidden in the storeroom.'

'The one in the office is on the wall, easy to spot if it had been tampered with,' offered Bowen.

'It's the one inexpertly hidden in the props room that's been broken into?' confirmed Hudson.

Bowen nodded. 'But the padlock to the door of the room hasn't been tampered with.'

'So, someone stole the keys from a hidden box through a padlocked door that hasn't been forced. They've used them to access the wardrobe area and steal a monk's habit, trash the place and leave that door open. Then used others, presumably to access the building, to attack Carole Morgan and lay out her body under the stage. After which, they shut the trap door, let themselves out and locked up the building.'

'They even set the burglar alarm,' added Sara. 'Lindie Howes was the first one in that morning, and she's adamant that she had to turn it off as usual.'

There was a stunned silence. Each officer turned the idea over in their minds. It seemed ridiculous.

'Whoever it was certainly knew the place really well,' said Hudson. 'How are we doing with those lists, Aggie?'

'I have a staff list,' replied Aggie. 'The remarkable thing is that they've all been there for years. Even the part-time cleaner has worked there for over five years.'

'And the people who might have acted with Carole?'

'Potentially hundreds of them,' sighed Aggie. 'She's been there for more than thirty-five years. Some she would know well, and some might only have done one or two shows before moving on. They don't even have to be a member to act there or help backstage, so not everyone would be in the records.'

Hudson screwed up her face in exasperation. 'So that's a dead end. We need to interview the rest of the staff and everyone at rehearsal that night. Aggie, you can set that up. How many people knew where this box was kept?'

'Only a handful, according to Ben Marsden,' replied Bowen. He looked sheepishly at his notebook before carrying on. 'He claims that Chris Webster may have seen it accidentally a couple of weeks ago.'

'My ex, Chris?' asked Sara carefully. Bowen nodded.

'We'll need to be careful with that interview, then,' said Hudson. She turned to the whiteboard and wrote *KEYS!* 'Let's track down all the sets and check they're with the people they should be with. What about Mrs Morgan's bag? We still need to find it, although it might not be so important if the murdering monk has acquired a set of master keys.'

'It's still missing,' said Sara. 'Forensics haven't mentioned it either at her home or in the theatre. We could search again now we've got a description.'

'Bowen, Noble,' sighed Hudson, 'you two pick that up. We're missing the bag, with one set of keys, and, I assume, the master set from the metal box?' Sara nodded in confirmation. Hudson moved on. 'CCTV, DC Noble?'

'There's none in Church Alley and none at the theatre,' said DC Noble apologetically, as if it were his fault. 'Not even the Drugs Team have anything covert that would be helpful. The council have cameras on Pottergate, as we know, and there are traffic cameras on the lights at Charing Cross, below the theatre.'

'Leaving a blind spot around the alley and the venue?'

'I'm afraid so,' agreed Noble. 'Using the council cameras on Pottergate, I've tracked Carole Morgan going to the theatre at about half past six. No sign of her after that.'

'Monks?'

'Four.' Noble smiled shyly. 'The ghost walk actor shows up twice, more or less when you would expect from the tour times. He's already changed into the habit before he comes along Pottergate. He's in a hurry and carrying a sports bag, which I assume contains his costume changes.'

'The others?'

'One person in a party group,' said Noble, waving at his computer screen. Sara moved over to have a look. Hemmed in by Hudson, Edwards and Bowen, she watched the grainy picture. It was dark and indistinct despite the street lighting. Noble clicked on it with his mouse, and the picture started to move. A group of nine people, all in Halloween costumes led by a zombie and including a monk with dark stains down his front, wobbled and joshed their way along the street and out of shot. It looked like a scene from a rather knowing horror film franchise. Sara didn't like movies like that.

'Some kind of birthday party?' suggested Edwards. It would be hard to get a decent image of anyone in the group with their costumes and make-up. 'Our perp could have insinuated himself with them to get away.'

'Timing wouldn't work very well,' said Noble, pointing at the time stamp in the corner. 'This one's more interesting.'

He opened another tab with a different section of the video. The restaurant on the corner was in darkness. The timestamp read 00:46. A couple staggered and wove their way into view along Pottergate.

The taller figure was wearing a monk's habit, the cowl raised to hide his face. They danced a few yards, the monk lifting the hem of the habit as he did so. A shorter figure with long dirty dreads, dressed in jeans and a torn anorak, wobbled after him. It was clearly a young female, as the anorak was swinging open to show a tight, revealing t-shirt and emaciated body. The woman was laughing at the monk's antics and shouted something. The monk turned around, wiggling and flapping the habit. Whatever he said, the woman screamed with laughter, doubling up for a moment and leaning on the spikey metal railings that surrounded the church. The monk figure said something else, which the woman didn't like so much. Suddenly, she stood upright and swung something at him. The object hit the monk on the shoulder, which he grabbed at in protest. The costume's hood fell as a short struggle ensued until the monk let go, and the woman staggered back against the railings, bumping her head. Suddenly, the monk was beside her, helping her up and offering an apologetic hug. The object lay on the pavement beside her.

'Can you zoom in on that?' asked Hudson. Noble clicked on the screen. 'Man's courier bag, with a long strap and fold-over flap?'

'Probably made of leather,' said Edwards. Noble zoomed in again.

'With a buckle fastening,' added Sara. 'Carole Morgan's bag?'

'And our perpetrator's costume?' suggested Edwards.

Noble set the image moving again. The couple appeared to make things up. The monk wound his arm around the woman's shoulder. She darted free before he could lead her away and grabbed the bag. Then she ran to hug him, and they moved away. At the end of the church, the entwined couple turned down Church Alley into the camera's blind spot.

'You know where I think they're going?' asked Sara. The others looked at her. 'How about the homeless group with their tents pitched in the church graveyard?'

CHAPTER 27

Nafisa and Ross had only hesitated for a few seconds, but by the time they raced down St Gregorys Alley to St Benedicts Street, Zach had vanished into the evening. She knew there were numerous side alleys and old courtyards, not least because the layout dated back to medieval times. The area was a warren. Nafisa had been to a party once in one of the old houses, squashed between a shop and a restaurant, with a tiny alley on each side to reach the rear of the properties. The place had effectively been one room wide, two rooms deep and four stories tall, including a cellar. To escape pursuit, Zach only needed to duck under an archway between the shops or run down the St Lawrence Steps, and they wouldn't be able to see him.

'I'm sorry,' said Ross. 'I didn't handle that well. But my boss, you know . . .'

'Doesn't sound like a very nice person, if I'm honest,' said Nafisa sharply. When Ross shrugged his shoulders despondently, she carried on. 'I'm guessing it isn't always easy to find work when you come out of the forces.'

'In your job, you must hear lots of stories about people coming out of prison and falling back into crime because they can't get an ordinary job?' asked Ross sourly. 'Well, coming out of the forces is a bit like that. At least it was for me.'

'Were you injured as well?'

'I got shot.' The café manager rubbed the side of his thigh. 'I was lucky, though. It wasn't a life-changing disability like so many have. Spent a few weeks in the hospital being patched up, then got put on desk duties until my term ran out. Couldn't wait to leave after that.'

'What brought you to Norwich?'

'My family still live here,' said Ross. His shoulders were hunched forward in defeat. 'I didn't get a trade when I was in there, and it took me a long time to adjust to normality. Couldn't get any sort of job.'

Nafisa looked at his toned physique in surprise. He was obviously also very bright. 'What did you do?'

'One of the chain coffee shops gave me a break. Some part-time hours. They trained me as a barista, and I've worked my way up. Trouble is, there are always a dozen people waiting to take your job from you and the owners all know it.'

'It sounds really tough.' Nafisa sighed and looked along the street. 'We can hardly go searching for him. You'd better get back.'

The young woman in the café had stored Nafisa's bags and laptop behind the counter. 'You never know who might walk past.'

Nafisa thanked her before heading for Castle Meadow and her bus home. To her, it seemed such a small incident that had sparked Zach's crisis. By the time she got off at her bus stop, she had already begun to trawl through the internet for information on PTSD.

* * *

It took hours to drill down the rabbit hole to real medical information on the condition, but when she left the house again on Saturday morning, Nafisa felt she was much better informed. Theoretically, she was going into town to meet her friend for lunch. In practice, she was a couple of hours early and fully intended to visit the tent city as her first port of call. It was Halloween today. The city buzzed with children's excitement at the promise of dressing up and too many sweet treats.

As she climbed the steps into the graveyard, the only sign of life around the encampment was the woman called Kells and the heavy sound of snoring from one of the tents. At first, Nafisa thought Kells was heading for the tree below Zach's tent to urinate until she heard the woman retching. Nafisa's stomach clenched with revulsion. After a couple of noisy minutes, Kells staggered back towards her tent.

'You okay now?' called Nafisa. She wasn't going to get too close to the vomit that stained the front of Kells's dirty hoodie. The woman looked up in an unfocused way.

'Oh, it's you,' she said disappointedly. 'If you've come for your money back, it's too late. I spent it.'

'What on?'

'Never mind, nosey bitch,' snapped Kells. 'Don't you judge me.'

Nafisa held up her hands, trying to placate the woman. 'I'm not trying to. I don't want my money back, thanks. I just came to see if Zach was here.'

'You got a thing for 'im, ain't ya?' Kells's face swung from suspicion to amusement with lightning speed. 'Fancy 'im, don't ya?'

'Not my type,' said Nafisa. Kells took several uneven steps forward. Nafisa knew she had to stand her ground or she would look vulnerable. Just for once, she wished that Russell was with her. He might be of little practical use, but at least she wouldn't be alone. 'Did you see him last night?'

'Nope.'

Kells dropped to one knee at the edge of the bonfire. She scrubbed around with her hands until she found a vodka bottle caught up in the trampled grass. Shaking it, she peered at the inside with bleary eyes. Roughly unscrewing the top, she drained the last few drops onto her extended tongue. When no more trickled down the neck, she shook the bottle again before throwing it heavily in Nafisa's direction. Her aim was bad, and there was no strength in the woman's arm. It fell into the ashes of the bonfire with a dusty thump.

'Fuck it. None left,' moaned Kells. She struggled back to her feet. 'What you waiting for?'

'I want to make sure Zach is all right,' said Nafisa cautiously.

'What's it worth?'

'Sorry?'

'This info? What's it worth?'

Nafisa was nonplussed. Even if the information was worth anything, she could hardly risk giving the woman more money for drink. If work found out, she'd be in deep trouble. She shook her head. 'I'm just worried about him.'

'Fuckin' do-gooders,' mumbled Kells, looking away. 'No use to anybody. And he said he would have some more good shit tonight.'

The woman began to retch again. Nafisa fumbled in her bag for a bottle of water. 'You want this?'

Kells looked at it uncertainly, then tottered around the bonfire and grabbed the bottle. Twisting the plastic top open, she took a long pull. 'Thanks, man.'

'Who said they'd have some more stuff tonight?' asked Nafisa, hopeful for a moment, although it wouldn't be good if Zach had turned to dealing to survive. That could screw everything up. She wasn't prepared for the reply.

'The monk,' said Kells. She swigged more water, then gave Nafisa a calculating look. 'Why, you want something?'

CHAPTER 28

Halloween was on Sara's mind as she darted across the road from the car park to the Rosegarden early on Saturday morning. As she was hoping to be at home this evening and there were several families with young children in Happisburgh, she wondered whether she should lay in a stock of mini-chocolate bars and a pumpkin. At least, one of those plastic ones, as there wouldn't be time to carve out a real one. She'd probably end up eating the chocolate herself if she bothered. With a shake of her head, she hurried up the front stairs to the theatre to try and concentrate on more serious matters. They were due to interview lots of people this morning, and she hoped to visit tent city later to confirm who had been wearing the monk's habit on the CCTV and where the bag was.

Lindie Howes was waiting for her in the lobby. 'The box office is open this morning, so I've set you up in the rehearsal room. I can bring people through as and when.'

In her usual efficient way, Aggie had spent much of Friday telephoning the cast members to ask them to give voluntary statements this morning. Lindie had a clipboard with a list of attendees and a pen.

'Was anyone unable to come in?' asked Sara.

'I'm pleased to say that everyone has agreed to help,' said Lindie proudly, checking the names. 'We all want to do what we can to find Carole's killer.'

There was something about the way she said it that made Sara take a mental step back. This was a murder case to the team. To the Norwich Players and theatre workers, their special place had been violated. It was a safe space that was no longer safe, and Carole was one of their own.

DC Bowen was waiting for her in the small studio which served as the theatre's rehearsal room. A table and chairs had been put out for them. Bowen was setting up a laptop to type electronic statements if people were willing to sign them.

'Morning,' he mumbled as he fiddled with the cable. 'Won't be long. Lindie says she's put the coffee machine on for us, just help yourself. The director's already here.'

They began with Glyn Hollis, who they had met before. Between his worries about the production being cancelled and his complaints about the disruptions, they managed to find out that he had worked with Carole several times and had nothing bad to say about her. As the morning wore on, it became clear that no one had anything bad to say about her. She was a trojan who worked tirelessly for the place. She was a dedicated, first-rate organiser who encouraged youngsters to join the venue. She was a great amateur actor with a real sense of authority.

'Turns out Carole was a real paragon,' said Bowen sarcastically as another of the actors left the rehearsal room. Sara gave him a weary glance before checking the list.

'People never want to speak ill of the dead,' she said. 'No matter what they thought of them in life. Bugger. Chris is next on the list.'

'Let's keep it simple,' suggested Bowen.

'What about the information we have on him?' asked Sara.

'Keep it in reserve to start with. You want me to lead?'

'Yes, please.'

Sara hadn't seen Chris for some time. They had lived in adjacent flats when she'd first arrived in the city, and things went from there. But their relationship had faltered after a while, as they sometimes do. Sara moving all the way out to Happisburgh hadn't helped. His loyalty to the Rosegarden had also been a factor. It was something she had never really understood.

He didn't look very different than she remembered when Lindie brought him in. His beard was fuller, and his hair had grown longer, but it had always varied according to which play he was in at the time. He was still handsome in her eyes, and he still had the muscular, trim figure with its barely contained lupine energy that she'd once found sexy. In fact, lots of women seemed to find him handsome and sexy. That had been the problem.

Both looked at each other warily until Bowen invited Chris to sit down. After he'd explained what they wanted, Chris settled in the chair, clearly prepared to be helpful. The usual eulogy about Carole followed. The woman was a saint if this lot were to be believed.

'What time did you leave the theatre?' asked Bowen. Suddenly, Chris looked uneasy. 'The director tells us that people were allowed to go when they had finished their scenes.'

'Well, no, I didn't go straight away,' admitted Chris. He glanced at Sara briefly, then turned back to Bowen. 'I waited.'

'Was there a particular reason that you stayed?'

'Sometimes I like to watch the other people rehearsing,' replied Chris. It was clearly an evasion.

'And that's why you stayed on that night?'

Chris looked embarrassed. 'Sort of.'

'Would you be able to expand on that?' pushed Bowen. 'We believe you waited in the gents' dressing room. Can't watch rehearsals from there, can you?'

Chris blinked at him. 'A camera on the balcony replays a live image to a television up there. So you can keep track of the show.'

Sara cleared her throat. 'Look, if you were waiting for someone, it's all right to say so. It's not going to be a problem to me.'

'Ah. Good,' Chris mumbled. 'I was waiting for Simone.'

Both Sara and Bowen checked their lists. Sara wanted to feel surprised, although she knew he had often made conquests or had girlfriends among the casts he acted with. Simone was playing King Lear. Wouldn't that make her a lot older than Chris? Wasn't the character supposed to be old? She pursed her lips to hold back the flippant comment that wanted to burst out.

'How long did you wait?'

Glyn Hollis's schedule indicated that Chris could have left about nine o'clock. They knew that the rehearsal had ended at ten fifteen. So, Chris had sat up there for at least an hour. Plenty of time to find the key box, break into the wardrobe, steal costumes and trash the place.

'Erm, it was quite a while,' he said.

'Was anyone with you? Could they give us times? Or did someone see you in the green room, perhaps?'

'No one. Just me. It was quiet.'

'It's just that it seems someone got into the wardrobe that night and vandalised it,' said Bowen carefully. Chris jerked upright, obviously surprised. 'Did you know that?'

'Not at all,' said Chris defensively. 'Why would they do that?'

'We can't tell you,' said Sara, suddenly overriding Bowen. 'My problem is this. The wardrobe was locked up. Whoever got in knew where to find the keys. We've been told you know where there's a spare set.'

'That would be Ben Marsden, no doubt,' snapped Chris. 'He screwed up a couple of weeks ago for the photo shoot, and I caught him getting a set out of his props room.'

'Screwed up is a harsh term, isn't it? He just needed access to the weapons box, didn't he?'

'He's always cocking stuff up. The way people go on about him, you'd think he was irreplaceable. But he's not as good as he thinks he is.'

'Most people here seem to be verging on sainthood,' replied Sara. 'Take Carole, for example.'

'She's done more for this place than Marsden ever has,' snapped Chris. 'Besides, he never liked her.'

'Ben Marsden didn't like Carole Morgan?' Bowen broke in.

'Well, he wouldn't, would he? They had a serious falling out a few years ago, and they've barely been on speaking terms ever since.'

CHAPTER 29

Ben didn't know what to make of the phone call requesting him to attend Bethel Street Police Station to make a formal statement. It sounded far too official for his liking. He'd been at home, attempting to clear up the kitchen, which needed it after several days of neglect. It was, technically, his day off as he had to work on Sunday this week, assuming that the show was still going ahead. The Trust had met to decide, but, as usual, no one had bothered to tell him what was happening. Ben knew that the police were interviewing cast members at the theatre that morning and was surprised they wanted to speak to him elsewhere. He abandoned the cleaning and headed into the city.

The entrance to the police station was on one side of Norwich City Hall. Ben had never been there before, although he knew where it was, like most locals. They didn't keep him waiting long at reception. DC Bowen appeared through a lockable door to take him to an interview room. It made Ben uncomfortable to hear the door slap shut behind him.

'I'm going to record our conversation,' explained DS Hirst as he settled across the table from her. She waved at a recording machine on the table. 'We'd like to ask you some questions about what you've already told us.'

'Are you arresting me?' asked Ben jovially. 'Do I need to call a solicitor?'

He'd intended it as a joke. The detectives didn't seem to find it funny. Neither looked like they would crack a smile, which worried Ben even more.

'You can if you wish,' said Bowen in formal tones. 'We haven't charged you with anything, so it's classed as a voluntary interview. You should know that anything you say today can be used as evidence later if required.'

Ben felt a cold sweat break out on his back, matched by the feeling of dread in his stomach. Obviously, this was no longer him trying to help out. They suspected him of something. The atmosphere in the room was frigid. It was just like the last time, and he knew he had to be cautious. Did they hope to charge him? Did they think he'd killed Carole? Why would they think that? He racked his brains, unable to settle on the things he'd already said that might incriminate him. His overactive mind settled on television detective dramas. Like most people, he'd seen enough of them to know that he didn't have to answer questions if he didn't want to. He'd also seen enough true crime documentaries to suspect that the pair of them were capable of fitting him up. He shivered.

'Mr Marsden, would you like a solicitor present?' asked Hirst. Her tone was tense. Ben was unsure what to do. If he said yes, it made him seem guilty. If he said no, then was he being a fool?

'No,' he said, hoping he wouldn't regret it. 'I haven't done anything to be worried about.'

They hadn't offered him a drink, he noticed.

'The last time you saw Carole Morgan was when you left the theatre on Wednesday night?' asked Hirst. 'Did you see anyone who could vouch for you after that?'

'No, why would I need to?' Ben was beginning to panic. 'Look, I was parked in the multi-storey across the road. I've probably still got the receipt in my car. I just chuck them in the glove box in case I need to claim the cost. That would say what time I left.'

'No one at home?' persisted Hirst.

'No. But you'd be able to get me on the traffic cameras, wouldn't you? I can give you my route home.'

The two detectives shared a look.

'You told us about the monk in the yard as you left,' Bowen moved on. 'The wrong actor in the wrong place at the wrong time, you suggested.'

'So?' Ben shrugged.

'We only have your word for it that there was anyone else there,' said Hirst. Ben felt like he was watching a tennis match as his attention swung between the pair. Now, he was sure they were trying to catch him out.

'Chris and Simone left a couple of minutes ahead of me. They might have seen him.'

'Are you sure that the building was secure when you left?' Bowen again. They were deliberately trying to confuse him.

'Pretty much. Lindie had done a routine lock-up before she went home. The only access was through the stage door and the front door. I'd put the chain and padlock on the stage door before I spoke to Carole. We did the secondary routine checks and I dropped the latch on the front door as I left.'

'But, as we know, the spare keys from your hiding place could have been stolen by then. Whoever had them could easily have got in.'

'If you say so. I can't be sure when they went missing.'

'What did you think of Carole?' Hirst suddenly asked.

'Sorry?' asked Ben in surprise.

'It's a straightforward question,' said Hirst. She was watching him closely, and it made him even more panic-stricken. Obviously, someone had said something. Almost certainly Chris Webster. But what?

'She was a good actor,' he replied carefully.

'I meant on a personal level.'

'Erm, well . . .' Ben struggled to speak. 'Let's just say she wasn't everyone's cup of tea.'

'All the people we've spoken to this morning seemed to think she was the heart and soul of the theatre.'

'She liked to think so,' snapped Ben, then he bit his lip. Damn! He shouldn't let them rile him.

'She used to be head of children's social services, didn't she? Do you know much about her work?'

'Not really.'

'Used to being in charge? Could she be a bit bossy?'

'Some people thought so.'

'Did you think so, Mr Marsden?' asked Hirst softly. 'Was she bossy with you?'

Ben looked between them. It was hardly grounds for murder if he did think the woman had been bossy. 'No comment.'

'How long had you known her?' Bowen picked up the interrogation again.

'Ever since I started working there.'

'How long is that?'

'About fifteen years.'

'And Carole had been an active member all that time?'

This felt like slightly safer ground. 'She'd been less active since James became unwell.'

'Carole used to do more?'

'She was chair of the Trust for a couple of years,' said Ben. He opened his mouth to explain what that meant, but Hirst jumped back in before he could carry on.

'Then, technically, she was your boss. You worked for her.'

'It's not as simple as that. Technically, I work for the company. Every member is my boss.'

'And was that the time when you and she seriously fell out?' Hirst ignored his explanation.

Ben slammed his mouth shut. This had to be Webster. It was a time he didn't like to think about if he could help it. Now, it had obviously made him a suspect.

'Mr Marsden, why did you fall out? What did you fall out about? Did you hold a grudge against her for what happened then?'

'It was years ago. I don't want to talk about it, and if you insist, then I want that solicitor. I'm going home and you can't stop me.'

CHAPTER 30

Unwilling to be drawn in further, Nafisa refused Kells's offer of 'something' and left the graveyard as quickly as she could without looking rattled. She called at the Wizard's Lounge to check with Ross. He hadn't seen Zach since the previous evening.

'I did go for a walk after work,' he told her. 'Checked some of the backyards and alleys where people sometimes sleep rough. No luck, though.'

It would have been dark last night when Ross searched. If she went poking about in those places during the day, it could cause trouble. There were a couple of places that Ross might not know about; she had better try them.

The official night shelter was at the bottom of Westwick Street. Nafisa had previously spoken to the manager over the phone on behalf of clients. She was grateful he was on duty this morning and recalled her name. They checked the register, but there was no record of Zach. It had been the least likely option anyway. She suspected he would want to be alone, not in the often noisy shelter on a busy night.

She cut across the river at the bottom of New Mills Yard. You could walk either way along the riverside from here, and there were lots of little areas of garden or shed doors to shelter in. You could hide there for a few hours if you were frightened.

The night had been dry, if chilly. Survivable to a hardened street warrior like Zach, even without his blankets or tent. Riverside Walk ended after a few hundred yards if she turned left, so she turned right onto the longer part of the path. If you knew what you were doing, you could get all the way to the railway station on the far side of the cathedral on this route. All she could do was walk gently along, looking for signs of someone bedding down for the night in the side alleys or garden back gates. Winding past the Playhouse Theatre, she worked her way towards Fye Bridge. It had already taken her nearly an hour, and she would have to give up soon, or her friend would be waiting for her at the restaurant. On the opposite side of the river, she could see the backs of the Tudor buildings that lined Elm Hill.

Nafisa paused to look across the water to a small garden area behind several old houses without spotting anything. As she walked on, raised voices made her look again. Two men were having a heated argument. She felt sure that one of them sounded like her missing client. She began to run, her bag banging on her side, across the bridge and up Elm Hill. There was a small side alley between two buildings that led down to the river, and in the middle of the alley was Zach, with a smart young man in Lycra exercise clothes. He had Zach pinned up against the wall while the former army sergeant was trying to cover his face with his hands. The gist of Exercise Man's invective seemed to be that Zach had made a mess of the garden, and he had clients due. Nafisa hurried to join them.

'Can I help you at all?' she asked breathlessly. She waved her work pass card in its lanyard. 'Zach, are you all right?'

'You know this vagrant?' snapped Exercise Man.

'He's a client of mine,' she said.

The man grabbed her pass and read it. 'Then you should be keeping a better hold on him. He's been kipping down in the garden behind our canoe shed. There's shit all over the place.'

Nafisa didn't ask if he meant literally or just empty food and drink packaging. Zach mumbled something and hung his head.

'What's that? Speak up, you cretin.'

'That's enough now,' said Nafisa quietly. 'Let me take him. I can get him back to his belongings.'

'Be my guest,' snapped the man. He swung Zach around and pushed him heavily. Caught off balance, Zach flailed his arms as he crashed onto the cobblestones. 'Filthy bastard.'

Exercise Man stomped away down the garden, muttering curses. Nafisa let him get out of earshot before she bent down to help Zach get to his feet.

'I'm sorry.' His voice was muffled as he was staring at the floor. 'I'm not sure how I ended up here. I don't usually make a nuisance of myself like that.'

'I know,' sighed Nafisa. It was one of the reasons she wanted to help the man. Underneath all the issues, he was a decent human being. 'You had a PTSD episode last night.'

'How do you know?' Zach looked up in surprise.

'I saw you. I'm so sorry. We were trying to have a coffee at your chum's café. Then you ran off.'

Zach shook his head. 'I just don't remember.'

It was lucky, Nafisa realised, that he hadn't simply run out in front of a vehicle and been hurt. 'Do you know who I am?'

'Yes, I think so.' Zach crinkled his face in concentration. 'Nafisa. Muslim. Social worker. Coffee drinker.'

'And cake eater.' Nafisa smiled. She tugged at her headscarf to keep it straight, briefly wondering if his tours of duty were why her religion had been so high on his list. 'You got me in one.'

'How did you find me?'

'Sheer chance,' she said. 'Would it be better to get back to your tent? Would things be clearer there?'

'I guess.' Zach yawned widely. They walked in silence up Elm Hill. He didn't seem willing or able to go very quickly. 'Chance? Really? You must have been looking for me.'

'I suppose.' Nafisa glanced sideways at him.

'I'm grateful,' he said. They'd reached St Andrews Hall, and he looked at it with growing recognition. 'Kells, right?'

'The young woman at the tent city,' suggested Nafisa.

'You bought that bag from her,' he said more decisively. Zach looked at Nafisa with a frown. 'She spent the money on drugs, you know. I'm sorry.'

'And, at a guess, a large bottle of vodka. They made twenty quid go a long way.'

They walked faster along St Andrews Street to the traffic lights at the multi-storey car park. Zach seemed to know where he was going.

'It wasn't just your money,' he said as they waited for the crossing to change. 'They'd been emptying a purse earlier. I guess that might have been in the bag. I should have realised.'

'Most people don't carry much cash these days,' Nafisa pointed out.

'Cards are still worth a few quid in the right pub,' replied Zach. 'Phones too. They would have been waiting for the monk to come back.'

This must be the dealer Kells had mentioned. Dressed up for Halloween. Idiot. 'Come back?'

'He's been visiting the graveyard ever since we started camping there,' nodded Zach. 'He only started wearing that stupid bloody costume a few nights ago.'

CHAPTER 31

'It doesn't seem enough to warrant him murdering her now,' said Bowen to Sara as they headed back into the office. 'I had a quiet word with Lindie before we left the theatre. She said this all happened a couple of years ago. Claimed she had also been in the firing line. Some unidentified member had made allegations against both of them for different reasons. She told me nothing was proven, although it was difficult.'

'Carole was in charge of this Trust committee at the time?' asked Sara.

'She was, and apparently, both felt that she should have stopped it. They thought that it was just sour grapes over some casting or other. Our victim resigned from the committee shortly afterwards, because of her husband's health.'

'Chris definitely had it in for Ben Marsden, so why would that be? Is Chris hiding something, or is that also something to do with a part he didn't get?'

'Who knows?' replied Bowen as they climbed the stairs to their room. 'Marsden and Howes would have had opportunities to make life uncomfortable for Carole Morgan at any time, wouldn't you think? So why do something now?'

'Something else happened?' Sara dropped her car keys onto her desk and slumped into her chair. 'He felt under threat from her? How would we find out?'

'You could ask another committee member,' suggested Aggie. She was watching the coffee pot fill with a fresh brew. 'I have a list for all of them. There's coffee-and-walnut cake in the tin. I thought we all might need a treat as it's weekend working.'

'Expecting a visit from Dr Taylor?' asked Sara with a smile. It was his favourite flavour. Aggie blushed slightly.

'He'll be here soon. The post-mortem results are in, and he wants to go through them with us.'

The whole team had gathered by the time the pathologist arrived. Aggie put a slice of cake on a plate for him, blushing at his compliments. The rest had to manage with the usual paper napkin, even her husband. A plastic container with a gluten-free brownie waited on the spare desk for DCI Hudson and her allergy. These days, Aggie even brought in soya milk for the DCI. Sara suspected their admin liberated that from the canteen downstairs, but the cakes were always homemade.

'Before Dr Taylor gives us his report, what else have we learned today?' asked Hudson, levering the lid from the pot and scooping up the brownie.

Bowen and Sara detailed their interviews.

'Let's double-check if Marsden is under any threat,' said Hudson. 'Noble, give his socials a look, will you? Aggie, find a Trust member to ask. What else?'

'I've been checking the CCTV from the traffic lights and on St Benedicts Street from the evening of the attack,' said Noble. 'There isn't much to see once the ghost walk party go past until about half past twelve. Then a tall, thin male in black trousers and hoodie comes past the theatre and turns up Charing Cross.'

'And then?' asked Hudson.

'Nothing,' said Noble with a frown. 'There's another gap in the coverage there. The street cameras pick up at the bottom of St Benedicts Street, up St Gregorys Alley or down Westwick Street. He isn't on any of them. No time gaps and no missing footage. He just vanishes.'

There was a short silence. The team knew that Noble was unlikely to have made a mistake.

'Are there side streets? Any flats or houses?' asked Hudson.

'There's the Strangers' Hall Museum,' offered Bowen. 'The courtyard door would be locked at night, and it's solid, thick wood. No other way in from that road.'

'Yes,' said DI Edwards suddenly. 'There are three flats in an old warehouse conversion. Easy to overlook.'

Noble clicked on his keyboard. 'Street view. Double grey doors. Flush into the opening and to the pavement.'

Sara looked at the picture. Between the shop on the corner and the museum's windows, there was a cream wall with windows. Possibly an old merchant's house. 'I've walked down there hundreds of times and never noticed that place. You couldn't get in there easily, could you?'

'Not without a key,' agreed Edwards.

'Can we identify this man?' asked Hudson.

'Nope,' said Noble with a sigh. 'Hoodie's up, so you can't see his face.'

'Let's just bear the vanishing man in mind, then.' The DCI was anxious to move on. 'Dr Taylor, what have you got for us?'

'Not much that's helpful,' said the pathologist, wiping cake crumbs from around his mouth with his napkin. 'The official report and the forensic team's investigations should be in your emails. They're still working in the wardrobe, but it is used heavily, like everywhere else in the building. Unfortunately, I've had to make a few leaps of faith in my analysis.'

'What can Carole tell us?' asked Edwards.

'There's damage to the back of her head,' began Taylor. 'The skin on her shoulders and elbows was scraped raw. I'd suggest that she was knocked over and fell on her back.

Bashed her head as she landed. Forensics found blood and hair traces on the carpet near the door to the auditorium. I think it belongs to Carole, although it had been too contaminated by people unknowingly walking over it before we found her to be certain.'

'So, she was standing in the aisle, and someone pushed her backwards onto the floor?' confirmed Hudson.

'Indeed. The damage to the back of her head suggests she landed heavily. She would have been disorientated or possibly knocked out. Although I have found some traces under her fingernails.'

'Traces? Human?' asked Sara quickly.

'Unfortunately not,' replied Taylor. 'Tiny fragments of fibre. They've gone for full analysis to check for possible DNA, but it's unlikely.'

'What kind of fibre?' interrupted the DCI.

Taylor looked blandly at Hudson. 'I'm getting to that. Black, part wool, probably. I asked the wardrobe mistress to send me a sample of the other monk's habits, but I think it will prove to be from our so-called ghost monk's costume.'

'Was this blow enough to kill her?' asked Sara. 'Was it an accident?'

'No, it wasn't,' replied Taylor. 'There are marks on the insides of our victim's thighs and to her throat. The blood vessels in her throat have been ruptured, and her hyoid bone is fractured. Someone knocked her down, knelt on her legs to prevent her from moving and strangled her with their hands. She tried to resist briefly, hence the little bits of fibre.'

Sara heard Aggie stifle a sigh. Although she never liked to listen to the details of the deaths they investigated, Aggie always sat through these conversations, partly out of respect for the victim. Sara admired her for it. Bowen twisted his chair round and put a consoling hand on his wife's clenched fingers.

'Would she have known what was happening?' asked Noble quietly.

'I doubt she was knocked out when she fell,' explained Taylor. 'Or she wouldn't have pulled at his clothes. Even so, she would lose consciousness within a few seconds. Death by strangulation can take up to a minute, but Carole wouldn't have known about most of it.'

'Long enough to be frightened?' asked Hudson. 'Or recognise her attacker?'

'To be frightened, yes. If this character had his hood up, I doubt she could see his face.'

The team took this in.

'Bastard,' Hudson said quietly. 'Terrifying an old woman like that.'

Sara doubted any of them disagreed. 'Did that account for her look in the grave?' she asked, tensing herself for the reply. The vision of Carole's screaming face was still raw.

'I can't be definitive, but my experience would suggest post-mortem relaxation of the face muscles. That's why people used to tie a bandage around the head and jaw in the old days. Like Marley's ghost in *A Christmas Carol*.'

'Too much talk of ghosts in this investigation,' said Hudson sharply. 'No ghost did this to our victim. You sure it was a man?'

'Given the size of hand indicated by the damage on her neck, I'd say male,' said Taylor. 'After our victim died, I suspect our attacker dragged her down the aisle and then carried her up to the stage. Given the sequence of the bolts and locks, I suggest he went backstage, pulled out the under-stage panel and accessed the grave trap from underneath. Then, he could dump and arrange Carole in the grave void with gravity on his side. We've taken samples throughout the route, trying to get some DNA.'

'Is that likely to yield anything?' asked Hudson.

Taylor shook his head. 'I'm sorry. Everywhere we looked were such high-traffic areas that it's unlikely. Even under the stage.'

'We need to look harder at the people belonging to the building,' said Hudson. 'Our attacker knew where to find a full set of keys, how to find the costumes in the wardrobe and all about the under-stage grave void. They even knew the alarm code, for God's sake. It has to be an insider, doesn't it? Who might have a grudge against Carole? Who hated the place so much they would deliberately do these things there?'

'If we could find this costume, would there be any traces on that?' asked Sara suddenly.

'Strangulation tends not to leave many traces, although we've swabbed Carole's neck for foreign DNA.'

'That's my first call tomorrow,' said Sara determinedly. 'Tent city and our homeless friends from the CCTV.'

CHAPTER 32

Although she knew she could handle herself, Sara was glad to see DI Edwards waiting at the bottom of Church Alley on Sunday morning. There were likely to be quite a few residents in the encampment, and she hadn't fancied tackling them alone. The city was quiet as most shops didn't open until after ten. The only real sound was the cathedral bells rippling across the empty streets, calling people to morning worship. She remembered hearing them when she had lived in the city centre. It had seemed such a quintessentially English sound.

Sara had checked their systems and discovered that an eviction order was booked to be activated on the graveyard crew at seven the following morning.

'Good job we decided to come here today,' said Edwards when she told him.

'I'm not sure what we can do if they saw anything,' she admitted. 'I mean, how do we keep them as witnesses? Even if we can temporarily hold up tomorrow's eviction, they'd wander off long before we got to trial.'

'I know,' murmured Edwards. He led the way up a small set of stairs to the graveyard.

The encampment had seven tents around an area that had been used for a bonfire. An old tomb had a ramshackle lean-to constructed out of cardboard. A pair of feet encased in mud-encrusted boots stuck out of the end to prove occupation of the temporary structure. Between the tents, there were piles of rubbish and bags of possessions. There were rucksacks, carrier bags, sports bags and even a broken wicker basket. They all looked filthy and spewed clothes or towels or other basic necessities. The rubbish piles reeked of rotting food. There was a pervading odour of the latrine, despite being open to the sky.

'Careful where you walk,' said Edwards, his nose wrinkled in disgust.

'Yes, boss.' Sara was already concentrating on where her feet fell.

'Wake up, you lot,' Edwards shouted. His voice bounced off the surrounding buildings and echoed eerily off the church's flint-filled walls and diamond-paned windows. 'Come on, out you come. Knock, knock!'

Sara looked at him in surprise. Behind her, the feet in the cardboard shack twitched suddenly. A faint female shriek issued from one of the tents. It turned into a moan of complaint.

'What the fuck?' the voice whined.

'Out you come, miss,' called Edwards. He took his pick of the tents, striding over to a dirty, dark blue one-man affair. He bent over to unzip the front flap. There was a thump behind Sara.

As she turned, she watched the lean-to begin to fold in on itself, the damp cardboard sagging with rain and dew. The pair of feet vanished, and a muffled voice began to curse. Before she could step forward to help, a hand pushed violently against the box which formed the roof, smashing it open. A bedraggled, old-fashioned man of the road emerged from inside like a nightmarish jack-in-the-box. Clutching a bottle of booze firmly to his chest, the man blinked blearily around the graveyard. As he swayed, Sara took in his begrimed face, unkempt hair and tangled beard. The stink of him was offensive even at twenty paces. The cardboard collapsed around him. His eyes focused on Sara.

'Fuckin' hell,' he snarled. 'Pissin' coppers. Look what you done.'

Sara was about to apologise, pointing out that she hadn't been near the construction. But the tramp subsided onto the pile of cardboard, losing focus and interest. He twisted the lid off the bottle to take a swig. She walked carefully over to join Edwards.

'Come on out,' called Edwards. His voice wasn't loud. Another whine answered him.

A head of matted hair shivered just inside the flap. In the semi-dark beyond, a slight figure occupied a dirt-covered sleeping bag. A pile of items lay on top of the woman for warmth. Sara thought she recognised the dreadlocked hair from the CCTV footage Noble had shown them. She tapped Edwards' arm to get him to move away.

'Better let me,' she said. He nodded. 'Miss, could you get up for a minute or two? We need to ask a few questions.'

The woman raised her head gingerly. 'Ah, fuck me. Police.'

'I'm afraid so.' Sara held up her warrant card.

'You here to move us on already?' The woman yawned. 'Too tired.'

'Not us,' said Sara. 'Just a couple of questions.'

'Give us a chance,' muttered the woman. It took her several tries to untangle herself from the sleeping bag and covers. She crawled out of the tent, pulling a fleecy blanket with her to wrap around her shoulders. It might once have belonged to a baby with its teddies and rocking horses. Now, it was covered in stains that Sara refused to think about identifying.

'I'm DS Sara Hirst,' she said as the woman settled on an upturned fruit box to roll herself a cigarette. Sara squatted down next to her. 'You are?'

'You can call me Kells.' The woman lit up and took a soothing drag. She looked directly at Sara, then peered around her to size up DI Edwards. 'Him?'

'He's the boss,' replied Sara. Edwards waved his warrant card, although Kells showed no interest in it.

'Must be serious, then. They don't normally send detectives for the likes of us. Something about whatever was going on in that place?' Kells pointed over her shoulder at the white theatre building.

'You know about that?'

'Saw you all there. Interviewing folks. Forensic vans. All that. Murder, was it? Exciting.' Kells didn't look excited. She sounded sarcastic, and looked bedraggled and depressed.

'We think you may be able to help us,' said Sara.

'Oh gawd,' said Kells with a shudder. 'You're gonna pin it on one of us. At least we'd get fed regular inside.'

'We think we may have seen you on CCTV the night it happened.'

'Yeah, yeah. Big Brother is watching you, eh?'

'I'm afraid so,' said Sara. 'Did you and a friend find some items that night?'

'Items?' parroted Kells in a high-pitched voice. 'Did we find some items?'

Sara waited until the woman had taken another soothing drag on her roll-up. 'After midnight. We think you and a male friend were on Pottergate outside the church.'

'Probably,' conceded Kells. 'It's easier to go bin-diving after the restaurants have shut. Food, y'know.'

'Who was your friend?'

Kells looked upwards. Her lip began to tremble. 'That'd be my Tam.'

'Tam?'

'My boyfriend.'

'What had you and Tam found, Kells?' pressed Sara.

'I found a bag,' said Kells with a sigh. 'Tam found this costume thing. Been wearing it on and off ever since.'

'What was it?'

'Freakin' monk's outfit,' said Kells to the sky. A tear began to drizzle down her cheek. 'He put it on. Said it was for Halloween. That he was dressed the same as the dealer. We thought it was a laugh.'

'Where is it now?' asked Edwards.

Kells looked at him blearily. 'Don't know. He was wearing it when he fell over the wall.'

'Kells, what about this bag?'

'Damn bag.' Now tears were streaking through the grub on the woman's face. Snot was gathering in bubbles on the tip of her nose. Sara dug in her pocket to find a packet of tissues, which she held out. When Kells didn't respond, she dropped them in the woman's lap.

'What happened to the bag, Kells?' asked Sara. 'This might be important.'

'Sold it.'

Sara sighed. She felt sure that the bag must have belonged to Carole Morgan. 'What about the contents?'

'Weren't much. Tam flogged them. In the pub down St Benedicts.'

Edwards leaned towards them. 'Can you remember who you sold the bag to?'

'Zach's mate. That woman with the headscarf.'

'Headscarf?'

'Yeah. You know. Muslim religious shit.'

Sara kept her look neutral. There was no point in taking the woman to task about her choice of words. It wouldn't make any difference. 'If we bought you breakfast, could you tell us all about it?'

'No,' snapped Kells. She snatched at the tissues and blew her nose noisily.

'It would be really helpful.'

'Don't wanna help you.' Kells threw the blackened tissue towards the bonfire ashes. 'You lot don't think enough of us to help catch that bastard.'

Damn, thought Sara. *Thought I was getting somewhere.* 'What bastard?'

'That other fuckin' monk. The dealer. The one who pushed Tam over the wall last night.'

CHAPTER 33

It had been a long night at the hospital. Nafisa had managed to grab a couple of hours' doze lying across some visitors' chairs in A&E. Zach could sleep sitting up, a skill many homeless people developed. She hadn't needed to stay at all. In fact, she need never have been involved. But when Zach rang her in a panic just before midnight, she got dressed, caught a taxi on Unthank Road, and met him at the hospital. The victim was Kells's boyfriend. Apparently, he was called Tam, although neither knew his surname. When the incident had happened, Kells had run away, screaming about murder. That left no one to go with the injured man, and Zach said he'd felt responsible and couldn't let Tam be put in the ambulance alone. He'd called Nafisa from a payphone in the waiting room. The doctor declared Tam out of immediate danger just after Nafisa had won the struggle with the coffee machine to get them a couple of drinks. They waited ages for a bus to take them back into the city. It was Sunday morning, and buses were rare.

'I'm sorry I dragged you into this,' said Zach as the bus meandered past the endless parked cars on Earlham Road. There weren't many other passengers, and they had chosen seats as far away from Zach as possible. Nafisa had braved sitting next to him, even though the smell and the motion of the bus made her feel nauseous.

'I don't mind,' said Nafisa. She was breathing through her mouth in an attempt to feel better. 'Look, I never did get to talk to you yesterday. There's something I need to tell you. How about a breakfast bap?'

At ten o'clock on Sunday morning, few options were open in Norwich's centre. One of the hardworking food stalls at the back of the market was cheerfully functioning. Nafisa bought a couple of baps and big mugs of tea, and the pair settled on two tall stools on the edge of the kiosk.

'Go on, then,' said Zach through a mouthful of bacon and bread.

'I spoke to the Luke Project about housing, and they may have a temporary placement coming up.' Nafisa didn't want to overpromise after her meeting with the difficult administrator. Egg yolk and tomato ketchup dribbled out of her vegetarian bap, and she licked it up appreciatively. Honesty seemed the best way forward. 'He wasn't best pleased that you didn't turn up last time, I'm afraid.'

Zach munched on his roll until it was finished. He wiped his fingers and straggly beard with a paper napkin. 'Did I cause you much trouble?'

'A bit.'

'I'm sorry,' he said. 'Even though I've been clear of the booze for nearly a year, I felt one of my episodes coming on and needed to get away.'

'If you really want me to pursue it, then I will.' Nafisa slurped her tea. 'They might not give you a second chance though, and they certainly wouldn't give you a third.'

'I get it,' nodded Zach. He looked reflectively at his dirt-engrained hands holding the tea mug.

'The problem is this,' said Nafisa in a low voice. 'Can you keep a secret?'

'Wouldn't have survived two tours in Afghanistan if I couldn't,' said Zach.

'You can't use this information in any way. If you do, I'll get the sack.'

'They're coming to evict us, aren't they?' Zach gave her a piercing look. He was used to all this, Nafisa realised. They all knew they would be moved on before long. 'You can trust me. How soon?'

'Very soon,' said Nafisa. She dropped her voice to a whisper. 'Tomorrow morning, first thing.'

'I'm so tired.' Zach's head slumped forward as he sighed deeply. Nafisa waited. Eventually, the veteran raised his head again. He drained his mug of tea. 'Can you get me in tomorrow?'

'I doubt it,' she said apologetically. 'I've checked another short-term option if you want me to keep trying with the Luke Project.'

When Zach nodded, she outlined the local Winter Shelter scheme. He ran a trembling hand down his face and pulled at his beard. 'I'd like to get off the road. I think it's time.'

It was the admission that Nafisa had been waiting for. 'That's good. Let's see what we can do.'

'I'd better get back to my tent,' he said, slipping off the stool. 'See if Kells has turned up again.'

'I'll come with you,' said Nafisa.

Zach didn't object. As they walked away from the stall, Nafisa glanced back to see the stall owner advancing on the stools with a cloth and anti-bac spray to fumigate the seats. He removed both tea mugs and dropped them into a waste bin. Nafisa strode out to catch up with her client.

It was only a few minutes' walk from the market to the church. Nafisa was pleased to see Kells when they climbed the steps to the graveyard. She was less pleased to see that the woman was talking to a tall, smartly dressed woman who exuded the authority of a police officer. The pair were looking over the graveyard wall, and Kells was pointing. A man in a warm overcoat was watching them closely. Nafisa wondered what a pair of detectives could want with the homeless crew. Her own dealings with the police were often antagonistic, as the officers she spoke to had a very low opinion of the people Nafisa was tasked with trying to help. Of course, that was nothing compared to the way the police sometimes treated the homeless themselves. Nafisa pulled up the zip on her coat until it almost reached her chin and fiddled with her headscarf. Both things she only did when she was feeling uncomfortable. Zach was already striding in to do battle, and she walked reluctantly after him.

'I don't know,' she heard Kells say. 'I was frightened. Thought he'd hit me an' all.'

'What did you do?' asked the woman.

'I ran off.'

'You don't know what happened to Tam?'

'I do,' interrupted Zach. He stood squarely between the woman and Kells. 'Who are you?'

The woman produced her warrant card. 'DS Sara Hirst. Kells was just telling me about the attack last night.'

'Yeah?' said Zach. His tone was packed with distrust. 'Why?'

'We'd like to help if we can,' said Hirst. 'And I think your monk is also of interest to us in another enquiry.'

'There's been a murder,' said Kells with naive enthusiasm. She pointed at the theatre. 'At that place. We're gonna be witnesses.'

Nafisa watched Hirst glance at the other detective and roll her eyes before turning to Zach. 'Did you see the incident with Tam?'

'I did. I've been at the hospital with him all night. He's in a poor way.'

'Oh, I didn't know,' Kells babbled guiltily. 'I thought he'd be okay. Thought that bastard was gonna punch me too.'

'It's okay, Kells,' said Zach, patting the woman's emaciated arm. 'It was a frightening situation.'

'Can you tell me what happened?' asked Hirst.

'This bloke has been coming here selling fixes,' said Zach shortly. 'Been wearing a monk's habit for some reason. Maybe he thought it was a joke.'

'And he attacked Tam? Why would he do that?'

'Tam had found a habit of his own in the dumpster last week and put it on. He was teasing the dealer about it. Said it was Halloween for us too, so he could wear a costume if he wanted. The bugger didn't like it. It got a bit heated, you know.'

'Yeah!' interrupted Kells. 'He didn't have the right to say them things. We're the customers, ain't we?'

Zach shushed the woman. 'Then that ghost walk tour thing arrived over there. Tam thought it would be funny to go and be another ghostly monk. Started making "woo-woo" noises from behind that headstone.'

'He didn't like that.' Kells shook her head vehemently. 'Neither of them did.'

'Neither of them?'

'The dealer or the chap leading the walk,' said Zach. He glanced back at Nafisa. 'The man down there started shouting at Tam. It riled him, and he started swearing. Then, the dealer barged into Tam from behind and knocked him over the wall. Fell on the pavement. Head first.'

'Is he badly injured?' asked Hirst.

'Yeah,' said Zach. 'Brain injury. In intensive care. We've just been sent away from the hospital.'

'We?' The detective was fast on the uptake. Nafisa had to give her that.

'Me and Nafisa,' said Zach. He turned and pointed.

'The woman with the headscarf, if I'm not mistaken,' said Hirst.

Suddenly, Kells burst into tears. 'It should 'ave bin me. He's gonna die. I can't bear it.'

She surged forward, evading Zach's grip, then raced towards the graveyard wall and the drop to the pavement below. Kells jumped.

CHAPTER 34

Storming out of the official police interview had not been the wisest thing he'd ever done in his life, Ben realised. He hadn't learned his lesson from last time, and he'd allowed the pair to get to him. Well, he wasn't going to help them or let them fit him up for Carole's death. There was also the question of who had told them about his fallout with Carole. That had to be Chris Webster. It all came back to that old case because Chris had been involved with that too. Sometimes, Ben wondered what had happened to Scooter, his erstwhile apprentice. He'd lain awake most of the night worrying away at his problems, and now he was tired before the day even began.

Because the theatre had amateur casts, rehearsals were done in the evenings. When a production was almost ready to open, it transferred to the stage and had extra rehearsals at the weekends. Sunday was technical rehearsal day. Ben's one chance to make sure everything was in place before the show opened. A phone call from the Trust chair the previous evening had brought Ben up to date with the plans to continue the show 'in tribute to Carole Morgan'. Her part had been taken over by another actor, who was trying to catch up on the line learning. Inevitably, today would be about getting her up to speed, and Ben's technical requests would be ignored. He was feeling deeply grumpy as he opened up the theatre.

The place felt cold and gloomy despite it being Sunday lunchtime. As he put on the working lights, Ben overrode the heating to fire it into life. No point in them all sitting there shivering all afternoon. He was heading for the gents' toilets near the foyer when he heard the front door bang. A quick glance was enough to know it was Chris and Simone, who nodded and headed to the dressing rooms.

Ben slipped into the gents. It was obvious that these two had begun an affair during rehearsals. He could understand the attraction for Simone. Chris was handsome and charismatic and twenty years her junior. He wasn't sure where the attraction lay the other way around. None of his business, he knew, as he washed his hands. Was it Chris riding high on the fumes of a new sexual affair that had made him so cocksure? Or had he always been like it? With a sigh of exasperation, Ben went through the auditorium to the green room.

'There's no hot water,' was the complaint Ben faced as he stepped through the door. Chris was standing by the water urn with two cups in his hand.

'Give me a chance,' said Ben. He brushed past Chris to turn on the plug. 'I've only just got here myself. Give it ten minutes to warm up.'

'Typical,' said Chris. He kept his voice low but clear. 'You can't even get here on time to look after the green room.'

Ben had been walking away, looking for the next key he needed from his large bunch. He swivelled sharply. 'What's that supposed to mean?'

Chris dumped the cups back on the kitchen work surface. 'Why isn't anything ever ready when you run a show? It's your job, isn't it?'

'Indeed it is,' said Ben. He looked pointedly at the clock on the green room wall. 'Which is why I'm here on time and opening up. Could it be that you two are early?'

Chris blushed. 'We care about our performances, even if you don't. We like to be here early to get into character.'

'What? "An actor prepares"?' asked Ben. He couldn't keep the sarcasm out of his voice as he referenced the famous Russian director Stanislavski. Many professional actors swore by his 'method' acting. Ben had always felt it had no place here, and saying things like that made Chris sound pretentious. 'Please, spare me.'

'Oh, I will,' said Chris. He turned on Ben. 'When you're doing what you're paid to do or when you've left.'

Ben felt his hackles rising. Mentally giving himself a shake, he selected the next key to keep his eyeline down. He wasn't going to let the little shit get to him. 'What's got into you? Was it you who told the police about that complaint against me?'

'Why shouldn't I?' demanded Chris. 'You tried to lay the blame on me!'

'I only answered the questions they put to me.' Ben spoke carefully. He looked up and waited to see how Chris would react.

The actor angrily screwed up his face. He clenched his hands, balling them into fists. 'You deserve everything you get.'

'Why?' Ben really didn't understand. Suddenly, he felt defeated. After everything he had done for this place, for the company and all the shows he had worked on, it only took one spiteful person to cause all this heartache. 'Did you really think I could have killed Carole?'

Chris spluttered. 'No, hell, not that.'

'Wasn't it enough that you complained about Lindie and myself two years ago?' The actor looked at him, eyes wide, jaw clenched. 'It was you, wasn't it?' When Chris didn't reply, Ben continued. 'Do you have any idea what you put us both through? Why would you do such a thing?'

'You interfered,' snapped Chris. 'You stood in my way. You had no right. Either of you. You think you're gods around here.'

'Are you seriously standing there and telling me that you put in two complaints about members of staff because you didn't get a part?'

'You needed taking down a peg or two. You deserved to feel as humiliated as I'd been made to. Besides, you left me to do your dirty work.'

'What are you talking about?' snapped Ben. Suddenly, he guessed why the actor disliked him so much. It all began to make sense.

'Jesus, Chris,' said a woman's voice behind Ben. He wasn't sure how long Simone had been standing in the stage doorway or how much she'd heard. 'I always wondered who'd done that. And it was you.'

'They earned it.' Chris pushed past Ben to Simone. When he tried to take her hands, she slapped his away. 'Don't you see?'

'No, I don't,' she replied. 'I knew I wasn't your first conquest here and was unlikely to be your last, but I didn't think you were so spiteful.'

'I'm not!'

'And if you did that, who else have you complained about or to?' asked Simone. Her lip curled in disgust. 'What else have you done?'

'I think we should all calm down,' said Ben, trying for a hint of normality. 'There's a lot to get through this afternoon.'

Simone ignored Ben. Chris stepped towards her, trying to pull her into his arms. She violently pushed him away, making Chris stumble backwards and into the far wall. His head clanged against the plaster. He let out a groan and put a hand on his scalp

'Did you have something to do with Carole's death?' demanded Simone. 'I wouldn't put it past you.'

'You bitch!' shouted Chris.

He strode towards Simone, his hand raised to hit her. Ben grabbed at him, pulling his arm and shouting, 'Chris, stop it!'

The actor spun to hit Ben instead, raising his fist to punch downwards, when a voice stopped him.

'Am I interrupting something?'

With considerable relief, Ben recognised the efficient tones of Detective Sergeant Hirst.

CHAPTER 35

Sara led DI Edwards swiftly into the room. They'd heard the raised voices from the auditorium as the show director, Glyn, was escorting them backstage. She wasn't surprised that one of the belligerents was her former boyfriend. They'd often had rows while together, and she was well aware of his fiery temper. He was also ill-equipped to accept responsibility for the results of his tantrums or when caught out in bad behaviour. Nor was she surprised that a woman might be involved in the argument, as Chris flitted from conquest to conquest, herself included. Given the angry look the woman on the steps was giving them, Sara assumed she was more than a witness. Ben Marsden had been about to get a black eye or lose a tooth when her arrival pulled Chris up enough to prevent his intended blow landing.

'I'm guessing this is none of my business,' she said sarcastically. 'At least, not yet.'

Chris turned away, muttering under his breath. Marsden turned to look at her, clearly relieved.

'DS Hirst, I wasn't expecting you today. How can we help?'

'We were hoping to ask a favour.' She indicated to her boss, who had moved beside her. 'There was an incident in the alley last night, and we could do with interviewing a couple of people about it. Is it possible to borrow your rehearsal room for an hour?'

'That would be fine,' said Marsden. 'I'll just put the heating on for you, or it will be cold.'

He took Sara and Edwards back through the auditorium. The table and chairs they'd used the previous day were still in the same place. The stage manager busied about, clicking on two space heaters and rearranging the furniture.

'Are you happy to look after yourselves?' he asked. 'Lindie isn't in today, nor are the box office volunteers. You could come to the green room if you need a drink.'

'It's all fine,' nodded Edwards. 'We won't be long.'

'If you could let me know when you're finished,' said Marsden. 'Just so I know who's in the building, for fire security and all that.'

Sara agreed she would, and he bustled out. 'I wonder what all that was about.'

Edwards shrugged. 'Lucky for him we arrived when we did. Let's get her in.'

They had left Zach at the encampment, helping Kells to limp back to her tent after the jump had sprained her ankle. He was also explaining about Tam's diagnosis. She was still crying.

Sara had rung Daryl Stone, who was on his way to meet them. The social worker had also agreed to talk to them before she left and was hovering outside near the front door. She looked pleased to be invited inside.

'Sorry about the wait,' said Sara. The tiny woman was shivering. 'Can I get you a drink or anything?'

'No, thanks. I'd just like to get on with this, as I could do with getting home. It was a long night.'

Sara set up her mobile phone to record and explained what she was doing. 'Could you just give us your name?'

'Nafisa Ahmed. I'm a social worker for one of the county council's abuse and dependency teams.'

'You've been working with the homeless people in the graveyard behind St Johns church?' asked Edwards.

'Just one of them. Zach. He's an army veteran, and I've been trying to get him a placement with the Luke Project.'

'Have you had any dealings with the others?'

'In passing,' she said.

'The woman called Kells says she sold you a large leather bag,' said Sara. 'Is that true?'

'Yes, on Friday afternoon.'

'Do you have it with you?'

'Just my handbag.' Ahmed shook her head, then adjusted her headscarf nervously. She patted the small blue bag which she had put on her lap. It's long strap hung to one side. 'I left the leather bag at home.'

'We need to see the bag and possibly run some forensic tests. It's quite important.'

'I guessed she might have stolen it,' admitted Ahmed. 'Shame, it was useful.'

'Was there anything in it when you bought it?' asked Edwards. She shook her head in reply.

'Can we collect it from you?' asked Sara. 'Or could you bring it in today?'

It was already past lunchtime. The social worker yawned heavily. 'I've been up all night, and I need some sleep. Can I do it tomorrow?'

Sara glanced at Edwards, who nodded briefly. 'I can arrange a pick-up first thing. But please don't do anything to it overnight. Can I have your contact details?'

Ahmed gave her home address and opened her purse to extract a business card. 'This is work in case you need it.'

Sara thanked the woman and took her to the front door. With a wan smile, she went down the steps. The vision that was Daryl Stone in full flow passed Nafisa Ahmed in the courtyard. His long black coat flapped behind him like a crow's wings. The deep-brimmed black hat seemed to have acquired more feather trimmings. Was that eyeliner he was wearing? It made his eyes look large and appealing. As Stone saw Ahmed, he halted, swept off his hat and bowed, making the tired social worker smile broadly. Then he strode up the steps to greet Sara cheerily.

'Thanks for coming in,' she said with a glance over the man's shoulder. Ahmed was standing transfixed, watching the striking man with obvious pleasure. There was no denying his charisma. 'This way.'

'No problem,' said Stone.

They were soon settled in the rehearsal room. Sara explained again about recording with her phone.

'We can do a more formal interview later,' said Edwards. He sounded to be growing impatient. Perhaps he thought this was all just a sideshow, whereas Sara was convinced it was important. 'We wanted to ask you about the accident last night.'

'Poor man,' said Stone. 'I was sorry I couldn't stay with him. The other homeless man said he would wait. It seemed they knew each other. Luckily, I had my actor with me. He took the tour people away while I called for the ambulance.'

'You were storytelling last night?' asked Sara.

'Alec was doing the costumes on the second walk,' agreed Stone with a nod. 'I was doing the stories.'

'Can you tell us in your own words what happened?'

'We'd done the jump scare,' said Stone. Edwards looked sideways at Sara.

'I'll explain later,' she said. 'Go on.'

'Alec had gone up the alley to collect the costume bag. He normally stashes it behind the ivy on the wall up there. Then, that other chap appeared up in the graveyard. It's so much higher that it looked like he had suddenly appeared above their heads. The people on the walk thought it was another part of the performance. They laughed at first until he started to get lewd.'

It was an old-fashioned word. 'In what way?'

'Oh, you know. Grabbing at his crotch, waggling his tongue like he was . . .' Stone stalled in his description. Sara kept her face passive and nodded. 'He started to say weird things. I guess he thought he was being funny. My party were starting to get uneasy, so I shouted to Alec.'

'Where was he?'

'Under the arch.' Stone pointed up the alley. 'He came back, and we both told the guy to, well, bugger off, basically.'

'Did that help?'

'Unfortunately not,' said Stone with a wince. 'He started shouting something like, "The monks are coming to get you," and making "woo-woo" noises. Pissed as a fart or high as a kite, probably both. Alec was rounding up the group to move on when we heard a scream. The guy toppled head first over the perimeter wall and crashed onto the pavement.'

'He tripped?' asked Edwards.

'No way,' insisted Stone. 'He was pushed. By the other monk.'

'There was someone else in the graveyard in a monk's habit?' asked Sara. 'Two of them? You sure he pushed the first man?'

'Absolutely,' nodded Stone. 'The guy that fell was a big fella. The other one was taller and thinner. He must have charged at him to get him to fall like that.'

'Did you get a look at him?'

'Briefly. All hell broke loose on our tour, of course. I shot over to look at the one on the floor, but he was out cold. The other bugger stood there, staring down at us. They had that damn bonfire going again. What with the flames behind him and the street lamp in the courtyard, he looked more demonic than anything we would ever dare to put on our walks. We could hear a woman getting hysterical. She came up behind him, and he swung round to slap her. Then his hood fell down, and they both ran off.'

'Would you recognise him again?'

'It was dark,' said Stone, frowning in concentration. 'But I think so.'

CHAPTER 36

The technical rehearsal had gone on for far longer than it should have. Glyn had ensured that Ben had his moment to solve issues, but most of the time had been given to the replacement actor, as Ben had suspected it would. Ben had loaded himself up with strong, sugary tea to stay awake. His bad night was partly to blame, that and the boredom. It was gone nine o'clock when he had shooed the last of the cast and crew out into the alley and begun his lock-up routine.

Ben's thoughts turned to the missing keys. *An entire set gone from the cabinet.* Whoever had them could still get in, since they hadn't gotten around to changing the locks. The cost of this would be significant, with a hundred or more keys to be cut, and he was waiting for the Trust to sign off on the expense. The alarm code was due to be changed by the security company in a couple of days. There wasn't much else Ben could do in the meantime . . .

He checked the dressing rooms were empty and turned off the lights. In the green room, he made sure the water heater was off and the dishwasher was running. Lights down. His feet echoed into the barrel roof of the auditorium as he checked the downstairs fire exits were sealed. Next, he climbed the stairs to double-check that the wardrobe door was locked, feeling a pang of sympathy for Rachel, who would be embarking on her clean-up tomorrow morning. He crossed the gallery, his feet clumping on the wooden floor. The fire exit was shut tight, and the storage rooms were locked. He yawned widely as he turned to leave.

A shadow flickered in the corner of his eye. The hair on the back of his neck rose instantly. Dropping quietly down the steps to the front row of seats, Ben held onto the barrier and leaned over to look into the auditorium below.

'Who's there?' he demanded. There was no reply. He held his breath for a moment, listening hard. Nothing.

Now, he looked keenly at the stage. His skin crawled with the sensation of being watched, although there was no sign of anyone on the stage. No random actor that he'd missed and locked in by mistake. There was a gallery above the stage, just as there was in Shakespeare's Globe. It was on the same level as he was, and he ran his eyes carefully around all four sides. Nothing. Of course not. He edged across the front row of seats, concentrating on his feet. His breath was getting short with fear.

'Nonsense,' he scolded himself in a low tone. 'You've never believed in ghosts.'

The sound was more like a breath than a whisper when it came.

'Marsden.' A male voice. 'Leave me alone.'

Ben skidded around, almost overbalanced, which would have been fatal if he hadn't grabbed the barrier in front of the seats. If he fell over the guard rail onto the seats below, he would almost certainly be dead.

'I can hear you!' he called. His voice wavered this time. 'Who are you? Stop fucking about!'

There was no reply. His eyes strained around the gallery again. Nothing. Or was there? Was he hearing things now?

At this level were two pairs of mullioned faux-Elizabethan windows, one on either side of the stage. Part of the original design, there were usually black flats in front of them. Glyn had decided to use them in his version of *King*

Lear, and the designer had opened up the facade. With a gasp, Ben realised he could see a figure standing behind one of them. Or could he? Was it just his imagination going wild? There were no lights on back there, so how could he see anyone? As he gazed at the stage-left window, the figure moved closer to the glass. He could barely see the outline, though he easily guessed it was their errant monk.

'I can see you!' he shouted. 'I don't believe in ghosts, you bastard!'

If there was someone there now, perhaps he could catch them. He might even be a hero. Whoever it was might know the theatre well, but he knew it better than anyone. Heart thumping, breath racing, he scrabbled along the side gallery, his back pressed against the storeroom wall, and ducked into the small gap at the end. It had brought him backstage six feet from the window. If there had been someone, they were no longer there. The light switch for this area was down a flight of stairs. Ben unhooked his torch from his belt and turned it on. The tiny beam swivelled rapidly around the rarely used area. He checked for footprints in the dust. Nothing.

Taking a deep breath to calm himself, Ben headed down the stairs and out through the green room.

'Just your mind playing tricks,' he tried to reassure himself.

Everywhere was in darkness, and he didn't bother switching on any lights. Completing the circuit to the auditorium, he collected his backpack with its script and tools. Flicking off the working lights, he padded through the foyer to the gents' toilets. Being the last in the building had never bothered him. He never got the sense that he wasn't alone or anything stupid like that until tonight.

He had a nervous wazz, washed his hands and collected his bag. The lights went off as he left. The ladies' loo was also in darkness. He let himself into the office and flicked on the lights. Reaching up to the panel on the wall behind Lindie's desk, he set the alarm. It began to beep rapidly at him. *Beep-beep-beep.* Thirty seconds. The noise had never worried him before. In theatre, thirty seconds was a luxurious amount of time to do a set or costume change. All he had to do was get out of the front door and hit the button to finalise the setting procedure. Tonight, Ben's heart was in his mouth as he strode out of the office, locking it behind him. Turning out the foyer lights, he opened the front door to let himself out. *Beep-beep-beep.*

Ben stepped outside and dropped his bag to free both hands to fasten the final locks. His hand grasped the front door rail as he pulled it closed as he looked through the glass into the foyer. *Beep-beep-beep.* With a cry of fear, he jumped backwards. It was there. The monk was there. Standing immediately behind the door. Its hands were held up in prayer. They dripped with blood. The hood, which totally obscured the face, slowly rose. For a terrified moment, Ben was sure that the face underneath wasn't flesh and blood. It was skeletal. The mouth opened slowly. It must be Ben's imagination. The skull was glowing.

He tried to turn and run. Fear locked his legs, making him clumsy. *Beep-beep-beep.*

Then, with an inhuman roar, the monk rushed forward, wrenched open the door and hurtled into Ben. The stage manager staggered backwards, twisted sideways and stumbled down the outside steps to land heavily on his knees in the courtyard. He felt the figure rush past him. Footsteps echoed around the yard and raced along the alley. Ben collapsed into a heap.

Inside the theatre, the alarm failed to set properly. *Beeeeep!* Now Ben was in all sorts of trouble.

CHAPTER 37

A police car had turned up at the house that Nafisa still shared with her parents at seven on Monday morning. She'd handed over the leather bag, which the officer had put in a large evidence bag. Quite what forensic traces they expected to get from it after it had been, at least according to Kells, shoved in a rubbish bin, then dragged around the city by Nafisa and finally left on her bedroom floor for three nights, she couldn't imagine. The bag had proved so useful that she promised herself a trip to the local leather goods shop in the city centre to see if they had anything similar.

The Monday morning team briefing began early, as the team had busy schedules. Russell Goddard slid into the seat next to Nafisa with a shy smile. When he thought no one was looking, he slid a flimsy paper bag beside her hand with a nod. There was a small Halloween-themed box of chocolates inside.

'Trick or treat,' he whispered.

'Treat,' she replied quietly. Nafisa couldn't resist a smile, although it was more from embarrassment than pleasure.

Team leader Samantha brandished a list. 'We need to go through our caseloads, as usual. But first of all, I need to let you know about our friends in the graveyard tent city.'

Nafisa steeled herself. They had been due to be evicted at seven this morning at the same time that the police had collected the bag. She wondered if the homeless crew had been allowed time to gather their belongings or if they had been manhandled back onto the streets.

'There's been a stay of execution,' said Samantha. 'At the request of Norfolk Police's Serious Crimes Unit. Apparently, Nafisa has been helping them with their enquiries. So perhaps you can fill us all in?'

'There have been two incidents,' said Nafisa. 'A murder in the Rosegarden Theatre last week. You may have seen it on the local news. Then, one of the tent people was seriously injured in a violent incident on Saturday night. Zach rang me after it happened and asked me to go to the hospital with him. The victim was in intensive care. I agreed to keep him company for a while.'

'First cardinal rule of social work,' Samantha reminded Nafisa and the rest of the team. 'Never get personally involved. Is that why you spoke to the police yesterday?'

How had she known that? Nafisa nodded. 'Anyway, the remaining crew might be witnesses in both investigations, so I assume that's why the police need them to hang around.'

'Hardly ideal witnesses,' frowned Samantha. 'They were likely to be high or drunk.'

'I guess they want to take statements or something,' mumbled Nafisa. 'I don't know, really.'

'Well, that's their affair,' said Samantha. 'The eviction order won't be activated until Friday at the earliest. Which gives us more time to try to extract your veteran client. Let's make that a priority.'

Nafisa nodded, grateful that the bag she'd foolishly bought hadn't come up as Samantha moved on to case reviews. An hour later, they were back at their own desks.

Russell arrived bearing a cup of instant coffee, which Nafisa hated. He plonked it on her desk, and the grey, scummy liquid slopped over the side onto her papers. She pulled a tissue from her trouser pocket to mop up with as he hovered.

'Thank you,' she said. Now, she either had to drink it or wait until he was out of the room to throw it away. Nafisa opened the box of chocolates, selected a brown shape that might have been a witch on a broomstick and offered him the box. 'Help yourself.'

His hand wove over the little plastic tray until it dived onto a white chocolate skull. If it was as tasteless as the brown stuff she was trying to swallow, Nafisa felt sorry for him.

'That was a kind thought,' she said. 'What have you got on today?'

Russell ran through his list of calls and interviews before shuffling nervously. 'I was wondering . . .'

When his voice trailed to a halt, Nafisa rushed in. 'I've got to go out for a couple of home visits. So, I'll be out all day.'

'Oh, I see.' Russell licked his chocolatey fingers. 'What about later? I mean after work.'

Oh lord, here it came. 'My parents will be expecting me home.'

'Any night this week, perhaps? I thought we could go for a drink or something.'

'I don't drink,' sighed Nafisa. 'And I don't think it's a good idea for work colleagues to start dating.'

Russell blushed bright crimson. 'I didn't mean anything by it. Anything serious. I'm sorry.'

'That's all right,' said Nafisa brightly. She picked up the telephone and checked her notepad for a number. Russell didn't take the hint until Nafisa waggled the handset in a businesslike manner. 'I must get on. Thank you for the chocolates, they're lovely.'

She watched him walk dejectedly back to his desk. What was she supposed to do? There was no way she wanted to encourage him.

With a tug at her headscarf, Nafisa dialled her contact at the Luke Project, determined to move on the situation for Zach before she tackled her other clients. The reluctant project worker agreed to another meeting that afternoon, adding the warning, 'I'll need to check with my manager first.'

It was a concession, which Nafisa intended to capitalise on at four o'clock when they met again. If he said no, she would just turn up anyway. At least Zach could stay in the graveyard for now, although that was hardly ideal. With any luck, by teatime, she would have better news. *Unless he's already moved on*, she suddenly thought. With a wobble of panic, Nafisa realised that he might have returned to the encampment and told everyone to clear out before the police came to evict them in the morning. She'd asked him not to, but that didn't mean he wouldn't have taken himself off and vanished again.

'Bugger,' she breathed, checking the time on her mobile. She had less than an hour before her next client appointment. Was there time to get into the city to check on Zach before she had to be out at Mile Cross? Her stomach knotted with frustration. Not being able to drive was a pain in the arse sometimes. Perhaps she should get around to doing something about it. That wasn't going to solve her current problem.

'Russell?' she called to her erstwhile suitor. 'I don't suppose you could run me into the city, could you?'

'Yes, of course,' he replied, and his face lit up with renewed hope. Nafisa sighed inwardly and gathered up her bags.

CHAPTER 38

'You seem to have had a busy time yesterday,' DCI Hudson said to Sara as the team gathered for their morning briefing. 'Perhaps you'd better go first.'

'Thank you,' said Sara. With a glance at DI Edwards, she opened her notebook, which was full of scribbles and crossings out. 'Better start with Saturday night.'

She described the interview with Daryl Stone, adding other details about the incident from Nafisa Ahmed. 'After we finished with them, I went to speak to this Zach character. He wasn't around, so I carried on to the hospital to ask about the injured man. He was still out cold when I got there. His head injury is severe, according to the doctors. He's in intensive care and may be moved to Addenbrookes, which has a specialist brain injury unit. His system was full of a cocktail of LSD, psilocybin and marijuana, which accounts for the behaviour and the lack of control. It doesn't help the doctors who are trying to treat him.'

'They're all drugs designed to make life seem a little more rosy and less horrible,' murmured Bowen.

Edwards gave him a nod. 'Not good if taken together.'

'The hospital had stripped Tam and kept his clothes,' said Sara. She pointed to some folded black fabric in an evidence bag. 'I brought it in for Forensics, just in case. Although, given that he's worn it several times and it's been lying around the graveyard for days, it may not be helpful in Carole's case. It might be if we're going to investigate this dealer monk.'

'Rachel in wardrobe said that two habits had been stolen,' Bowen reminded them. 'Could have got rid of one in case it had evidence on it and started to use the other. Tam must have found the original.'

'I think we have to include that,' said Hudson firmly. 'What are the odds of two incidents like this, both involving habit-wearing assailants, happening within yards of each other? Assuming Tam was pushed, then it's attempted murder. If he dies in intensive care, we will be upgrading it.'

'He can't tell us much at the moment,' said Sara. 'We have Daryl Stone's testimony, and we could ask his actor what he saw.'

'Definitely,' said Hudson. She wrote *TAM* in big letters on the whiteboard. 'I'll put that on your to-do list, Bowen. Aggie, can you dig around in Tam's background? Bowen, Noble, try and get a statement out of this junkie girlfriend and the other homeless man who both witnessed it.'

'Then all we have to do is find this monk,' said Bowen in a low voice. 'Piece of piss.'

Hudson shot him a venomous look. 'Noble, have another go at the CCTV for Saturday night. See if this bloke was wandering around in the outfit. I know it was Halloween, but he had to get into the graveyard from somewhere.'

'Samples from the theatre wardrobe of other monk outfits for comparison are due this morning,' said Edwards. 'At least we might be able to be reasonably sure where the one Tam was wearing may have come from.'

'Good work,' said Hudson. She pointed to the other evidence bag. 'And the bag?'

'We got lucky,' said Edwards. 'Nafisa Ahmed had bought it from Kells. When we interviewed her, she agreed for a uniform to collect it from her this morning. Again, it's been used since it went missing, so there may not be much forensic evidence to be found. She was clear it was empty when she acquired it.'

'Let's get them down to the lab and hope for the best,' sighed Hudson. 'We don't seem to be having much luck with Forensics on this one. Good old-fashioned police work will have to do. What other progress?'

'I managed to get hold of another committee member yesterday afternoon,' offered Bowen. 'He assured me there were no outstanding complaints about any staff member and that Carole had taken a back seat recently because of her husband's condition. Her freedom to act there was rare now, and the cast and crew had been rallying around to support her. No reason for Ben Marsden to be worried about her.'

'It would seem that my ex-boyfriend isn't a fan,' said Sara quietly. The team turned to look at her. She looked back at the DI, who filled them in on the argument they'd stumbled into the previous day. 'He was also rude about Marsden when we interviewed him.'

'Perhaps Mr Marsden isn't as popular as it appears,' suggested Hudson. 'But is all this enough to warrant him murdering someone? Opportunity, yes. Motive, not really.'

'Means? Any able-bodied man with a penchant for dressing up and with access to the stolen keys,' added Bowen. Sara couldn't help smiling at his intervention. He carried on in a fake horror film voice. '*The Attack of the Rosegarden Monk. A ghost seeking revenge from beyond the grave.*'

'No ghosts allowed,' said Hudson. They dutifully smiled at her attempt at humour. 'Let's keep Chris Webster on our radar. Perhaps he knows or suspects something that we don't know yet.'

'If the staff are all long-term and all seem to get on with each other, it has to be something else to do with the place itself, doesn't it?' asked Sara. 'Perhaps something that's happened in the past. Have we ever been to an incident there, or has anyone from there been in trouble with us?'

'Fair point,' nodded Hudson. 'Aggie, check the system for any previous mentions. If you have no luck, ask Drugs and Vice if they have any ongoing operations around the area.'

'There is something else,' said Noble quietly. The team turned to him, expecting more CCTV or mobile evidence. 'In your report of Stone's interview yesterday, he said he thought he might be able to recognise the second monk. The one who pushed Tam over the wall.'

'It was only a fleeting glimpse.'

'Didn't Mr Morgan say something similar about the monk who broke into their house and trashed the place?' Noble was clicking on his computer to pull up another report. 'When you spoke to him the morning after at his daughter's place, he claimed he recognised the voice, although he was naturally upset and confused then. Did the FLO get any more out of him about that?'

'I'll check,' said Aggie. 'She's been putting in daily short reports. I'll go through them.'

'Tracey is bringing Helen Morgan-Harris to the mortuary this morning,' said Sara. 'To officially identify her mother. I could go over.'

'Good idea,' agreed the DCI. 'Anything else you've noticed, Noble?'

Noble shook his head. 'I'm still puzzled by the vanishing man in black on Charing Cross. Perhaps we should ask at that set of flats to see if they've seen anyone.'

'You think it might be significant?' asked Hudson.

'I don't like CCTV blind spots,' replied Noble. 'There's several of them around this area. Down the alley past the theatre. On Charing Cross. I found another one between Charing Cross and St Gregorys Alley. It's called St Gregorys Back Alley. The area is riddled with these medieval cut-throughs, which gives our monk plenty of get-outs.'

'You and Bowen can get down there and have a scout around,' agreed Hudson. 'See what you can find. All right, lots to be getting on with. Get to it.'

Hudson strode back to her office as Sara's desk phone rang.

'Good morning, DS Hirst. Officer Shepherd from Bethel Street here.'

'Good morning. How are you?'

'Not bad, thanks,' the young officer replied. 'Given what's going on at the Rosegarden Theatre, I thought I ought to let you know about a couple of new incidents logged this morning.'

'Two?'

'One was an accident involving an IC1 male falling out of the graveyard and being seriously injured on Saturday night.'

'We're onto that one. What's the other?'

'I'm just on my way down to interview an employee called Ben Marsden,' he said. Sara could hear paper rustling in the background. 'Ah, here we are. The alarms at the place were triggered last night, and we had an automatic call-out. The officers who attended say he was attacked as he locked up the theatre after rehearsal.'

'Inside or outside?'

'Not sure,' said Shepherd. 'The thing is, he's claiming that it was someone dressed in a monk's outfit.'

CHAPTER 39

Ben realised he should have expected them to arrive mob-handed as he returned to work on Monday morning. A uniformed officer called Shepherd from Bethel Street said he was there to sign off the paperwork from the automatic call-out. Detective Hirst was there again, this time playing second fiddle to the DI. He was suspicious of them all now after they'd tried to trap him during the interview on Saturday. Not to mention, they'd caught Chris giving him a hard time yesterday.

'I was just following my usual lock-up routine.' All three were sitting across the table from him in his own rehearsal room. It felt like an invasion of his privacy and deliberate intimidation. 'I was the last one in the building, as usual on a Sunday tech rehearsal.'

'Had you seen everyone else leave?' asked Shepherd.

'Mostly,' replied Ben. 'People leave when they've finished. We were the only set in the building, so sometimes I just hear people leave as the front door slams. I go around all the dressing rooms, everywhere backstage and upstairs. Since whoever is doing this broke into wardrobe, I even check the doors that are supposed to be already locked, just in case they aren't. There didn't seem to be anyone here until I thought I saw this damn monk upstairs. It made my flesh creep, I can promise you.'

'Where was he?'

'Backstage on the balcony. I tried to get at him, but I wasn't fast enough. The dressing rooms were still locked, so he couldn't be there. I went round the other downstairs rooms afterwards, and there was no sign.'

'Is there anywhere else he could have hidden?' asked DS Hirst.

Ben knew he looked uncomfortable. The memory of the ghostly figure, which seemed to vanish backstage only to reappear in the foyer, made him edgy. He must have missed him somehow. But the man was wearing a black costume backstage in the theatre, where everything was painted black, and Ben had turned off the lights. It was hardly surprising. He thought hard. 'I didn't check under the stage. The panel was in place, so I didn't think about it.'

'You set the alarm as usual?' Hirst checked.

'Yup, then went out of the front door.' Ben waved behind him. 'I have thirty seconds to get out there and press the release button. There are three deadlocks I have to activate. That's when I saw him. Standing in the foyer. I nearly wet myself. He pulled open the door and pushed past me. Knocked me down the steps.'

'He actually pushed you?' asked Shepherd. He was scribbling in a notepad. 'Not a ghost, then?'

'Thumped me hard. I've got the bruise on my shoulder to prove it. Not to mention the ones on my knees where I fell. Want to see?'

None of the officers did.

'There's another thing,' said Ben. His voice dropped, and he shivered. 'His hands were covered in blood. I saw it dripping when he held his hands out. He could have got at my stock of Kensington Gore, of course.'

'What the hell is that?' Edwards asked.

'Theatrical fake blood. I'd just got a bottle in. We need it for *King Lear*.'

'Have you checked?' demanded Shepherd.

'Not yet,' replied Ben, his temper beginning to fray. 'You haven't given me a chance.'

'Did he touch anything apart from you?' asked Hirst, standing up.

'Handrail on the inside of the door.'

Hirst strode purposefully out of the room, the door banging shut behind her.

'Anything else, Mr Marsden?' asked Shepherd.

'Well, yes. The thing is, if anyone was in here, the alarm shouldn't have set. It should have warned me if a room was in use.'

'Motion sensors? In all the rooms?'

'More or less,' nodded Ben.

'Are some not covered?' asked DI Edwards sharply.

'The ladies' dressing room and the lighting store on the balcony.' Ben shrugged. 'The storeroom is always locked, and I'd checked it was secure.'

'The ladies' dressing room?'

'It's an anomaly. Technically, the room is part of Strangers' Hall Museum.'

'Sorry?' DI Edwards looked confused.

'It's at the rear of the stage. Our building backs onto Strangers' Hall. Back in the day, when the chapel was converted to a theatre, a deal was made with the house owner to use one of their rooms as a dressing room. Access to the old house was blocked off. The hall was given to the city as a museum shortly after that, and we kept the room. It's probably easier if I show you.'

Ben led his interrogators through the green room. DS Hirst rapidly joined them.

'Bloody cleaner has already wiped it,' she muttered to Edwards. 'No chance of fingerprints. I've asked Aggie to organise a swab just in case of DNA.'

Edwards cursed. They followed Ben.

Three steps led through a door and up to the stage level. Immediately to the right of this door was a second one. Ben fiddled with his keys and found the one which opened the padlock to the heavy wooden door. It was painted black, as was the back wall of the theatre. Ben patted the wall.

'This is the end of our building.' He opened the door and went down three steep steps into the well-appointed and airy ladies' dressing room. The police followed him. Turning to them, he held out his hands. 'This room is part of Strangers' Hall.' He pointed to the high ceiling. 'One of the exhibition rooms in the museum is above our heads. You can sometimes hear visitors walking about, oblivious to the fact that we're down here.'

A set of double-height Tudor mullioned windows filled the wall at one end of the room. Light flooded through the ancient glass onto the dressing room stations in front of them. Lined tapestry curtains fell from floor to ceiling to cut out the light if required.

'Don't the ladies worry about being seen getting changed?' asked DS Hirst.

Ben shook his head. 'Only on a matinee day. Hence the curtains.'

'What's beyond there?' asked Shepherd. 'I thought I knew this city, but I'm lost.'

'Strangers' Hall Museum gardens.' Ben smiled at having caught them out. 'It's a walled garden with a period flower collection.' He reached across a low window ledge to open one of the windows. 'This is the fire escape. We've never had to use it. The ladies are supposed to climb out here and wait by the boundary wall of the museum for rescue.'

DI Edwards let out a low whistle. Hirst pushed past Ben to look out. After inspecting the window briefly, she climbed into the flagged courtyard beyond. Her footsteps receded.

'This place is a warren,' said Edwards. 'How do you cope?'

'You get used to it,' replied Ben with a shrug. 'It's a unique site.'

Shepherd took a turn to inspect the window. It was simply sealed with an old-fashioned latch and groove in the frame. He leaned out of the window and checked the frame outside.

'It looks as if someone might have been tampering with this recently,' he said. 'There's paint missing and fresh wood showing. Is it possible that your monk is getting in this way?'

'He could be,' said Ben in surprise. 'The room is locked on the outside once the ladies have left and kept that way most of the day, so even if he did get in this way, he would find it hard to get any further.'

'He could hide in here when it was empty,' suggested Edwards. 'Then let himself out that way when you'd all left.'

'I'd already locked this before I saw him on the balcony,' said Ben quietly. 'There was no time for him to unlock it, and how would he have locked it after himself in any case?'

'Is there any way in and out of the garden?' asked Shepherd.

'There's a gate in the wall. The museum keeps it locked. The wall is about ten feet high.'

'It's fifty metres or more to the gate,' said Hirst as she ducked her head back into the room. 'A fair distance from the building if it's on fire. I reckon a fit bloke could climb over the wall if they tried hard enough.'

'Is there any other way in from next door?' asked Edwards.

'None at all.' Ben pointed to the floor this time. 'The undercroft for the museum can't be accessed from this room and doesn't go under the rest of our building.'

'Undercroft?' asked Hirst sharply. She eased her way back through the window. 'What's that?'

'There's loads of them,' said Ben. He frowned. The woman couldn't be local. 'Most of this area is medieval. The street plan hasn't changed in hundreds of years. This area was full of merchants' houses, and most had undercrofts dug into the chalk below.'

'Medieval warehouses,' said a voice from the door. Shepherd turned sharply. Rachel stood on the top step, holding the door open with one foot, her arms full of costumes. 'Protected by the house or shop above it. They're all over this part of the city. In the old days, some of them even joined up. We don't have one, more's the pity. We could do with the storage space.'

Ben pushed past DI Edwards to help Rachel with the pile of costumes. 'Just hang them on the rails?'

'I'll do it,' she said, glancing at the officers. 'When the room is clear. By the way, is there a problem with the under-stage access?'

'Why?' asked Ben. He felt three sets of ardent police eyes and ears zooming in.

'You usually keep it locked, don't you? When I walked past just now, I caught it with that pile, and it fell open with a thump. Really made me jump!'

CHAPTER 40

There was an almost comic struggle in the doorway to get past Officer Shepherd and be first at the access for the understage area. Falling to her knees, Sara pushed her head and shoulders into the void to look. There wasn't much light under there. She flicked on her torch app and swung the light from her mobile around. The grave pit had its wooden cover in place. The little piles of rubbish still lay where they'd been before. Her beam swung on. There was no mistaking what she saw. A body lay crumpled on the dusty floor towards the front of the stage. Its back was towards her, the legs splayed, one arm under the torso, the other flung above its head. Whoever it was wore trousers and a sweatshirt, but that didn't immediately indicate gender. From here Sara could see a blood-drenched wound in the matted hair. She heaved herself backwards and knelt up.

'There's someone under here,' she snapped to Shepherd. 'Clear the place. Lock the building down. Get the teams in and call an ambulance, just in case.'

As Shepherd pounded away, speaking rapidly into his radio, she heard Rachel in the dressing room saying, 'Oh my God! Oh, that's awful,' before bursting into tears. Ben Marsden was trying to comfort her without much success.

'You'd better have a look, sir,' she said, standing up to make room for DI Edwards to peer inside. After a moment, he also squirmed backwards.

'Marsden!' he called loudly. There was an answering grunt from the dressing room. 'How do you open this grave trap affair from above? We need to get at them. They may still be alive.'

'If it's not locked underneath, it's this way.' Ben Marsden stomped up the wooden steps to backstage, then around to the stage-left wing. They both followed him onto the stage, ducking past a piece of set for *King Lear* and across to the grave trap. A solid brass handle was sunk into the wooden floor, which he lifted and pulled. The trap door came up in his hand, and he dropped the lid with a crash on the stage. The three of them crowded around the gap. Sara was the first to react.

'Fucking hell,' she muttered. Her skin went cold; sweat broke out on her forehead; her knees softened as she stepped back. With a ragged grunt, she collapsed onto her bottom and hip, her legs caught underneath. Before DI Edwards could move to help, she had rolled onto her back, her head thumped on the floor, and a scream formed on her lips but caught, gurgling, in the back of her throat. Coughing out the phlegm, she managed, 'It's Chris.'

* * *

The rapid response paramedic hadn't been needed. Chris was cold and stiff. He had been dead for some time. Officer Shepherd had been a marvel of efficiency, with a good deal of help from Lindie Howes. They had managed to get everyone out of the building, apart from Marsden.

Shepherd had raised uniformed staff to close down the alley and found Bowen and Noble, who were making enquiries a few streets away, while DI Edwards had rung Dr Taylor.

'The gang's all here,' the DI said sarcastically when the two DCs turned up.

Lindie had plied Rachel, Sara and even Ben with the universal comfort of strong, sweet tea before persuading Rachel to go home. She'd put a message on the box office answerphone saying the venue was temporarily closed. Now, she was in the office, making emergency calls to various theatre and committee people.

Ben Marsden sat alone at the back of the auditorium. His mug of tea was balanced on the back of the seat in front of him. It rattled occasionally, Sara assumed with nerves.

Her nerves were also in pieces. It was the nature of the job that she'd seen many a cadaver in her time, but finding a former lover's dead and twisted body was a first for any of them. The mug of hot tea wobbled and slopped liquid onto her smart jeans despite holding it with both hands. The image of his head, turned at an extreme angle to stare up at them, his jaw open in a scream, played in front of her eyes like a still from a shock-horror film. Tea washed around her gums unswallowed. She almost snorted it up her nose as she shook herself. Swallowing with a gasp, Sara coughed loudly.

DC Noble sat in the theatre seat to her right, Bowen to her left. He gently levered the mug from her grasp. 'Breathe. Slowly, one at a time.'

As the coughing fit subsided, she tried to focus on the organised mayhem that once more engulfed the stage. The three team members sat halfway up the auditorium, giving them a premium view of the stage.

Forensics officers in their coveralls were arranging lighting stands or taking photos or laying out kit. Dr Taylor kept half appearing, then vanishing again as he worked inside the grave trap. The lights were up on the stage to help the investigators, but those in the auditorium were only at half-strength.

'Looks like a play, doesn't it?' asked Bowen quietly. Sara had to agree. A very gruesome kind of play.

DI Edwards was busying himself on the stage, talking to Dr Taylor as he bobbed up and down.

'Any idea how long he's been there?' asked Edwards. He had his back to them, and he was speaking quietly. Sara realised the acoustics in the place were amazing. They could hear every word he said.

Dr Taylor pulled himself out of the trap to stage level. 'Rigor mortis is well set in. Overnight, I'd say. Has nobody missed him at all?'

'I'll give the missus a call,' said Bowen. As he stood up, the theatre seat tipped up with a bang. 'She can check the reports this morning.'

He eased sideways along the row of seats and headed towards the foyer. Noble offered Sara her mug of tea back.

'He lived alone,' said Sara. Her voice was ragged from the coughing fit. She sipped at her drink. 'At least, as far as I'm aware.'

Taylor looked at Edwards, who nodded and said, 'It would seem his current girlfriend wasn't best impressed with him yesterday. I suspect she went home without him.'

'How do you know that?' asked Taylor in surprise. Edwards told him about the fight they had interrupted in the green room. 'Was he prone to fighting?'

'Not when I knew him,' admitted Sara. 'Why?'

'Because it looks like he was in a fight very recently.' Taylor glanced down into the grave trap. 'I need to get him on the slab, obviously.'

'And the way he's lying?' asked Edwards.

'Again, I need to do the post-mortem to be sure. It looks like he's been dumped down there in a hurry. However, the angle of his neck looks more deliberate. That may have been staged.'

'Might it be an accident? A fight that went wrong?' asked Sara. Taylor squinted out at his audience.

'Unfortunately, I doubt it. There's significant damage to the back of the skull.'

'He was murdered?' asked DI Edwards sharply. 'Like Carole Morgan?'

'Give me a chance,' replied Taylor. 'I've still got lots of work to do. Definitely a suspicious death at the moment. Who was he fighting with?'

Ben Marsden spoke quietly from the back of the auditorium. 'That would be me.'

CHAPTER 41

Russell dropped Nafisa off at Charing Cross to save him from having to find a parking space. She hurried around the corner into the alley only to find her way barred by a police cordon. Cutting across the narrow road on the other side of the graveyard, she spotted Zach standing with several tent city residents staring over the wall. They were watching the theatre with renewed interest. Luckily, he spotted her.

'Mind the brambles,' he said as she struggled in by the secret entrance, her arms full of bags again.

'What's going on?'

'Not sure,' said Zach. He helped her with her bags, which they hid temporarily in his tent. She squeezed into the curious group and peered over the wall. 'About half an hour ago, several police cars appeared, making their usual racket. They shut off the alley again. Some forensic vans turned up after that. My money is on another murder.'

'Another one?' Nafisa was shocked. Until this week, if anyone had told her that the Rosegarden Theatre even existed in Norwich, she wouldn't have known what they were talking about. Undoubtedly, the latest events would give them a notoriety that would be hard to live down. 'What on earth could anyone have done in a theatre that merits two murders?'

'Who knows?' Zach shrugged. 'I haven't been in a theatre since I was a kid.'

'I've never been,' admitted Nafisa.

'Not even to a panto?' asked Zach. He sounded almost shocked.

Nafisa shook her head. 'I went to the Castle once on a school trip. Does that count?'

'Probably.' Zach smiled. He led Nafisa away from the group. 'Did you want something?'

'I just wanted to make sure you were still here,' she admitted. She lowered her voice to a whisper. 'They've held the eviction order back until Friday, and I have another appointment with the Luke Project this afternoon. I thought you might have moved on, and I'd missed my chance.'

'Your chance?'

Nafisa blushed. 'My chance to give you a chance. Please don't leave, I'm so close to finding you a solution.'

'And what about the others?' Zach gestured to the other tents. 'Can you do anything for them?'

'Perhaps, if they wanted me to.' She looked at the temporary encampment and frowned. 'Have some of them already moved on?'

'Kells and Tam,' nodded Zach. 'Well, technically, just her. He's still in intensive care, I think. She walked up to the hospital last night to see him.'

Nafisa was impressed. It was a good four miles away. 'How is he?'

'They wouldn't let her in.' Zach was visibly annoyed. 'I'm guessing because she looked homeless and didn't need help herself.'

'Then she walked back? Good God!'

'Got back after midnight. Most of us were settling for the night. She was knackered.'

'I'm not surprised.'

'She was up before dawn, though. Packed up both tents. Piled most of their stuff behind the bushes up there.' Zach pointed to several unkempt shrubs that stood against the back wall of the church. They were grimy with city dirt, barely distinguishable from the dark, shiny flints of the wall. 'Then she took off with a rucksack of stuff. Haven't seen her since.'

'Where has she gone, do you think?'

'Hospital, I'd guess.'

'I hope they let her in this time,' said Nafisa. 'Perhaps I should go up and help her?'

'Kells can take care of herself. Don't worry about it. And she missed the other bit of fun,' said Zach.

Nafisa looked at him. 'What?'

'There must have been something going on at the theatre yesterday. Just after nine, that bloke who works there, the one who sometimes brings us cups of tea, must have been coming out. He got knocked down the stairs by someone leaving in a hurry. Someone dressed as a monk.'

'Bloody hell!'

'We were by the fire when we heard the bloke shout. I ran to the wall just in time to see the pillock run off down the alley.' Zach laughed. 'I tried to run after the bugger, but it was no use. Then an alarm went off inside and all hell broke loose. Fire engines and police cars. Blues and twos, shouting and carrying on.'

'He got away from you?'

'I didn't think I could jump over the wall without hurting myself,' admitted Zach. 'Not much of a soldier anymore. By the time I'd got down the steps, he was at the corner.'

'He was too fast for you?'

'Not exactly. I can still run pretty good, and it's downhill. I thought I could catch him. He turned left, but he'd vanished by the time I'd got to the corner. I don't know how.'

'Did you see his face?' asked Nafisa urgently.

'Yeah, I did,' nodded Zach. 'Think I'd guessed who he was anyway.'

'We should tell the police immediately.' Nafisa grabbed him by the arm and attempted to drag him to the graveyard steps.

'He's a dealer,' said Zach, resisting her tugging. 'A new one. I don't remember him from before.'

'You might be able to identify him though.'

'He might not be on their books. New kid on the block.'

'He might have something to do with these murders,' said Nafisa urgently. 'And you've seen his face.'

'I don't want to get involved,' said Zach, nodding at the theatre. He pulled his arm away and planted his feet firmly. There was no way that Nafisa could move him physically.

'It has to be worth a try, doesn't it?' she wheedled.

Zach looked unconvinced. 'If I go to the police, he'll figure out I've seen him. That could make trouble for me. I don't want to be the next one, do I?'

Nafisa knew it was the code of the road that you never shopped anyone. Not even dealers. A little light bulb flashed in her head. She looked at Zach in what she hoped was a stern fashion. 'It's your duty to help the police. You did your duty in the army. Now you need to do it here.'

'I don't even know his name.' Zach wavered a little. 'Not his real one. Kells called him Walter. But what sort of name is that? He can't be more than in his late twenties. No one that age would have such an old-fashioned name.'

'Well, Walter might be a murderer,' said Nafisa firmly. 'I'm going over there to tell them what you've told me. You gonna come with me or not?'

She had marched almost to the top of the stairs before she heard Zach catching up with her.

'All right, all right,' he said. 'Just don't change your mind about this placement, will you?'

'I wouldn't do that,' she replied curtly. 'Now, let's both of us go and do our duty.'

CHAPTER 42

They were once again in the temporary interview room in the rehearsal studio. DI Edwards had tried to prevent Sara from taking part. She'd insisted, and they'd compromised with her sitting at the back of the room, banned from speaking. Edwards and DC Bowen faced Ben Marsden over the table.

'You say that you saw someone in the auditorium as you were locking up,' said Edwards. Marsden nodded. 'You thought you were alone?'

'I was, apart from whoever it was, dressed as a bloody monk, yes,' snapped Marsden.

'No one can corroborate what you've told us.' The DI was keeping his voice level. 'How do we know you're telling us the truth? What if it's just your imagination?'

'There was definitely someone,' replied Marsden. His body was tense and rigid. 'It was no ghost who pushed me down the stairs.'

'Perhaps you tripped,' suggested Bowen. 'Did you bang your head when you fell?'

'Just my hands and knees.' Marsden held up his hands to show them the palms. They were scuffed and raw. A couple of pieces of grubby sticking plaster were partly peeling off. They looked less than hygienic.

'The problem is this,' said Edwards. Sara winced. The boss was using his 'reasonable' tone, which always signalled trouble. 'You were the last one to see Carole Morgan alive.'

'Not true,' sighed Marsden. 'I was the last one to see her in the building. I don't know if anyone saw her after that, apart from her killer.'

'And now,' said Edwards, ignoring the interruption, 'you're the last one to have seen Chris Webster alive.'

'Also not true,' said Marsden. He folded his arms defensively across his chest. 'I last saw him heading for the dressing room. I didn't see anyone after I locked up backstage.'

'Apart from this ghost,' said Bowen. He sounded as if he were sneering.

'You can't have even started your investigations yet,' pointed out Marsden. 'So how do you know if or when he left. You don't know anything.'

Sara longed to interrupt. The stage manager was right. They didn't know anything of the sort. Someone knocked at the door.

'You can see my difficulty,' said Edwards. He nodded to Bowen, who went to open the door. 'We have evidence that you didn't get on with Carole. Myself and DS Hirst caught you in the middle of a fight with our second victim. It doesn't look good.'

'Sir,' Bowen interrupted. Sara could see Shepherd hovering outside. 'Someone is insisting on speaking to us, and I think we probably should.'

Marsden sighed in relief as Edwards switched off the recorder on his phone. 'Wait here, Mr Marsden.'

Without being asked, Sara hurried out of the room with them. Shepherd led them to the theatre bar. Another uniformed officer stood talking to two people: the social worker they'd interviewed yesterday and the homeless man from the churchyard camp. Edwards waved the officer away.

'We've been looking for you,' Edwards said to the man. 'We need a talk about Saturday night.'

The DI turned to the social worker. 'What can I do for you?'

He indicated some easy chairs, and Nafisa Ahmed sat down. Zach stood behind her protectively.

'I assume you have another incident here,' said the woman. 'Something that happened last night?'

'I can't prevent you from assuming anything,' said Edwards cagily.

Nafisa frowned. She leaned back in the chair and eyed Edwards. 'Zach saw someone last night. I think you should listen to what he has to say.'

Sara watched the homeless man as he shuffled uneasily.

Edwards turned his attention to the man. 'Zach? What's your full name, Zach?'

'Zachary Wilson,' insisted the man. 'I've been just Zach for years. You should call me that.'

'Zach was in the army,' interrupted Nafisa. 'I think his full name has unwelcome associations. Oh, I'm sorry, Zach. I shouldn't have . . .'

'That's all right,' said Zach. He placed a dirty mittened hand on her shoulder and patted her. 'My past isn't a secret. It's just something I don't like to talk about much. I was pensioned out, Inspector.'

He slowly pulled off his outer coat and the padded anorak underneath it. There were two more jumpers under that. Zach pushed up the sleeves on his right arm and held it out for inspection. Sara could see ragged, silvery scars criss-crossing his lower arm. Looking more closely at his neck and face, she could see other old red scars, livid against his pale skin. The arm hair refused to grow on the scars, curling over the old battle wounds. The veteran traced one of the wider ones with his fingers.

'IED. Afghanistan.' Zach re-dressed himself carefully. 'I was lucky not to lose an arm or leg. I was lucky not to die.'

Bowen mumbled a rude word, and Sara felt it was probably justified. Whatever their job might bring them, terrorist bombs were not a common hazard for the police here in rural Norfolk.

'What did you see, Zach?' asked Edwards. 'And when?'

'Last night. Just after nine.' Zach glanced out of the long glass window towards the city hall clock, barely visible above the roofline outside. 'Heard a shout in the courtyard. There have been so many problems, I thought I'd better look. I saw that nice chap who works here lying on the ground and this dealer, in his monk's habit, running off down the alleyway.'

'Did you do anything?'

'Ran after him. When I got round the corner, he'd vanished.'

Sara glanced at Bowen. It was the same phrase Noble had used. This monk seemed real enough. Then, he could vanish as quickly as any spectre.

'You said dealer? What do you mean by that?'

'It's okay, I'll tell them if you want me to,' said Nafisa.

Zach shook his head. 'You know what they get up to around the tents,' he said to Edwards. 'Whether you believe me or not, I don't indulge. I have my own demons, but that shit isn't one of them.'

'We have a pretty good idea what they get up to,' agreed Edwards. *At least he used 'they'*, Sara thought gratefully. *Let the man talk*.

'There's plenty of people in the city you can buy from, or so they tell me. This bugger was different. Turned up the day after we'd set up. Came into the graveyard, bold as brass and offered cut-price baggies.'

'Two weeks ago?' asked Bowen.

'About that,' nodded Zach. 'He didn't dress up at first. Had a black hoodie on instead. Had some good stuff, the others told me.'

'When did he start dressing up? What was he wearing?' Bowen sounded excited.

'That damn monk's robe thingy. Started about a week ago.'

'Last Tuesday?'

'Might have been Wednesday. It's not easy to keep track of time in our situation.'

'Go on,' encouraged Bowen.

'He'd done a good job hiding his face,' Zach considered. 'Apart from on Saturday night.'

'When Tam got pushed over the wall?' Sara suddenly asked.

'Yeah. Then. His hood fell down. He legged it afterwards.'

'And have you seen him since?'

'Not for dealing. Last night, when that theatre fella got knocked down the stairs, I saw him then. Still in his bloody monk's outfit, though he could run fast.'

'How can you be sure?' pushed Sara. 'Did he have the hood up?'

'Yes. Thing is, as he ran towards me, he was pulling something off his head, and he knocked his hood down. I'm sure it was the same bloke.'

'Did you see him clearly enough to recognise him again?' Sara held her breath in anticipation.

'Perhaps.' Zach thought for a moment, then squared his shoulders. 'Yes, I reckon I can.'

CHAPTER 43

For some reason, to do with the homeless man from the tents and his social worker, Ben was dismissed without explanation or, in his opinion, the apology that he was due. The building buzzed with forensic people, and a police cordon once again cut them off from the city. He was glad that he'd had the foresight to put his clothes from last night into the washing machine at home. The monk had left bloody marks on his sweatshirt as he'd pushed past Ben outside. Something else they could use to frame him. His flesh crawled with paranoia.

'There's nothing I can do,' he said to Lindie. She was in the office, filing contracts into the outside show cabinet. 'They won't let me anywhere near backstage.'

'I think you should go home,' said Lindie. She sounded sympathetic. When Ben looked at her, she also seemed paler than usual. The contracts in her hand were shaking, and she was leaning on the side of the cabinet for support.

'I think we both should,' he said.

'I'm waiting for the Trust chair to turn up.' Lindie slumped into her chair, dropping the papers onto her desk with a weary gesture. 'He can deal with it after that. I can't imagine they'll want to keep *King Lear* going.'

'Oh, they might,' nodded Ben. 'One of Shakespeare's hardest plays, and it will sell like hotcakes, just so people can be in the place where two murders happened.'

'We'll be shut until the Christmas show, if you ask me,' said Lindie. 'Go on, get off home. If I hear anything, I'll send you a text.'

Ben gathered his stuff and went over to the car park. He couldn't really remember much of his drive home. It must have been autopilot and self-preservation that got him there. Still on automatic, Ben dropped his rucksack on the hall floor, made a cup of tea, and turned on the gas fire in his living room. He only became aware that he was sitting in his favourite armchair when the lunchtime news music thumped out of his television. They ran the usual headlines, followed by the local ones. The theatre was mentioned, with a familiar reporter at the top of Church Alley spouting sensationalism. He looked to be relishing it. Ben flicked the sound off.

'It's just like last time,' he muttered. A wave of depression threatened him, only that wasn't Ben's nature. 'Come on. Do something. Think it through.'

Surely, it wasn't the same as before. To start with, the other problem had been handled by the police with very little publicity accruing to the theatre. These last few years had made a lot of difference. Back then they had treated the place with the respect due to a venerable Norwich institution, although they had got their man and jailed him. Nor had it been for a murder, let alone two.

Social media hadn't been so strong a player then, either. As Ben flicked through the search engine on his mobile phone, it was clear that the theatre was being subjected to a barrage of idle gossip and conspiracy theories, most of them centring around the fantasy that the murders were being perpetrated by a ghost. Suddenly, the ghostly Rosegarden Monk was an internet sensation. He sighed with frustration.

Ben didn't believe there was no such thing as bad publicity. Stories like this could actually kill the place as stone dead as their poor victims. He shuddered with revulsion. What if this was as much a part of the monk's intention as the actual deaths? What if he didn't just want to kill? His victims weren't random. They were both deeply involved in the place. And what if he didn't just want to demonstrate that he was, or had once been, one of their own? What if the mad bugger wanted to bring the whole place down? To destroy it?

Ben chewed his lip thoughtfully. Who could feel as strongly as that about an amateur dramatic company, even one as well-endowed as the Rosegarden? Of course, there had been rows and fallings out over the years. Only one person might feel as strongly as that about them all. A youngster who had been on his mind for days now.

Ben searched on his phone again. It took a while, but eventually, he turned up an old newspaper report. A photo of the young criminal headed the page. Tall and gangly, with a teenager's physique, he glared angrily at the photographer as if he couldn't believe that he'd been caught, let alone sentenced to nine years.

Ben remembered him and the investigation all too well. The pretty, young DC who clearly saw this case as her route to promotion, who had hassled Ben to say something incriminating about the youngster. It was the root of his mistrust of the police. Ben had never seen the lad taking or selling drugs at the theatre or anywhere else. He wasn't going to say he had just to get him put away, which the DC had suggested was what was needed. *Get one of the little buggers off the street* was the phrase she'd used. Ben was not going to lie for her.

He felt the same suspicion of this set of detectives, who might be trying to set him up for the fall rather than leave the case unsolved. God only knows what they had been trying to persuade some of the others to say about him.

Reading over the news report reminded him of the court case. He had refused to attend himself. It was Chris Webster who had given the most damning evidence, who had sworn he had seen the trainee selling baggies to the other ghost walk man in the courtyard. The one who had died suddenly.

Then there had been the row with Carole, who had taken the police's side. They had never made up their differences after that. The latter complaint from Chris had only compounded their antipathies.

But here was the problem. The lad had been just seventeen when he was caught. His sentence had begun seven years ago. Even with probation or some other sentence-reducing tactic, he couldn't be out yet. Could he?

CHAPTER 44

Zach's vague statement was enough for DC Bowen and DI Edwards to bundle him into a car and head off to Wymondham to arrange a trawl through the suspected local dealers with the help of the Drugs Team. DC Noble walked off to do more checks around Charing Cross. Nafisa Ahmed had suddenly sworn when she'd realised the time.

'I should have been at an appointment ten minutes ago,' she said, gathering her bags.

'Where?' asked Sara. 'Can I give you a lift?'

'Mile Cross,' replied the social worker. She tugged at her hijab in frustration as the strap of her laptop bag caught it. 'Can you do that?'

'Sure. I've got to go to the hospital anyway. It's on my way.'

Nafisa scurried after Sara as they crossed the road to collect her car from the multi-storey. 'Nothing serious, I hope?'

She frowned for a moment, then smiled. 'Not for myself. There's an identity viewing at the mortuary, and I'm going to support the family.'

* * *

Sara was early enough to grab something to eat and a coffee in the café bar, but by the time she'd found an empty seat, her appetite had vanished. She moodily picked at the packaging holding the tuna-and-mayo sandwich. As she took a bite, bits of tuna fell onto the table, where they lay looking unappetising. The food was hard to swallow. She swigged her drink to wash it down. Her stomach grumbled at her, threatening to give the mouthful back. There was little doubt why she was feeling this way. It was the shock.

Her relationship with Chris had finished a long time ago. There had been no reason for her to meet him after that, and she hadn't even run into him in the street. If asked, she would have said that she'd moved on, not least to the next short-lived affair with Dante Adebayo.

Seeing him again in the theatre had been difficult enough, despite the fact she'd known about it in advance. Somehow, seeing Chris twisted up under the stage, staring up at her, had shocked her to the core. How did you cope with that? The man who'd welcomed her to Norwich. Her lover and, she'd thought, her friend. Now he was dead. Murdered by someone dressing up as a ghost. Perhaps it would be better if she pulled herself off this case. DCI Hudson might insist on that anyway. She sighed.

'Sara?' The voice was familiar. Tracey Mills, the family liaison officer, waved at her from the glass entrance doors. She must be taking Helen Morgan-Harris down to the viewing. They were also early. Sara raised her hand in reply, stuffed the limp sandwich into the rubbish bin, swigged her coffee and threw the cup away.

'Thought it was you,' said Tracey as they met. 'Would you recommend the café?'

'Not really,' Sara admitted. 'Coffee's okay. We could go straight down if that's all right with you?'

'Just waiting for Dad,' said Helen, to Sara's surprise. She hadn't expected James Morgan to be part of the visit. 'He doesn't like us going in the loo with him. It helps keep his dignity for a while longer.'

He emerged from the accessible toilet a couple of minutes later. He was leaning on a walking stick and shuffling slowly across the foyer. It took him several seconds to recognise his daughter among the hurrying people. His face was grey and drawn with stress, although it lit up with a smile when Helen reached him.

'I didn't think you would bring him,' Sara whispered to Tracey.

'He insisted,' shrugged Tracey. 'It's his right. The daughter seems to think he won't believe Carole is dead unless he sees her. Keeps saying she's sitting in the bedroom at night.'

'He's seeing her ghost?' asked Sara. She didn't mean it seriously. Or did she? A shiver ran down her spine.

'It's the sort of dementia that he's got,' said Tracey quietly. 'With Lewy body, you get hallucinations. Seeing people that aren't there is not unusual.'

'He didn't imagine whoever it was that trashed their home,' said Sara. 'He was real enough.'

Helen was watching them expectantly. Tracey smiled and went over to them. 'It's this way.'

It was slow going. Despite the stick, James walked stiffly and slowly. Gradually, they passed the various wards and crossed the atrium. The number of staff and visitors dwindled until they reached a set of doors that said *Staff Only*. A pass card would be needed to go any further. Sara spoke briefly into the access phone. A few minutes later, a mortuary assistant let them in.

'Dr Taylor has just got back,' she said to Sara. 'He asked that you wait with the visitors.'

Sara's heart sank. She could guess why. They must have brought Chris into the examination room when they returned.

With a sympathetic smile, the assistant led them into the waiting room and flicked on the lights. There was no daylight here. It felt as if they were underground, although they weren't. Sara assumed this was for privacy. One wall contained several windows. Curtains were drawn closed on the far side, so visitors couldn't see the room beyond.

'You have a choice in a moment,' said the assistant quietly to Helen and James. She indicated the curtained windows. 'Your loved one is waiting for you in the next room. You'll be able to see her well enough if you wish to remain here. I can also take you into the next room if you wish to be closer to her. However, I would respectfully ask that you don't touch her at this time. That will be possible later on. I'll give you a few minutes to think.'

Helen struggled with tears as she tried to explain this to James. He looked at her in confusion and began to shuffle his feet anxiously. Tracey moved to Helen's side.

'Unless you need to be closer, may I suggest that staying here would be easier for Mr Morgan? It's a strange environment for us all.'

'I'm not sure he understands what he's insisted on doing,' sighed Helen. 'Yes, let's stay in here.'

There was a polite knock at the door. Dr Taylor stepped into the room in clean scrubs. Tracey gave their decision.

'If you care to step up to the windows, I'll open the curtains for you.'

He went out again, and a few seconds later, they heard the curtains being gently moved aside. Dr Taylor walked to the far side of the trolley, where someone lay under a pristine white sheet. He looked at Helen, who nodded. Dr Taylor lifted the top of the sheet with great care, revealing Carole Morgan's head. He folded it gently at her neck. Time suspended, even for Sara. It was always difficult to be with family at these personal moments, far removed from crime scenes or post-mortems.

'Yes, that's Mum,' said Helen quietly. Her arm was laced through her father's. James Morgan was rigid as he gazed through the window at his wife. 'Is that enough, Dad? Shall we go now?'

The pair turned away. As Tracey helped them towards the door, Helen was crying helplessly. Her father hugged her to his chest.

'We'll be all right,' he said to her. 'We've still got each other.'

He sounded so lucid, so capable. Sara felt tears prickle in her eyes, which betrayed her usual professionalism. She ground her teeth silently to help herself get a grip.

'You think that man who came to our house did this to my Carole at the theatre?' James asked.

'It's too early to be sure,' replied Sara.

'I couldn't see his bloody face,' he said angrily. 'But I recognised his voice. I can't remember why he should be at the house, damn it. I can remember where I know him from, though. He was a troublemaker for Carole and almost destroyed the scheme she'd set up. Just before she retired, he ended up in court. I went to support her, and that's why I know his voice.'

CHAPTER 45

Nafisa felt that her client hadn't forgiven her for being late. The woman was difficult with her despite the offer of help that Nafisa had brought. The teenage daughter was out, supposedly at school, although they both knew that she was truant more often than she attended. Nafisa left the house and trudged to the nearest bus stop just as it started to rain heavily. The sky was dark with clouds, and the evening was drawing in early now with the autumn clock changing.

Nafisa shivered under her umbrella. It was only three o'clock. Her work papers, which were once more in a supermarket bag-for-life, were getting damp. With a sudden rush of determination, she took the bus to the city and headed for the expensive leather goods shop just as she had promised herself. She rarely indulged in treats, using much of her income to support her now-retired parents by paying them a high rent and extra for her keep. This afternoon, Nafisa took her time selecting a large, dark brown leather courier-style bag with a deep flap and clip fastening. Then she dug out her bank card and resolutely paid for it.

The case worker at the Luke Project had confirmed their meeting, and Nafisa had decided to take Zach with her. Neither man knew what she intended. Carefully storing her work papers inside the new bag, she splashed through the puddles to the graveyard. The wind tugged at the hood of her coat, grabbing at her headscarf and throwing spiteful cold shards at her skin.

The miserable weather had almost emptied the city. Only the occasional pedestrian hurried past her, head down against the drenching sheets of water. The shops and cafés looked temptingly warm with their bright lights, but most of them looked empty, and some were already shutting up for the evening, as more customers seemed unlikely.

The night had settled in early as the city hall clock struck half past three. The alley past the theatre was still cordoned off. A couple of police officers sheltered under the church arch, gloomily looking out at Pottergate. Forensic vans lined the small street of Lower St Johns. Nafisa rolled up her umbrella and used it to force her way up the 'secret' entrance steps to the graveyard.

It was silent. Rain lashed across the headstones and box tombs. Slippery mud streaked the grass where the tent city people had walked or camped. Intermittent shafts of street light flickered through the blustering trees. The bonfire was a murky mess of soaking grey ash and a half-burnt pallet. Only three tents remained, one of which was Zach's. None of them looked occupied. The temporary cardboard shelter lay where it had collapsed; the occupant had vanished, the board melting under the pounding rain.

Nafisa decided to look around as best she could in the indifferent light. As she skidded past the bonfire, a single heavy step made the hairs on her neck stand up. Pulling up sharply, she looked around. No one was there as far as she could see, although it was difficult to be sure in this light. Her breathing quickened as her heart rate climbed with anxiety. The tree branches sent shadows jumping across the headstones, momentarily highlighting a carved skull and crossbones on one and a weird angel motif on another. They plunged back into darkness, and she shuddered. The bulk of the church rose at the top of the graveyard, its flint-covered walls shining like mourning jet. More shadows chased between the unlit windows.

Zach's tent was zipped shut. He must still be helping the police. She hoped he was being treated like a witness rather than a suspect. He wouldn't take kindly to the latter. Hovering between the two remaining tents, she called a greeting. There wasn't even a moan in reply.

The rain had penetrated her coat, and she could feel the cold wetness dripping down her back. Her dark woollen trousers hung limply against her legs. The chill on her skin raised goosebumps, and she shivered with growing fear. She had never felt less like going to a business meeting in her life.

A metallic clatter from the theatre courtyard made her jump, almost literally. She shrank back against one of the trees. Someone had dropped something. Glancing over the cemetery wall, Nafisa watched a forensic officer in a coverall gather up the things he had dropped and store them back in his toolbox. Clipping it shut, he walked down the alley. She watched his head go around the bottom of the graveyard, knowing she could hardly appear down the overgrown steps while the man was there. She wasn't supposed to be here.

Besides, Nafisa felt she couldn't move at all. Her feet were glued to the oozing turf. The tree behind her gave a tiny amount of shelter, but the bark dug into her back through her wet clothes. It felt unreal to be standing there, watching him, knowing he was unaware of her. Momentarily invisible in the world. Almost as if she were out of time altogether. The sensation of being watched seized her. Panic rose in her throat. Still, she couldn't move.

The man unlocked one of the forensic vans and put the box inside. He stripped off his coverall, crumpled it into a ball and threw it into the back with the box. The back doors slammed, and the man hurried through the streaming rain to the driver's door. Nafisa waited until the engine fired and the van moved away down the little hill.

Reluctantly, she moved away from the shelter of the tree. Carefully stepping around the grey muck of the bonfire, Nafisa felt her heart pounding again. Pausing by the mushy cardboard shelter, she looked around uncertainly. Surely there was no one here. Gathering her courage, she moved again. Police officers were at the top of the alley, and forensic people all over the theatre. How could she really be in danger?

She took no more than three paces past the chest tomb when she sensed, rather than heard, someone behind her. A hand grabbed at the strap of her new bag and pulled sharply. Nafisa felt herself being spun around.

Shock made the blood roar in her ears. Her eyes could barely make out the tall, thin figure dressed all in black. The hoodie that sheltered his face blew down in the wind. She was horrified to see a skull grinning at her. Her mouth opened, but the scream wouldn't come. Her bags were ripped from her body and thrown across the graveyard. Strong hands gripped her arms. Nafisa was lying on her back on the water-logged earth in less than a second. Her beautiful, bright headscarf instantly soaked up the muddy water. Someone was kneeling on her thighs. Hands pinned her arms to the ground. Revulsion gripped her, and she struggled wildly.

The figure sharply raised one hand, and before she could take advantage of her free arm, the hand ricocheted across her face. The pain was more intense than anything Nafisa had ever known. Now, the hand clamped over her open mouth.

'No screams, no shouts,' hissed a voice close to her face. The man's weight on her legs was brutal as he leaned forward. 'You interfering bitch. You're going to pay for what you've done.'

The hand swung again, this time hitting her on the side of her head, and Nafisa sank into darkness.

CHAPTER 46

Aggie was brandishing a sheaf of printouts when Sara returned for the evening briefing. 'We've found it. There was a case several years ago. Drugs dealt with it.'

DS Ellie James occupied the seat at the spare desk. She had been a DC in the SCU team when Sara first joined Norfolk Police. Ellie had moved into the Drugs Team when she was promoted to sergeant. She and Sara had struck up a friendship in the early days, which survived despite the arrival of new relationships and Sara moving to the coast. Gone were the days when they went clubbing together. Ellie now lived with her partner, Cara, in Norwich, where they spent their spare time volunteering for the annual Pride parade activities. Ellie gave Sara a knowing grin.

DCI Hudson settled in front of the whiteboards and waved Aggie forward. 'What have you got?'

'Carole Morgan was a career social worker,' said Aggie. She began to put various newspaper articles up on the board. 'She rose to head of Children's Services at the county council. During her time there, she instituted a lot of changes.'

'Sounds like she had a talent for getting things done,' suggested DI Edwards.

Aggie nodded and continued. 'One major project was to create links with local businesses and community groups to give youngsters in their care some work experience or help them find new hobbies. The thing of interest to us is the connection with Mile Cross High School.'

Mile Cross was a Norwich council estate with a difficult reputation, unearned in Sara's opinion. It was a lightweight problem compared to some places Sara had been when she'd been an officer with the Met. There were also some lovely 1930s houses, which were the envy of other tenants. She pursed her lips in annoyance when Bowen snorted his derision. He opened his mouth to say something as Aggie frowned at him, and he subsided obediently.

'Carole's friend was head teacher there,' said Aggie. 'They created opportunities for several pupils to gain experience beyond the confines of the estate.'

'Was one of those at the theatre?' asked DC Noble.

'It was,' nodded Aggie. 'Here's an article from about eight years ago, when young volunteers from the school started doing weekly sessions at the Rosegarden.'

She pointed to a photo of a group of smiling teenagers standing in the courtyard with the head, Carole and Ben Marsden. Carole looked proud; the youngsters looked pleased; Marsden looked grumpy. DC Bowen joined his wife by the board.

'This is the young man of interest,' he said, picking out a tall, skinny teenager. 'This is where it gets really interesting. This is Edward or Eddie Kenyon. Also known as Scooter. The Drugs Team have more than a passing knowledge of Scooter.'

The team turned to look at Ellie, who stood up and held up a file. 'Young Scooter was a bit of a wag. He had bags of confidence and some talent for acting, which he used to his advantage as a minor drug dealer at school or around the estate.'

'Did Carole know about that?' asked Sara.

'She always said that she didn't,' replied Ellie. 'I'm not so sure. She claimed it was her friend who recommended Scooter for the Rosegarden sessions. He was on our team's radar, but he was such a minor player that they mostly watched him hoping to find bigger fish to arrest.'

'Further up the supply chain.' Noble nodded reflectively. 'Did it work?'

'Interestingly, only for a short while. At first, getting involved at the theatre seemed to be the boost he needed.' Ellie pointed to the article. 'He'd be fifteen in this picture. In fact, he took to the place so well that he stopped dealing altogether for several months. He acted in a couple of shows, and left school at sixteen to start an apprenticeship with the venue to learn backstage skills. Scooter appeared to have landed in the right place with the right support, vindicating Carole Morgan's scheme.'

'But it didn't last?' asked DI Edwards, full of cynicism. Ellie shook her head.

'About six months into the job, Scooter reconnected with his supplier and began to deal again.' She laid the file on the desk in front of her and pulled out various reports. 'We picked up on him again when he contacted a known mid-chain dealer for class-A baggies. Unluckily for him, the timing was terrible. We had an operation planned to bring down the whole line, and Scooter was scooped up with the rest.'

'Surely he wouldn't get much time for that? He was only a street dealer.' Sara was confused. Ellie shrugged.

'He was at the dealer's house when we went in. Scooter tried to do a runner out the back door, pursued by a couple of the team. He'd been sampling some of the goods and was in a fighting mood. Broke Jake Wood's nose and gave Yvonne Bexter a black eye.'

Noble sighed. 'So, they threw the book at him.'

'Yup. He got nine years. Seven for dealing, and a further two for assault. Not concurrent.'

Bowen whistled. It wasn't usual.

'He was held in Norwich Young Offenders to begin with. Shipped up north after a few months.'

Sara pulled the file towards her and checked the arrest sheet. 'He was tall, even then. Skinny, but plenty of room to muscle out. How did he take to prison?'

'According to the psychologist I spoke to, very angrily.' Ellie pushed a copy of another report towards Sara. 'He spent most of his sessions with her blaming everyone except himself. She says it was a borderline obsession. She also thought he might be at risk of sexual abuse, given that he was quite a pretty boy when he went in. HMP Deerbolt is a mixed prison and YOI, although the youngsters are kept separately.'

'Was he?' asked Edwards. 'Abused?'

'The other way around, it seems. His tallness gave him an advantage in the young offenders' institute. Became obsessed with working out. His size and age gave him *droit de seigneur* within a few weeks. Got two further years added to his sentence for it. So eleven years in total.'

There was a cagey silence as the team passed photos of Scooter between themselves. The raw anger showing in his arrest photos had settled into a deep-seated hatred in the picture taken when he'd been found guilty of abuse in Deerbolt. The venomous stare was unmistakable despite a floppy fringe half obscuring his eyes. As were his handsome features.

'He'd be what now? Twenty-four or more?' asked Hudson. 'He's got another four to go. Why is he of interest?'

'The staff and some of the actors at the theatre and Carole Morgan were all interviewed when he was arrested. One admitted they'd seen him dealing in the gents' dressing room. Another claimed they'd seen him doing it one evening outside the courtyard.'

'Ben Marsden?' asked Bowen. 'Was it him?'

'No. Marsden claimed he'd never seen Scooter doing anything like it. Got quite upset by it. Refused to give a statement.'

Sara frowned. 'What about Carole Morgan?'

'It seems that Carole went to his trial,' said Ellie. 'Gave evidence for the prosecution, saying he'd let everyone down, although her chum, the head teacher, said he came from a good family and had been a reasonable pupil.'

'Was that true?'

'The good family bit was. They moved away afterwards. Didn't want to stay around here when his younger brother and sister might have to go to the same school. It seems they were as shocked as Carole claimed to be. His school records showed him to be an average pupil but not especially badly behaved.'

DCI Hudson pinned a picture of Scooter on the whiteboard. 'So, Scooter knew the theatre intimately, worked closely with Ben Marsden for at least six months and had reason to hate the place if others there had given evidence against him.'

'Agreed,' said Sara with a frown. 'That might explain why Carole would be attacked. It doesn't explain why Chris was killed.'

Ellie looked slightly sheepish as she flipped open another page in the file and pointed. 'Unfortunately, it does. He was the one who said he'd seen Scooter dealing in the courtyard.'

Sara read the page and looked up. 'Selling drugs to one Stuart Stone. Daryl's father, I assume.'

'I'll double-check,' said Aggie, scribbling herself a note. Hudson nodded her approval.

Sara looked closely at the custody pictures of Scooter. 'Where is he? Please tell me he's still in the prison system.'

'I'm afraid not,' said Ellie. 'He was let out on licence four months ago on condition he stayed near Deerbolt in the Barnard Castle area. Was in a bail hostel and attended his sign-ins until six weeks ago.'

'When he vanished?' supplied Sara.

Ellie nodded gravely.

CHAPTER 47

When his mobile suddenly woke him, Ben realised he must have nodded off in his armchair at least a couple of hours ago. The fabric of his trousers was hot to the touch, where he had stretched out in front of the gas fire. His tea was stone cold, and it was dark outside. Rummaging down the side of his armchair, he unearthed the phone as it trilled at him. The number was the theatre office.

'I'm sorry to disturb you.' It wasn't Lindie. He yawned as he tried to answer the chair of the Trust committee.

'S'okay,' he mumbled. 'What can I do for you?'

'We wondered if you could come in. We need to discuss the situation,' said the chair. It wasn't an invitation; it was definitely more of an order. Ben winced at the man's cut-glass tone, and his assumption that Ben had nothing better to do with his time off. Even so, he agreed, wondering as he drove in if he would be quizzed about his interview.

The police and forensic people had gone, and the alley was clear when he crossed from the car park. The temporary cordon tape had been yanked down, leaving a torn ribbon which flapped manically in a gust of wind as he passed it. Rain drummed heavily on the tents in the graveyard. The people up there were in for a bad night.

To Ben's surprise, the committee wanted his input on whether the show should proceed. Lindie was also there. Ben suspected the poor woman hadn't been home as he watched her struggling to keep her eyes open. Director Glyn Hollis sat fidgeting with his pen and notepad as the debate wandered back and forth.

The Trust seemed unable to make a decision. One half of the committee was reluctant to lose the undoubted income that continuing would bring, while the other agreed that it was impractical to go on. As usual, it was a compromise. Put the play back until a slot could be found in the next season, then do it as a tribute to the two victims.

'I'll put together a press release tomorrow,' said Lindie in conclusion. She turned to Glyn Hollis. 'Is that enough time for you to contact the cast?'

He nodded. 'I don't think they'll be surprised.'

'Will you give details about ticket refunds and so on?' asked the chair. Ben thought Lindie did well not to roll her eyes. Of course she would. It was part of her job.

'I'll lock up,' he offered as the various Trust members hurried off into the wet and windy evening. 'You get off home.'

Lindie didn't need to be asked twice. She zipped up her coat and hurried down the front stairs. Ben completed his round of checks, grateful not to see another ghost or corpse. As the alarm set with a long beep, he shrugged up the hood on his jacket before crossing the courtyard.

'Here, mate,' called a man's voice. 'Can you help me?'

Grateful to be heading back to his warm living room, Ben stopped reluctantly. A figure stood in the graveyard clutching sheaves of wet paper. The man was bundled up against the weather, and the rain driving into Ben's face made it difficult for him to see properly.

'Yeah? What? You need a cuppa or something?' Ben moved closer to the wall. The man moved closer to the edge. 'Ah, it's Zach, isn't it?'

'Yeah. No, not a cuppa, mate, thanks.' Zach waved a fistful of paper. 'I'm really worried, and I could do with some help grabbing this lot before it all blows away.'

'Paper? Just paper? Christ!'

'Not just paper.' Zach shook his head. 'I recognise them. They're forms and reports. Social work stuff. I think they belong to Nafisa.'

The woman who had been with him that morning at the theatre, Ben remembered. Zach's face was crumpled with worry.

'Hang on,' Ben called up with a sigh. Shouldering his rucksack, he climbed up the steps to the graveyard. It was hard to see much in the dark. The street lights flickered in and out as the trees bent and swayed in the gusting wind. The rain had slackened a little compared to an hour ago, but it still gusted into Ben's face, half blinding him. He pulled out his backstage torch and flicked it on. Swinging the beam wide, he soon picked up Zach, striding towards him, arms full of sodden paper. They met by the box tomb. Zach dumped the paper on top, holding it down with both hands.

'Look at this.' He nodded his head at the pile, then flicked his head over his shoulder. 'Look over there.'

Ben shone his torch at the papers. There was little doubt they were official documents. Logos and departmental headings survived in the mass that was rapidly turning to pulp.

Ben stepped past Zach and let his torch rake the encampment. Only three tents remained, and one had collapsed in the weather. It writhed like a maimed animal in the mud. More paper lay in the puddles, scattered into the tree branches and trapped in the bushes. A carrier bag flapped angrily from the fork of a broken headstone.

'Why do you think this belongs to Nafisa?' he asked loudly, almost shouting against the wind.

'Handbag,' replied Zach. He gave up the unequal struggle with the paper, dumping it on the lee side of the chest tomb. Pages began to peel off and scatter immediately. 'Laptop and work bags. Over here.'

He led Ben past the grey remnants of the bonfire to his tent. Zach had been wise enough to pitch up in the protection of a set of thick bushes, so at least his tent was still standing. A small, bright-blue handbag with a long strap and a brown leather courier bag dripped by the front flap.

'You sure they belong to her?' Ben asked, although the little blue handbag looked alarmingly familiar.

'Checked inside,' said Zach quickly, holding out the handbag. 'Cards in her purse. ID with her photo.'

'And the other?'

'Receipt caught in the bottom. Her card, I think. Hard to be sure in this. She was going to visit to tell me about a placement meeting she had this afternoon. Although the police kept me late. I hoped she might still be around.'

'Where did you find them?'

'By the tomb,' said Zach. 'I'm really worried. Why would her work stuff be scattered all over the place? Why leave her purse or her laptop? Something's happened to her.'

'It could be an accident,' Ben suggested unconvincingly as he shone his torch around the grass. The ground was too trampled to tell him anything. The beam flickered up the side of the stone. The pious inscription about the occupants had long since faded. It wasn't just the rain that sent shivers down Ben's back. 'Damn. I think we ought to call the police again.'

CHAPTER 48

She had barely reached the ground floor of the building when Sara's phone rang. After the long silence, Adie was suddenly calling her. Folding herself into one of the sofa chairs opposite Trevor Jones's reception desk, her heart jumped in anticipation as she swiped to answer it.

'Hello,' she said in an unusually quiet voice. She held the mobile close to her ear to cut out the bustle of the home-going civilian staff. 'Adie?'

'Sara?' His plummy tones sent a warm quiver down her spine. 'How are you?'

'I'm all right. How about you?'

'I'm great. Are you free to talk?'

How dare he sound so upbeat when she'd been wondering where he'd been.

'Just about to leave work,' she said brightly, although her heart sank a little.

'I wanted to apologise for not ringing before.' Adie's voice began to cut up. His signal must be poor. 'Did you get my message?'

'No. What message?' Here it came. She gritted her teeth.

'I'm sorry. I tried to leave you one from the airport, but I wasn't sure I'd done it right.'

Sara knew that technology wasn't his thing. 'Airport? Which airport?'

'Schiphol. Everything happened so fast.'

'Amsterdam? What are you talking about? Where are you?'

'Nepal.'

Sara half stood up in surprise. 'Nepal? What? Why?' Her voice must have also gone up as Trevor Jones shot her a look of enquiry.

Adie's voice crackled. The line cut out momentarily, then back in. '. . . opportunity. College said I could use it as part of my final papers.'

'Adie, you're breaking up. I didn't get that.' She was getting frustrated.

'I'll explain when I get back. I'm on a plant-hunting expedition. A new species of rhododendron.'

Sara felt her jaw drop open. For once, she was lost for words.

'That's why I haven't been able to call you,' continued Adie. 'Only a satellite phone up there in the mountains. We just got back in range.'

'What's going on?'

'It all happened so fast.' He sounded anxious and elated at the same time. His words were becoming scrambled. 'I just prayed you'd got my message. It was a bit long. I haven't been ignoring you . . . sorry . . . miss you . . . wanted to ask you about Christmas . . . it was the chance of a lifetime, I had to come . . .'

His voice crackled, then vanished and the disconnect tone mewed in Sara's ear, leaving her frozen on the spot. Her brain refused to process the last few moments as she stared at the glowing phone in her hand. What was Adie doing in Nepal? What was a plant-hunting expedition? If that was what he'd said. It was winter. How did you hunt plants in the winter? What mountains, come to that? What the actual . . . ?

'Are you okay?' asked Trevor Jones. His voice was kind and genial and much closer than expected. Sara twitched as she turned to face him. 'Not bad news, I hope?'

'Trev, what's a rhododendron?'

The sergeant looked perplexed. 'It's a big shrub, isn't it? Bunches of pink or purple flowers in the spring. You see them in the grounds of those big houses a lot.'

Sara was no clearer than before. 'And Nepal?'

'Nepal? North of India somewhere, if I remember rightly.' Jones snorted in amusement. 'The missus wanted us to go on an adventure holiday there. See the temples and all that. Not bloody likely, I said.'

'North of India. So, the mountains would be the Himalayas?'

'I think so. Why?'

'I'll have to look it up.' Sara tucked her phone into her pocket. 'It would seem my friend has gone there on a plant-hunting expedition.'

'Lucky bugger,' nodded Jones. 'Keen gardener, is he?'

She ignored Jones's assumption that her friend was male. 'Very keen. Even more keen than I'd begun to realise.'

Shaking her head in disbelief, she felt the phone vibrate again. Half hoping it was Adie trying again, she felt disappointed when the screen displayed a number she didn't recognise. It took her a moment to make out the voice when she answered it.

'DS Hirst?' The wind gusted in the background, interfering with the voice. She could hear heavy footsteps on the pavement. Whoever it was must have found shelter as they were suddenly clearer. 'It's Ben Marsden. From the Rosegarden.'

'What can I do for you?'

'I think you need to return to the theatre,' he said. 'Zach, the homeless veteran you interviewed, has found some stuff in the graveyard belonging to Nafisa Ahmed.'

'The social worker?'

'That's right.' The tone of the stage manager's voice changed as he went indoors. Sara could hear an alarm beeping in the background. 'It's her work bag and her handbag.'

'Outside in the graveyard? In this weather?'

'Her papers are all over the place.' Marsden was breathing heavily as he punched at a keyboard. The alarm stopped beeping.

'Got it,' he muttered. 'Look, I've just opened the theatre again, so you can come straight here if you want.'

'Has she had an accident?' Sara glanced out at the gusting rain.

'She might have,' said Marsden cautiously. 'It looks like this stuff has just been abandoned. I thought you ought to know immediately, with everything else that's been going on. It doesn't look good to me. What if she's been attacked?'

A door banged in the background. Sara heard Marsden swear and call out, 'We're not open, sorry. Hang on, DS Hirst. I'd better see who that is.'

His boots thumped across the office floor, and she heard the door squeak as it opened. The phone was still in his hand, she realised. She could hear what he was saying distantly. 'Can I help you?'

Whoever it was didn't reply. Marsden drew a noisy breath. There was a clatter as the mobile hit the floor, followed by a fleshy thump. Something heavy fell over with a crash.

'Mr Marsden?' Sara called hurriedly. 'Are you there? Mr Marsden?'

There was no reply from the man, but Sara could have sworn she heard footsteps. Suddenly, the mobile cut out.

Sara looked around for help, happy to spot Aggie and Bowen coming down the stairs. They switched immediately back into work mode. Aggie rang for an ambulance while Bowen accosted a uniform with a police vehicle. Sara tailgated them into the city, both of them riding on blues and twos. Scattering the few pedestrians still on Pottergate in the awful evening weather, they drew up outside St Johns church and ran down the alley. A paramedic had beaten them to it. His mountain bike, with its green paniers, was propped against the entrance stairs. In the foyer, Ben Marsden sat on the floor, leaning against the wooden front of the bar.

'I'm pleased to see you conscious,' said Sara as she knelt down next to the stage manager. Holding up her warrant card, she looked at the paramedic for permission to carry on.

'I'm waiting for the ambulance,' the man said. 'I think Mr Marsden should get his head checked out. There's a nasty bump, and he was knocked out. Do you feel well enough to talk to the officer?'

Marsden nodded, then winced in pain.

'I'll keep it brief,' Sara assured him. 'What can you remember?'

'I'd been helping Zach in the graveyard,' said Marsden. He frowned to concentrate.

'You said there were papers?'

'All over, and some bags.'

'You decided to call me?'

Marsden tugged at his trouser pockets. A used handkerchief emerged. He looked around in confusion. 'Had your card somewhere.'

'I can give you another one,' said Sara gently. 'Where's Zach now?'

Marsden stuttered. 'I'm, erm, not sure.'

Sara turned away and gestured to Bowen. The DC immediately headed out of the theatre, and a few seconds later, Sara saw him through the windows scurrying towards the graveyard entrance steps.

'You told me you'd opened up the theatre for us. Then it sounded like someone else had come in behind you.'

'Yes! Yes, they did,' said Marsden excitedly. 'Thought it was Zach. But it wasn't.'

'Can you remember who it was? Were the lights on?'

'No lights,' he apologised as he struggled to sit more upright. 'Hadn't got that far. I know who it was.'

'You could see them?'

'Not exactly. Wearing black clothes and this strange balaclava under his hoodie.'

'It covered his face?'

'Had a skull on it. That boy's got much weirder since he's been away.'

'What boy, Mr Marsden? How could you recognise anyone with their face covered?'

'His voice. I'd know his voice anywhere. Besides, I reckon he's the only one with a big enough grudge.'

'Who?' asked Sara impatiently.

'Eddie Kenyon,' said Marsden. 'Everyone used to call him—'

'Scooter,' finished Sara. 'Are you sure?'

Marsden deflated. 'Absolutely.'

There was activity in the doorway, and two more paramedics came inside. Sara moved out of their way as a medical discussion kicked off around the grey-faced stage manager. Although he was reluctant to go to the hospital for tests, it sounded like the medics were winning the debate as she went outside. The uniformed officer from the car stood waiting.

'I think we should get Forensics back,' she sighed. 'Call it in and get the alley shut down. Again.'

With a roll of his eyes, the officer tugged at his radio to call control.

Sara walked rapidly along the alley and climbed the crumbling steps to the graveyard. DC Bowen was squatting down next to a box tomb, picking up papers, with a bedraggled-looking Zach beside him. The homeless man had a pile of documents by his feet. He rested one foot on it so it wouldn't blow away. He nodded at her as she joined them.

'DS Hirst,' he said. The wind blustered his words away.

Sara pointed to his foot. 'You think these belong to Nafisa Ahmed?'

'Yes. I've got her bags as well.'

'I've called in Forensics again,' she sighed.

'They'll be taking out season tickets,' said Bowen. He stood up and grunted as his knees cracked. 'Do you think we can get this stuff inside? It will all blow away if we don't.'

'Let's take it into the theatre,' suggested Sara. 'Can you help us with that?'

Zach nodded. 'I've collected as much as I can.'

They divided the soggy pile between them and took it inside. The ambulance crew helped Ben Marsden down the stairs. He leaned out to grab at Sara.

'Can you ring Lindie? Tell her I'm sorry, she'll have to come back to lock up.'

Sara gave him a curt nod. The place would probably be occupied for the next few hours anyway, and someone else from the theatre ought to know what was happening. Dumping the sodden mess on a bar table, she left Bowen to sort it out and followed Zach back to the graveyard. Skirting the muddy ash where the bonfire had been, they reached his tent. Unzipping it, Zach rummaged inside and extracted three bags. One was a small, blue-vinyl handbag. There was a black laptop bag, with its contents intact, and a dripping leather courier bag. Sara turned it over in her hands.

'You think this belonged to Ms Ahmed? We collected the one she bought from your fellow camper as evidence.'

'I can't be sure,' said Zach. He folded his arms and tucked his hands into his armpits. 'My fingers are too clumsy in this cold. I think she may have just bought it. There's a receipt in her handbag.'

'You better come inside out of the weather,' said Sara as kindly as she could. The man must be soaking and cold to the bone. At least the wind and rain seemed to be slacking off, as if the storm was blowing itself out. Carrying the bags and stepping carefully across the slippery turf, the pair reached the top of the steps.

Suddenly, the wind howled demonically. It whipped up into a vortex, almost pulling the pair over. Rending the fabric and smashing the metal poles with demon fingers, it dragged the remaining tents into its centre, whirling the debris into the dark sky. Watching in horrified fascination, Sara saw the mass spiral towards the church. As the mini whirlwind spun upwards, it reached the same height as the church roof, where a new blast of wind caught it. The debris seemed to hang in the air undecided for a moment before it hurtled ferociously back towards the earth.

Zach grabbed Sara roughly and shoved her down the steps in front of him. He pushed her against the nearby wall, throwing himself in front of her, pinning her to the brickwork as the debris hurtled over their heads and into the alley. Metal shards clattered around them. Tent fabric and lines writhed over the flagstones, whipping dangerously and heavy with rain. Clothes, cooking kit, plastic bottles and the rest of the homeless crew's possessions tumbled to the floor.

When the noise stopped, Sara became all too aware that Zach needed a bath. Her second thought was that they'd both had a very narrow escape. They could have been seriously injured. She heard Bowen and the officer racing to help them.

'Thank you,' she mumbled as the man stepped back, releasing her. It seemed inadequate. A third, rather late thought came to her. 'Where on earth will you stay now?'

Zach shrugged, although he seemed to be struggling to breathe, and his face was rigid with anxiety. 'I haven't got a fucking clue.'

CHAPTER 49

Her arms were trapped behind her back, her hands crossed and tied with something strong. She lay on her side, shoulder and hip aching, ankles crossed and bound together. Her head lay sideways at an unusual angle; the hood of her rain jacket smothered her face. Breathing was difficult. Her temples pounded with pain. Some disgusting cloth had been stretched around her face, pushing open her jaws and pulling up the skin on her cheeks. She could feel the knot at the base of her skull. The taste made her gag momentarily. A stink in the air reminded her of a rubbish-filled wheelie bin that had been waiting two weeks in the sunshine before the binmen arrived. It was rank with dead food, part-emptied takeaway containers and unwashed bodies. Nafisa shook with the cold that seeped through her wet clothing, through her skin and into her inner body.

She had no sense of time. How long had she been here? Nor could she see anything. Was it just pitch black, or had her eyes also been bound? Nothing made any sense. Arching her back, she wriggled until the hood on the jacket slipped backwards, and then she blinked furiously. Her eyes were definitely open. Tugging at her hands seemed to pull the binding tighter. The movement dragged at her hijab, pulling at the grips she used to keep it steady in bad weather. They tangled painfully in her hair and scratched at her scalp. Turning onto her back would trap her hands. Rolling onto her front would make breathing harder. Panting at the effort, Nafisa subsided onto the floor.

Try to think, she chided herself. Where on earth could she be and why? Fighting down the wave of panic that rose from her gut to her throat, Nafisa tried to organise her thoughts.

A cellar, perhaps? Allowing her head to drop to the floor, she sniffed as best she could. The place did smell of damp. No scent of earth, though. Rubbing the small area of bare skin between the gag and her hijab on the ground, she felt the rasp of cold stone. Definitely a cellar with a stone floor.

Remember, she commanded her brain. *You were in the graveyard, looking for Zach.*

In the wind and rain and dark. Someone had grabbed her from behind as she passed the box tomb. The thing was in the middle of the graveyard. It would be hard to notice something going on from the passages on either side unless you knew it was there. She'd been on the ground. There'd been a skull for a face and pain where they'd pinned her to the soaking ground by the thighs.

Can't really have been a skull, she reasoned. The pain in her head wanted her to stop thinking, to rest and drop back into sleep again. She resisted. *Haven't been asleep. The bastard knocked me out.*

No, it couldn't have been a skull, but it could have been one of those full-face balaclavas they sold in the army surplus stores. They sometimes had white skulls printed on them. Yes, that must have been it. Nafisa didn't believe in ghosts. Especially not ones that hit you hard enough to knock you out. Too physical to be ephemeral.

It was a man's voice; she was sure of that.

It had also been a man's physique. Although she never considered it an issue, Nafisa knew she was tiny and light in weight by modern standards. It was just the build God had given her. Unfortunately, adding that to the element of surprise, the man had been able to overpower her easily. He'd pulled all her things from her hands and thrown them away; she did remember that. The effort was too much, and her head was throbbing.

Fearful of overbalancing and further pain, Nafisa tried to voice a prayer. It stuck in her throat, little more than a gargle. She concentrated on saying her daily prayers in her mind. The repetition of something familiar gave her a moment's respite. A sense of comfort ran through her veins, and she offered a prayer of gratitude.

With a sigh, she felt her body relax. Until she could understand her situation better, maybe it was best to allow her body to rest as best it could. Someone would miss her soon. Her parents. Someone at work. She'd failed to turn up for that meeting for one thing. Her eyelids closed. It made no difference to what she could see. She began to sink into a doze.

Which made it all the more shocking when a square above her suddenly opened. Nafisa's heart raced, and she panted with fear. Could this be someone coming to help her? Or was it her attacker coming back?

Allah preserve me, her mind raced. *Allah protect me.*

Her eyes opened wide in the unexpected light. There wasn't much of it. She must make the most of the moment. Squinting, she looked around herself quickly. The walls glowed. Were they painted white? They were roughly plastered or painted-over stone. Dumped on one side, she could see piles of clothes, an old sleeping bag, filthy blankets, a rucksack and carrier bags of mouldering food. Ahead of her was a strange alcove halfway up the wall filled with a darker shadow to reveal its shape. She'd been right about the floor. It was covered with large flagstones. There were no doors as far as she could see.

The only exit must be through the trapdoor above her, where the light was coming from. An old-fashioned wooden ladder leaned below it. As Nafisa watched, someone descended feet first. Tall, thin and dressed entirely in black, the figure climbed into the cellar, pulling the trapdoor closed above them.

'Well now, isn't this cosy?' said a male voice. Nafisa recognised it from the graveyard. Her heart rattled ever faster; she began to suck noisy, bubbling breaths through her nose. 'You're awake, then.'

They were both in blackness until a sharp white light beamed out of the figure's head. It turned slowly towards her, pinning her in its powerful beam. She was dead after all, and this was to be her version of hell, her brain insisted frantically. The figure took several slow steps towards her. The corona from the light beam lit just enough of him to show the skull again. Nafisa's nostrils ran with mucus, and tears streamed down her cheeks. She would drown in the stuff soon. Maybe that would be for the best.

Not a chance! she screamed inside her head. *Fight! Fight! Don't give in.*

Now, the man was leaning over her. The beam was nothing more extraordinary than a strong head torch. As his face loomed closer, Nafisa realised she'd also been right about the balaclava. She forced herself to look back at him and watched him grin through the mouth hole.

'Aww, pretty lady's crying,' he said. He cocked his head to one side. Laughter bubbled under his words. 'Spoiling your looks. Can't you wipe yourself up? Oh no, you can't reach, can you?'

The bastard was enjoying having this power over her. What the hell could she do now? Accent! Was that a local accent? Or the remnants of it? Really? A hand reached around her head.

Focus, she swore to herself. *It's a white man's hand. Young.*

Her eyes flicked open with pain as the hand wound itself into the back of her hijab and tugged hard. The man had grabbed a length of her hair with it. As he pulled, Nafisa screamed in her throat at the pain.

'Aw, there, there,' the voice crooned. Her scarf was in his hand. He rubbed her face clean with it. Nafisa tried to wriggle away from his touch, prompting a laugh from her captor. 'You can't get away from me, my beauty. Let's have some fun.'

CHAPTER 50

Sara had finally reached home close to two in the morning. She must have been tired, as she didn't usually let these things bother her. But, though she was grateful to Zach for protecting her, she had trouble making herself want to help find him a bed for the night. Her skin crawled from the stink of his body odour, and she needed a long shower to get rid of it. Lindie had returned at half past ten and suggested he try the church scheme. Although he was supposed to have a referral from the council, a pleading call from DC Bowen had persuaded them, and Zach had walked off into the rain to find the church hall, promising to return the following morning.

Bowen had checked the hospital, and there was no one with Nafisa's description in A&E. Aggie had checked with her distraught parents, who had been expecting her home for her evening meal. Tracey Mills had been sent to sit with them. Officer Shepherd had arrived with several colleagues to begin a search of the alleys and back gardens around the area. They struggled through the rain and dark without success, and the search was called off for a few hours at one in the morning.

Zach climbed the steps to the theatre on Tuesday morning about five minutes after Sara and DI Edwards had arrived at seven. They encouraged him to sit in the bar to keep warm. Forensics were poking about in the graveyard across the alley but had declared the theatre clear for use. Nafisa's papers and bags had been removed for examination. Shepherd had returned with a fresh group of officers to repeat their search from the previous night now that they could see better.

DC Bowen arrived bearing two tins of cake from Aggie. 'DCI Hudson said to tell you that Ian is in the office, going through the CCTV from last night.'

Lindie had let them in, looking tired and rumpled. Her hair needed a brush, and her clothes looked crushed. She put on the coffee machine on the offer of some chocolate cake.

'Have you been here all night?' asked Sara, watching Lindie slowly running the vacuum cleaner around the bar tables. Lindie shook her head, turned off the cleaner and sat stiffly on a chair. Sara pushed a mug of coffee and a slice of cake towards her.

'I got a few hours' sleep,' said Lindie with a yawn. It clearly hadn't been enough. 'Poor Ben. He has been in the wars. Do you know how he is?'

Sara glanced at Bowen, who picked up his mobile to check with the hospital.

DI Edwards moved to a chair next to Lindie. 'Do you remember Eddie Kenyon? Were you here then?'

'Of course I remember,' said Lindie. She picked up the last cake crumbs by dabbing them with her long, elegant fingers with their silver skull and symbol rings. 'I've been a member here for over twenty years. Started work in the office about twelve years ago.'

'And this scheme that Carole Morgan set up. What did you think of that?'

'That it was a good idea,' replied Lindie. 'We survive on volunteers, and that means community involvement. The publicity was good, although not all the candidates proved useful.'

'Scooter was good?'

'Talented, actually. The makings of a very good actor. Quick to pick up on the technical side too. Bright lad. Apart from the, well, you know. Not so bright about that.'

'What was it like when he was arrested?' asked Sara. Aggie had looked up the case files and sent her a link. The contents seemed rather sparse compared to the evidence they'd have to put together these days. Something was nagging at her memory about the DC involved in the case.

Lindie frowned. 'There was a difficult atmosphere. Some people didn't believe that he'd done anything. Others were incandescent that a youngster had brought disgrace on the theatre.'

'Did you see him doing anything?' Sara pushed, although she knew the answer from the file.

'No, I never did. Despite being here more than most, neither Ben nor I ever saw him selling stuff.'

'How did you think the officers at the time handled it?'

DI Edwards spluttered out his coffee at Sara's question. 'DS Hirst, is that appropriate?'

'I think so, sir,' she replied firmly. Edwards nodded, then moved away to cut another piece of cake, so he wasn't listening.

'What did you think?' Sara turned back to Lindie. The office manager had gone bright red. 'You can be frank; this isn't a formal interview.'

'We were all interviewed, naturally,' said Lindie carefully.

'Who by?'

'There was a team like yourselves,' said Lindie evasively. 'I'm not sure I can remember.'

Sara flicked through an open document on her phone. 'DC Mollie Hart? Looks like she did most of the interviews. Yours and Mr Marsden's included.'

'That sounds about right.'

'What was she like to talk to?'

Lindie glanced around to make sure no one could hear her. 'She did seem to have it in for Scooter.'

When Sara pushed, Lindie refused to say any more. She stood up quickly and returned to her cleaning, the powerful drone of the vacuum disrupting all further conversation. When she hoovered towards Zach, he stood up to leave. Sara followed him outside.

The rain had stopped, and the wind had subsided. Banks of leaves were piled up in the corners of the courtyard, glistening wetly. Two workers from the council were loading up the broken tents and other items from the alleyway into trolleys to take it all away for disposal. Zach watched them with a dejected air.

'Have you been able to rescue any of your things?' Sara asked him. He shook his head. 'Is there anything I can do?'

'You can find Nafisa. I'm really worried about her.'

'So are we.'

'She was the only one who tried to help me. What about her colleagues?'

'We're going to speak to them after we've finished here. Can I ask you about the photos you looked at yesterday?'

'There were so many of them, I'm not sure if I could identify our dealer now,' said Zach. He sounded resigned. 'Go on, then.'

'How far back did they take you?'

After considering it for a long moment, he nodded. 'Some of the photos were quite old. People from years ago. You have someone in mind? Someone who's older now?'

'Perhaps,' Sara agreed. 'Would you be prepared to do a formal identity parade later on? It's all done on computer now, so you wouldn't have to meet the person.'

'If I'm still around.' Zach shrugged. 'Don't you have better things to be doing?'

'I do. One more question, then I'm off.' Sara pointed to the graveyard wall. 'When you saw the man running away after he knocked Ben Marsden down the stairs, you said you ran after him. Then he seemed to vanish. Exactly where?'

'I'll show you,' offered Zach. He limped out of the courtyard and down the alley until they reached the traffic lights. Standing next to the empty shop on the corner, he waved along Charing Cross. 'He turned left along here. I'm sure about that. By the time I got to the corner, he'd gone.'

'Could he have got as far as the alley beyond the pub?'

'Possibly. He was moving fast.'

Sara's phone rang. It was Tracey Mills, the family liaison officer. 'Excuse me.'

'Good morning. I'm not too early, am I?'

'Not at all. How are Nafisa's parents?'

'Terrified,' said Tracey. 'As you would expect. I thought I ought to let you know. Helen Morgan-Harris just called me. She said her father is at his best in the mornings, and today, he said he was sure the monk's voice belonged to Eddie Kenyon. Told me he never liked the boy; he felt he was likely to get obsessive. Does that help?'

'Thanks, Tracey,' said Sara gratefully. 'That's really great. All we have to do now is find the bugger.'

CHAPTER 51

DI Edwards and Sara walked swiftly across the city to reach the social worker's offices. Nafisa's boss, Samantha, was expecting them.

'Do you have any news?' she asked anxiously as she shook their hands and introduced herself. They settled at her desk. The office was open-plan, but an attempt had been made to provide a little privacy by dividing it up with filing cabinets and a tall bookcase.

'Not yet,' said DI Edwards. 'We have an ongoing search, and we're speaking to everyone who might know about her movements from yesterday.'

'I can tell you where she intended to go,' nodded Samantha. She clicked at her computer. 'I'll check her diary. We might need Russell to join us.'

She stood for a moment and waved at a young man across the room. He had clearly been watching proceedings as he was standing next to them within a couple of seconds. His face was twisted with worry. Samantha consulted her screen.

'You'll understand that at this stage, I can't divulge the names of clients,' she said. Sara nodded and pulled out her notebook. 'We had our morning meeting first thing.'

'Ms Ahmed seemed her usual self at this meeting?' asked Sara.

'Tired, I'd say,' said Samantha. 'She'd been at the hospital much of the night with a client.'

'Is that usual?' asked Edwards.

'No,' Samantha snapped. 'She gets too involved sometimes. We care for our clients, DS Hirst. Unfortunately, they don't often appreciate us in return. It's best not to get personal about any of it.'

'Nafisa is a wonderful social worker,' interrupted Russell. He shrank in size when his boss shot him a frown. 'She always did her best.'

'Nafisa had an appointment with a client in Mile Cross at one o'clock,' said Samantha. 'She doesn't drive, you know.'

'How does she usually manage?' asked Sara in surprise. Surely, a job like this entailed lots of home visits. 'I gave her a lift up the Mile Cross yesterday.'

'On the bus mostly, or a taxi here and there,' said Samantha. 'Sometimes we help out with lifts. She was too good at her job for me to penalise her for not having access to a car. That's why I asked Russell over. I thought you were going to give her a lift to Mile Cross yesterday. Didn't you?'

Russell looked in a panic at this question. 'Not exactly.'

Sara watched him turn bright red. 'You helped Nafisa yesterday?'

'I took her into town,' he nodded. 'Dropped her at Charing Cross.'

Samantha pursed her lips and sighed. 'Not to see her client?'

'She seemed worried about the army veteran and wanted to see him first.' Russell was twisting his fingers. He looked like a naughty schoolboy in front of a strict headmistress, caught out in a lie.

'Would that be Zach?' asked DI Edwards. Russell agreed it was. 'We've already met your client. He's been very helpful. Why is he on your books?'

'Nafisa was trying to get him a fresh-start place,' answered Samantha.

'Could you find out if she saw her clients in the afternoon?' asked Sara. With a glance at his boss for confirmation, Russell hurried back to his desk. 'Did she have any further appointments after that? Or was she due back here?'

Samantha scrolled further down the page. 'Yes, with the Luke Project at 4 p.m. I'll check.'

She picked up her desk phone and punched in a number. Her conversation was brief. 'I see. I'm sorry you feel like that. However, you should know that Ms Ahmed has been unavoidably delayed. I can't say more than that now, but please don't take this out on our mutual client.'

'She didn't make it?' asked Sara as Samantha put down the phone.

'I'm afraid not.'

Samantha pulled a face. 'Nafisa indicated that the man was less than enthusiastic about Zach. They'd offered him a place a few months ago, and he'd vanished before moving in. They probably have him down as a time-waster.'

Russell padded up to the desk. 'She saw them. Left about three, the client says. Went to the bus stop.'

Edwards turned to Sara. 'Give her half an hour to get into the city on the bus, and that gives us a starting time to search the CCTV footage. Give Noble a shout, will you?'

Sara walked past several empty desks to a quiet area on the far side of the office. DC Noble answered after one ring.

'Thank you,' he said gratefully after she explained the new details. 'The bus from there would drop her at Castle Meadow. I'll see if I can trace her after that.'

'She must have vanished sometime between three and four, when she was due at the Luke Project.'

'Good to have a tight window,' agreed Noble. 'The council are being helpful. They've already sent me footage for the whole day.'

When Sara turned, Russell Goddard was hovering a few feet behind her.

'Anything?' he asked anxiously.

'Not yet,' replied Sara. 'Russell, can you tell me if Nafisa took lots of papers with her?'

'She often did,' he confirmed. 'Carried them about in carrier bags. She shouldn't have been taking them home, really.'

'Not a big leather bag?'

He shook his head. 'She had one for a few days. Then you took it off her.'

Sara winced slightly at the accusation in his tone. 'It was evidence.'

'I know.'

'Did she say she might buy another one?' When he shrugged, Sara didn't pursue it. The window for purchase was small, and only a few shops might have such an item. It wouldn't be hard to trace. She would have rejoined Edwards, but Goddard reached out a hand to stop her.

'You will find her, won't you?' he asked gloomily.

'We're doing our best,' she assured him. 'Are you fond of your colleague?'

Russell's lips went white as he pulled them tightly shut. 'It's just that she's somehow got caught up in all these incidents at that theatre. What if she saw something? What if she's been murdered too?'

CHAPTER 52

Sheer luck had saved Nafisa. Above them, a door slammed noisily, and footsteps began to walk about on the floor, which was their ceiling. Her attacker had sworn under his breath and rolled away. He sat close, unmoving, waiting for several minutes. The feet on the wooden floor continued to move about. They heard a thump as bags were dumped. A television was turned on. A kettle was put on to boil.

'Fuck it,' swore Skull-man quietly. 'Flat was supposed to be empty.'

She lay as still as she could. The man leaned close to her ear.

'Lucky for you,' the voice snarled. 'It seems I don't like performing where I can be heard. Who'd have thought it? Once an actor, always an actor, surely?'

Skull-man moved away, his head torch flickering on the floor and walls. He scrambled on his hands and knees to the pile of bags in the corner. Without looking at her again, he shook out his sleeping bag. Nafisa whimpered as the cramp made her legs judder. Her shoes beat a tiny tattoo on the flagstones. Her attacker watched her impassively. Unable to control herself, Nafisa's feet made more noise. Skull-man stood up and reached into his pocket. There was a silver flash as he pulled out a serrated knife. Not large, but vicious. As he looked down at it, all she could see was the white hand and the sharp blade. Nafisa began to scream behind her gag as the vision moved towards her.

'*Is this a dagger which I see before me?*' intoned the attacker. '*The handle toward my hand.* Stop making that noise, or it's curtains for you.'

Laughing quietly at his joke, Skull-man put one hand around Nafisa's throat and squeezed. Her panic subsided as her breathing shortened. She sent up a prayer of supplication. If this was the end of things, she must surely qualify as a martyr. *Allah, let me die as one who has surrendered to You and join me with the righteous.*

She felt the man run his hand along her legs until he reached the ties. He slipped the knife between her ankles. Struggling with the plastic bond, he sawed away until it parted. Her legs juddered with pins and needles. He clamped his hand over her gag to prevent her from crying out. He rubbed her calves with his free hand until the sensation eased. Running his hand up as far as her crotch, he rubbed between her legs. Then he rubbed his own crotch. Close to fainting now, suddenly, Nafisa's bladder found relief too. She no longer cared; a different kind of darkness was racing over her. The head torch looked down at the growing puddle.

'A golden shower,' he muttered appreciatively and rubbed himself again. 'I do love a virgin who already knows how to play. You are a virgin, aren't you?'

Nafisa just stared at the skull, mesmerised.

'I bet you are,' he laughed. 'That must mean I've died and gone to heaven for my reward, right? That's what you lot think, right? If you blow yourselves up, you get virgins in heaven. Ha!'

Nafisa's skin crawled for more than one reason. *Allah protect me.*

There must have been no reaction from Skull-man's wayward body because he suddenly let her go with a grunt. Leaning close again, he said, 'There is one bit of good news for you. I don't fuck dead things. You won't die until after my dick is active again.'

He stood up and aimed a mild kick at her stomach. Nafisa passed out.

* * *

It was the pain that woke her. It pulsed all over her body. She couldn't tell how long she'd been lying there. There was no light. Nafisa tried to take stock of her body. Still bound and gagged. Still lying on the cold flagstones. The sour smell where she had wet herself. The memory dimly returned. It would be embarrassing under other circumstances. Now, she found she simply didn't care. All her clothes were clinging to her, cold and wet. Her skin was covered in goosebumps. She shook with cold. Blinking confirmed her eyes were open. Nafisa drew as deep a breath as she could and listened.

As far as she could tell, she was alone. If she was lucky, Skull-man had died. More likely, he had gone out while she was unconscious. Letting out the breath, she panted through her nose for a while. Her head spun at the effort. She waited for equilibrium to return.

Lying in the dark, it seemed to her that the old adage was true. Nafisa thought that she could hear better when the ability to see was removed. Straining to listen, there was little to latch on to. Was it night, and no one moving about much? Or were the floors above so thick that she couldn't hear any signs of the city life above her?

City life? she wondered sharply. *What makes me think I'm still in the city?*

Logic. Unless Skull-man had bundled her into a vehicle, he must have dragged or carried her after he'd knocked her out. If the latter, they can't have gone far without causing comment. She must still be in the city centre. If she could somehow get up that ladder, she would soon be free. Surely someone would help her.

Hope blossomed in her foggy brain. She focused on her legs. Twitching them, she found that Skull-man had made a mistake. He'd left them free. She could move them. The pins and needles returned as she bent them at the knee. Waiting for it to subside, she weighed her options. She had to take a risk. Skull-man might return at any moment.

Nafisa was lying on her right side. Using her left leg, she brought the knee over until it found the floor, then pushed. With a groan, she rolled backwards onto her arms and hands. There was a cracking sound, and pain shot up her left arm from her wrist. It made her dizzy. Had she broken her wrist? Or dislocated it? She had to keep going.

With a determination she'd never known she possessed, Nafisa pulled both legs up at the knees and pushed her heels into the flagstones until her body began to slide backwards. Each time she did it, she moved a few inches. Certain that she had been lying only a few feet from the cellar wall, she lifted and pushed until she felt her head make contact. Never one to go to the gym or exercise class, Nafisa doubted that she had any of that famous core strength. But fear is a great driver. She bent her knees, held her head up and pushed her feet. Screaming at the pain in her arm was a waste of energy. She still needed to move. Now, her head was bent at the neck, pinned against the rough stones. If she didn't keep going, she would suffocate like this.

Bend at the knees, hold at the core, push feet. Ignore the excruciating pain. Bend at the knees, hold at the core, push feet. Now, her shoulders were supported, and she could breathe better. Bend at the knees, hold at the core, push feet, shuffle bum. And again. And again. Finally, she sat upright against the wall. She would make the final effort and get to her feet in a minute.

She twisted to find a better position, and pain shot through her body from her wrist. Broken, it seemed. Nafisa's head dropped forward as she passed out.

CHAPTER 53

They returned to the office for an urgent team briefing. Sara was pleased to see Dr Taylor sitting at a spare desk. DS Ellie James followed hard on their heels, making straight for Aggie's cake tins. Bowen and Noble were rattling at their keyboards, and DCI Hudson came out of her office before Sara got her coat off.

'Let's see what we've got,' said Hudson, standing in front of the whiteboards. Front and centre of the information pinned there was the prison photo of Eddie Kenyon. 'How is the search for Nafisa going?'

Sara had been speaking to Officer Shepherd, who seemed to have volunteered to oversee the street search. 'They've gone through as many alleys, gardens and shops as possible around the theatre. They're expanding their activities to the city centre, including the riverside area.'

'Keep us updated,' urged Hudson. 'Dr Taylor?'

The pathologist nodded. He pulled a sheaf of paper out of his bag. 'I rushed it through as best I could. There's no doubt as to the victim's identity. Chris Webster, coffee shop owner and actor at the Rosegarden.'

Sara felt the team's eyes on her. She kept her head down and stirred her drink.

'His family have been contacted,' supplied Aggie. 'His parents live in Colchester and are on their way. They should be at the hospital by mid-afternoon.'

'We're ready for them,' nodded Dr Taylor. 'I didn't actually need to do much that was invasive. The cause of death was a heavy blow to the back of the head by a blunt instrument.'

'No shortage of those backstage,' murmured Bowen.

'We found it already,' said Taylor. He waved a photo. The dark object was square with a cut-out handle in the middle for lifting. The corners looked sharp. 'It had been thrown down the grave trap after the body. It's called a stage weight. They use them to hold down things like struts on scenery. Every theatre has them, apparently. Several were used on the *King Lear* set, and a pile of spares was in a corner backstage.'

'Easy to get hold of one,' said Hudson. 'How much do they weigh?'

'They're made of cast iron and weigh twelve and a half kilos.'

There was a collective release of surprised breath from the team. Sara almost choked on her coffee. 'You'd need to be fairly strong to lift them.'

'Especially if you lift it high.' Dr Taylor stood up and demonstrated. 'I think the attacker would have lifted it with both hands and swung it sideways to hit him with the point in the corner. There are three separate areas of damage to the victim's head. The first would have felled him to the floor. The other two were to make sure he was dead.'

'There must have been blood everywhere,' said a wide-eyed Noble.

'There was,' agreed the doctor. 'In the gents' dressing room. The forensic cleaners were moaning about it soaking into the emulsion on the walls.'

'All over the attacker's clothes too,' said Hudson. 'We need to find this costume.'

'The stage weight was a little gem of information,' added Taylor. 'There were lots of fingerprints, as you would expect.

Eddie Kenyon's are the clearest set, so he handled it most recently. There were traces of blood, brain matter and skull fragments from the victim in one corner. Smoking gun, in my professional opinion.'

'He'd changed into ordinary clothes, plus a skeleton balaclava when he attacked Marsden in the foyer,' Sara reminded them. 'He could have destroyed the costume by now.'

'Why hasn't he killed Marsden as well?' asked Aggie. She blushed when they turned to look at her.

'Perhaps because he was friendly with the lad back in the day,' suggested Sara slowly. 'Maybe he doesn't want to kill him, just shut him up.'

'Some humanity under all that rage?' pondered Bowen. Aggie smiled at her husband in relief. She always wanted everyone to have some saving grace, unlike the rest of the team, who knew that it wasn't like that in the reality of street gangs and drug dealing. Being hard was a survival tactic.

'I contacted the probation officer on Scooter's case,' said Ellie James. 'He'd been staying in a hostel for about three weeks. The manager said he'd been quiet until one evening when there'd been a row in the communal television room over what to watch. Scooter wanted to watch some Shakespeare play, but the others didn't. He had the leading objector on the floor and was strangling him. It took four of them to pull him off. Got given a warning. Vanished a couple of days later.'

'Given that we've had three people identify him,' said Edwards, 'plus the good doctor's evidence, there surely can't be any doubt who we're looking for.'

'No doubt at all,' agreed Hudson. 'He's also been dealing in the area again. Any news on that front?'

'DC Adebayo has gone off to chat with some lesser dealers on the Mile Cross.' Ellie glanced at Sara, who felt her shoulders rising to hide her embarrassment. 'He must have been getting his baggies from someone. That should give us another confirmation.'

Hudson nodded. 'Are we assuming that he's also attacked our social worker?'

'No doubt about it, and I'm really worried about her,' said Sara. Edwards nodded in agreement.

'She's been helpful to us prior to this,' added Edwards. 'I don't fancy her chances if Scooter thinks she's also seen something.'

'If he's killed her,' continued Hudson, 'what has he done with her? Why haven't we found the body? You say the city unit is checking the riverside? He could have thrown her in the water. Should we get a drag organised?'

There was a brief silence at this gloomy thought until Hudson tapped her marker pen on the desk. 'If he's attacked her, surely we'd see something on the CCTV? The window of opportunity is small, less than an hour. Noble?'

DC Noble had been patiently scrolling on his computer during the entire conversation. 'CCTV for yesterday arrived just before the meeting, and I'm just getting to the optimum time frame, ma'am.'

'He could have abducted her,' suggested Bowen. 'She could easily still be alive.'

'How far could he have got without being seen?'

'I've got them,' said Noble excitedly. 'Coming out of the bottom of the alley. It's on the traffic light camera. Yesterday at about three forty-five.'

They rapidly gathered around his chair to watch the screen. Although the evening had been dark and the storm was gusting rain in front of the lens, a pair of dark figures staggered around the corner. Sara pointed excitedly at them.

'He's supporting her. As if she'd passed out from drinking or something.'

'She couldn't walk unaided,' said Dr Taylor. He squinted hard at the image. 'Her feet are dragging on the floor. It's hard to tell if she's dead or unconscious.'

'Let's err on the side of unconscious,' said Aggie in a plaintive voice.

They all watched as the two figures moved out of range of the camera. Noble clicked impatiently between tabs on his screen.

'He's done it again,' he snapped in frustration. 'They just vanish in this camera blackspot on Charing Cross.'

'Which narrows it down, doesn't it?' said Bowen excitedly. 'Either he's holed up somewhere on that patch, or he's going back up that other alley with no cameras, into the Strangers' Hall gardens and back into the theatre through that window.'

'He'd have to drag her over that ten-foot wall,' Sara pointed out.

'Agreed,' said Hudson. 'Edwards, Hirst, you get up to the theatre pronto. The rest of you, let's go door-to-door immediately and see what we can find.'

CHAPTER 54

Ben had waited patiently in A&E for three hours before he was seen. A scan was recommended, and he was sent back to sit in the waiting room. To his surprise, the MRI scan was done quite quickly. The sensation of being slid backwards into the scanner and the loud noise as it made its circuit made him feel sick. When the doctor checked the scan, he was pleased to see no serious injury. Back in A&E, they suggested that Ben spend the night in a ward for observation if only they could find him a bed. At this point, ignoring all the warnings Ben discharged himself and got the late-night bus back into town to collect his car from the car park. Wincing at the cost of leaving it there for so long, he got home and groggily went to bed.

When he woke up late the following morning, a text from Lindie told him he had missed yet more fun and games at the theatre.

Was here for hours last night. More forensic people and coppers all over. When can you come in? I'm knackered!

It seemed that the theatre was empty of investigators now. It was almost midday, and the doors and box office window were open, indicating business as usual. Lindie was sitting with her arms folded on her desk, her head resting on top. She didn't look up when Ben opened the office door. The volunteer at the box office window smiled and winked, lifting a finger to her lips to shush him. He nodded, making his head throb. Quietly putting his bags on the spare desk, he went to the green room to make tea for all three of them.

Lindie stirred when he placed the mug on her coaster. 'Thank goodness you're here. Can I go home now?'

'As soon as I've caught up with the news,' he assured her. She smiled.

'Police have been and gone,' she yawned. 'After they found you last night, they sent in Forensics. Again! I was here until after two o'clock.' She yawned even wider to prove her point. 'I thought you'd be in hospital.'

'They wanted me to stay,' admitted Ben. 'I didn't see the point, so I discharged myself with the usual warnings.'

'How's your head?'

'Throbbing like a good 'un,' said Ben. He rubbed his forehead gingerly. 'They told me to take tablets if I needed to.'

Ben pulled a strip of paracetamol from his pocket and swallowed a couple. Lindie watched him as she sipped her tea.

'Those detectives were back this morning,' she said. Ben looked at her sharply. 'Asking more questions about the past.'

Lindie paused, giving Ben the chance to speak. With a sinking feeling, he knew he would have to say something. 'Was it about Scooter? You remember him? Eddie Kenyon.'

'How could we forget?' she nodded.

'I told them I recognised his voice when I was attacked. I think he's the one behind all this.'

'I think they agree with you, and that wasn't all.'

'Oh?' Ben felt himself beginning to sweat. Now what? Was he under suspicion for something else?

'They asked about the team that interviewed us. DC Mollie Hart?'

Ben couldn't stop himself from huffing angrily. 'I really didn't like that woman.'

'Did she ever . . .' Lindie's voice trailed off, unwilling to finish her sentence. Ben turned to her.

'Did she ever what? Suggest that I might like to see Scooter off the streets? Perhaps make a statement saying I'd seen something I hadn't?'

Lindie looked down at her tea mug with a sigh. 'You too? I thought it was just me.'

'Did you?'

'I said I'd think about it,' she replied. 'In the end, they never came back because Chris Webster had shopped him.'

'I told them where they could put it. She was too ambitious by half, that copper. Using Eddie to get a promotion, if you ask me. Why didn't you tell me at the time?'

'It made me uncomfortable; I didn't want to dwell on it.' Lindie frowned. 'It was such a shame. I really thought we'd made a difference to one person's life. Turned them around. I've always believed in the power of Doctor Theatre.'

'So have I,' agreed Ben. 'But people have to want to be helped. You can't force something on them. Do you think they got Chris Webster to lie? Do you think he really saw Eddie dealing?'

'Possibly.' Lindie considered it. 'Or maybe they put more pressure on him because we weren't cooperating.'

'That might explain why he was angry with us,' said Ben slowly. 'Did he come to resent the fact that he'd perjured himself and wanted to make our lives difficult because we hadn't done it instead?'

Ben started to say something else, but voices in the courtyard distracted him. He stood to look out of the window. 'They're back again. Look in a hurry too.'

DS Hirst and DI Edwards speeded up the outside stairs two at a time. The front door burst open, making the box office volunteer jump with surprise. Hirst bustled through the office door without waiting to be invited.

'Mr Marsden, you know the buildings around here as well as anyone,' she panted. Ben agreed that he did. 'Do you remember Ms Ahmed? The social worker who was here yesterday morning?'

'Of course.' Ben stood up anxiously. 'Those were her papers in the graveyard, then? Zach thought they were.'

'He was right,' Hirst hurried on. 'She's been missing since teatime yesterday, and we're really worried about her.'

Ben looked at Lindie. She looked confused. 'You think something happened to her?'

'We do. Have either of you checked the building today? Done a full search?'

'No reason to,' said Ben. 'Do you want us to?'

'I'll call in reinforcements,' said DI Edwards. He stepped outside the office, busily dialling on his mobile.

'We have good reason to think she may have been abducted and brought back into the theatre.'

Lindie screamed faintly as she slumped back in her chair. 'Not another dead body?'

The box office volunteer screamed more loudly before standing up and slamming the shutter down so no one outside could hear.

'We may be in time if we hurry.' Hirst was rocking back and forth in her agitation.

'Why do you think that?' demanded Ben. 'What makes you think someone would bring her back here?'

'CCTV from the traffic lights,' said Hirst. She waved towards the bottom of the hill. 'We found her being moved towards Charing Cross. Then, there's a blind spot in the camera network. She's just vanished between the shop on the corner and St Gregorys Alley. We thought she could have been brought here through Strangers' Hall gardens.'

'It's a long way to carry someone and over that wall,' said Lindie. Her face had drained of what little colour her gothic make-up allowed. 'Why not somewhere on Charing Cross?'

'It could be,' agreed Hirst. 'He goes round the corner and simply vanishes. I've got a team going door-to-door as we speak.' She leaned towards Ben, her voice taut and urgent. 'Can you think of any other building he could have access to? A bolthole? Anything?'

Ben looked at Lindie, and both spoke together. 'Birketts.'

CHAPTER 55

Ben Marsden rushed from the office and pounded across the green room to his storeroom with Sara in hot pursuit. She could hear him swearing and crashing around at the back of the store, where he had his supposedly secret key box. Sara climbed through the piles of props and stood where she could see the stage manager. He knelt by the broken metal box and rummaged frantically. Organisation was clearly not the man's strong point. By some miracle (or possibly due to a previous job incumbent), some of the old keys had labels attached by a string. Eventually, Marsden held up a handful of tangled labels and keys. Pulling them apart, he gave half to Sara.

'See if you can find one for Birketts,' he snapped, pulling at the cardboard and string in his hand. Sara began to flip quickly through them.

'Who or what is Birketts?' she asked as she twisted each label to read them.

'It was the building behind us,' said Marsden. He seemed to have no luck and returned to throwing keys out of the box. 'It's an old merchant's house which faces onto Charing Cross and backs onto us, next door to Strangers'

Hall. It used to belong to the council. For a while, we used it as a props store. I had keys.'

'You don't use it now?'

'Council sold it to a developer who turned it into flats. We moved out. Most of it's in here now.' He waved at the piles and stacked shelves around him.

'Didn't you give the keys back?' Sara finished her bunch without luck. 'Why did you keep them?'

'I just forgot,' replied Marsden excitedly. 'When the builders moved in, I assumed they must have changed the locks.'

Sara was getting really frustrated. 'Why do you want to find it?'

'It has an undercroft. The perfect hiding place. Scooter knew about it. He went in there with me several times. What if they didn't change the locks? What if Scooter found them when he took the theatre keys? Ah!'

He brandished a torn brown cardboard label clearly marked *Birketts Building*. Scrabbling more among the jumble of random keys, he gave up and looked at Sara. 'I can't see the key. The thing was old-fashioned, big and made of iron. It opened those outside doors. The ones that look like you could drive a horse and cart through them.'

'It's got to be worth a try,' she agreed. She climbed rapidly out of the room, Marsden following her, unwilling to be left out at this juncture. 'Show me.'

They ran down the alley, Edwards at the rear still talking on his mobile, and swung left at the shop. The old double warehouse doors were painted grey. Marsden slapped his hand next to the keyhole, which was buried in the centuries-old wood. 'Here. In here.'

Sara's heart pounded at the sight of them. The doors looked heavy. Surely, no one would hear them knocking. A shout from across the road disturbed her for a moment. Footsteps danced between the cars and bikes as DC Bowen abandoned his door-to-door calls and rushed to join them. There was a short exchange of abuse with a cyclist.

'Sarge? What's happening?' he panted.
'We need to get inside,' said Sara.

* * *

On a post to one side were four entry doorbells, with names next to them and an intercom speaker. Bowen pressed hard on the lowest one. They heard it ring through the ground-floor window to their left. There was no reply. Sara pressed it. The intercom crackled.

'All right, hold your horses,' said a grumpy man's voice. 'Who is it?'

'Police,' snapped Sara. 'DS Sara Hirst. We need to get inside the building urgently.'

'Fucking hell!' said the man, sounding startled. There was a buzzing, and a lock clunked. A dishevelled-looking thirty-something man in a dressing gown stood blinking sleepily at them.

Sara held up her warrant card. 'We need to get in.'

'Sure. Of course. In my flat?' He looked down at his lack of clothes. 'Sorry, I've just got back from abroad. My sleep clock is all over the place.'

He stood aside, and the three detectives piled inside with Marsden at the back. The outer grey doors protected a more modern-looking set of glass-and-wood doors. Immediately behind was the communal hallway. Metal post boxes were fastened to the wall with a table below them. A set of wooden stairs to the upper floors was on the right, and a short corridor ran to the left of this to the ground-floor flat.

'Undercroft?' demanded Sara. The man looked bewildered. 'What's that?'

'There's an undercroft in this building,' she snapped. 'How do I get into it?'

'I've no idea what you're talking about.'

'Marsden?' demanded Sara, swinging round to face him.

'It's all different,' he muttered, looking around him frantically. Bowen tutted anxiously. He pointed to the wall on his left. 'It was years ago. That wasn't there. The stairs were in the middle.'

Sara almost snarled in frustration. She wanted to scream at the man. Biting her lip, she watched Marsden waving his hands around, trying to make sense of the space. Then he pushed past Sara towards the door to the ground-floor flat.

'By the wall, the entrance was by the wall.'

There was a shadowy gap below the stairs with empty coat hooks on the wall. He scuffed his foot along the vinyl floor tiles until it caught on something.

Sara pushed Marsden aside and knelt down to examine it. It was an inset handle, the black pulling loop hidden in the tiles' design. She dragged at it, grunting with the effort of lifting the heavy trap door. Leaning it back against the wall, she peered down into the darkness.

'Isn't there a light down here?' she demanded. The man in the dressing gown was doing an impression of a goldfish.

'I didn't even know it was there!' he wailed.

Marsden handed her a small torch, its powerful beam already shining. With a nod of thanks, Sara shone it downwards. She ducked her head to look inside when they all heard a woman's muffled screams.

'Nafisa? Nafisa!' Sara shouted.

There was a gargle as the scream cut off briefly before starting up again.

'It's all right. It's the police. It's Sergeant Hirst. It's Sara. You're safe now.' Sara pulled her head back with a jerk. 'There's a ladder. I'm going down there. See if you can find the lights. Call for an ambulance.'

Putting Marsden's torch in her mouth, she went into the trapdoor feet first. Supporting herself with her arms on the hall floor, she dug around with her feet until they made contact with a wooden rung. More confident now, she looked down to light the way and clambered into the undercroft as quickly as possible. At the bottom, she rapidly scanned the place with the torch. The floor was made of stone flags, and the walls were painted white. There was a jumble of clothing near an old sleeping bag and piles of stinking rubbish here and there.

Nafisa was sitting against the far wall, her hands behind her back. Sara shone the torch at her, making the poor woman wince. A wide strip of grubby fabric was pulled across her mouth. She was hyperventilating, her cheeks puffing in and out as she tried to breathe, scream and cry around the blockage all at once. Sara strode to her side.

'Sorry,' she said, reaching down and tugging at a corner of the material. It gave suddenly, pulling away at Nafisa's jaw, making her cry out. 'It's all right now. We'll get you out of here as fast as we can.'

'He'll come b-b-b-back. I kn-kn-kn-know he will.' Nafisa's voice bubbled with fear. Sara put her arm around the woman's shoulders to help her up. Nafisa screamed in pain.

'What is it?' Sara carefully placed her back against the wall.

'I think I broke my wrist.'

'Can I do anything?' called Marsden, leaning down in the hole. He shone the torch on his mobile around the walls. It stopped by a light switch. The plastic cover was in bits, and a tangle of wiring poked out. 'The lights have been smashed. It won't work unless we get an electrician in. Can you hang on for a few minutes? I can get you some light.'

'Good. Make it quick.'

Marsden nodded, and he vanished.

Sara shone the torch around again. There was a strange niche on the wall opposite. She laid the torch in it so it shone at the wall above Nafisa, giving them some background light. Pulling a crumpled tissue from her pocket, she wiped Nafisa's face. The woman's breathing was settling down a little, although her eyes drooped and her body trembled.

'Help will be here soon,' said Sara. She rubbed Nafisa's legs to warm her. The fine woollen trousers were wet, holding the coldness of the undercroft against the victim's skin. By the smell of it, the poor woman had wet herself. Kenyon had clearly not even allowed her to move to go to the toilet, Sara realised angrily. It was, of course, dehumanising. Exactly his intention, she didn't doubt. It made Sara's blood boil and she vowed to herself that she was going to find the bastard and get him sent to Belmarsh.

'I've rung for an ambulance and for backup,' DC Bowen announced as he climbed tentatively down the ladder. 'Matey in the flat upstairs is putting on some underpants and keeping an eye out.'

'You'd be more comfortable if we could release your arms,' Sara told Nafisa. 'Can you sit forward a little?'

With a grunt of pain, the frail woman tried to lean forward. Sara supported her shoulders as Bowen shone his torch down her back. He shook his head. 'Bloody cable ties.'

Sara glanced where he'd looked. The things were impossible to undo, difficult to cut and had made Nafisa's wrists raw where they had rubbed into her flesh. Globules of dried blood stuck to the black plastic like garnets on a bracelet. Mindful of gathering evidence, Sara put her face near Nafisa's ear.

'Did he touch you?' she whispered. 'I mean sexually?'

Nafisa winced but shook her head. 'He wanted to.'

'But he didn't?'

'No.' Nafisa giggled hysterically. 'Couldn't.'

Sara pulled the woman gently into her arms for a hug. It was a small mercy. Feet thumped in the corridor above them.

'Can you take these from me?' called Marsden.

He held a pair of lanterns down into the gap. Bowen helped lay Nafisa back against the wall before going to the ladder. Marsden handed down eight of the things before swinging himself down into the undercroft. Picking up a lantern, he flicked a switch on the base. It began to pulse with an amber light. Bowen caught on quickly and began to pick up other lanterns. Soon, the undercroft glowed with a warm, flickering light, which was comforting or spooky, depending on how you felt. It was certainly better than nothing.

'Had them for a play last year,' said Marsden. 'Meant to look like candlelight but battery-powered. Best I could think of at short notice.'

Sara nodded. 'Do you have anything that will cut cable ties?'

Marsden frowned. 'Of course. I'm a techie.'

He reached into a pouch on his belt and extracted a Leatherman multi-tool. Sara helped Nafisa lean forward again while Bowen shone his mobile's light on her wrists. Marsden selected a strong snipper and pushed gingerly behind her back to have enough space to work. He pressed the tool, which didn't respond immediately. Marsden put both hands on the lever and pushed again. With a snap, the ties parted, and Nafisa's arms dropped to her sides. She moaned loudly with the pain.

Then, it all got complicated. There were lots of people clattering about in the hallway. They could hear voices shouting in the street outside. Two paramedics climbed down the rickety ladder to take over the patient, who sagged into the arms of one and fainted. DC Noble shimmied down the ladder to say that they had put a cordon around the area, much to the annoyance of the traffic, as the road led to one of the main car parks in the city. DI Edwards was outside calling for Forensics, he added, and the man from the flat had put the kettle on.

Sara stood near Nafisa, waiting for the organised chaos to get into order. In the flickering light of Marsden's stage props, there were several things she was desperate to look at. That pile of clothes, for one thing. Unless she was mistaken, there was a black woollen monk's habit screwed up among it.

'Try not to touch anything,' she muttered to the paramedic who was holding Nafisa up. She pointed at the clothes and the piles of rubbish. 'There'll be evidence in all of this lot.'

He nodded. 'We'll get her out as soon as possible, then it's all yours. Poor soul. Who could do such a thing?'

Sara didn't reply. She couldn't bring herself to. Anger tied her tongue.

'Can you stay here?' she asked Bowen.

'Yes, sarge,' he nodded.

For safety's sake, she took a few positioning snaps of the likely evidence on her phone, then climbed the ladder into the hall. Noble followed her. The front doors were propped open, and Sara was grateful for the fresh air that came through it.

Outside, DI Edwards turned away from an argument with a uniformed traffic officer with a curt, 'Just get a bloody diversion in place.'

Marsden followed Noble as they crowded out the door onto the pavement. All of them seemed grateful to be out in the daylight.

'Well done, you two,' said Edwards. He held out his hand to Marsden, shaking the stage manager's hand vigorously. 'Really good thinking.'

He turned to Sara. 'And she's going to be all right?'

'Who knows?' Sara shrugged. 'At least she's alive.' Lowering her voice, she added, 'Nafisa says he didn't rape her or attack her sexually. That saves her from one set of intrusive examinations. I'm going to get that bastard for all of this.'

DI Edwards nodded. 'And we're going to help you.'

CHAPTER 56

Ben watched as the paramedics assisted Nafisa Ahmed up the ladder and into the back of the ambulance. He thought that she looked weak, which was hardly surprising. She wore one of those paper boiler suits, which covered her body but left her hair exposed. If they'd have let him, he could have brought some spare clothes and a headscarf from wardrobe. One of the forensic team soon appeared with the woman's clothes in evidence bags, which went into a large plastic box for transport. The team had blocked the road and pavement with their vans as they started the detailed work in the undercroft. Ben didn't expect it to tell them anything they didn't already know. Eddie Kenyon, Scooter, had been the guilty party. Where the hell was the man now?

'I think we should let the forensic team get on,' said DS Hirst. She indicated the police cordon, manned with uniformed officers. 'Perhaps we can get another statement from you later, Mr Marsden?'

Ben nodded. The street was cut off on either side of the building. Lindie was exhausted and should have gone home, but curiosity had got the better of her and she stood behind the cordon at the St Benedicts Street end. Ben waved, and she waved back.

'I've left the volunteer at the box office for now,' she said when he joined her. 'I thought it might be nice to get a coffee away from the place for once.'

'Bloody good idea,' agreed Ben.

They walked up St Gregorys Alley to the Wizard's Lounge coffee shop, choosing a table in the window where they could see disgruntled pedestrians detouring around the street cordon and across the small green. The coffee was bitter and strong, just how Ben liked it. Lindie pulled a face. They dunked their croissants into the foaming cups. Ben felt himself relax, the tension seeping out of his back and shoulders as some semblance of normality returned.

The shop manager was standing watching the crowds through the other window with his arms folded and a pensive look on his face. Wondering what was attracting his attention, Ben shifted his position to stare outside, and Lindie did the same.

'Isn't that the chap from the graveyard?' asked Lindie after a pause. She pointed through the window to some metal benches on the far side of the green. Ben squinted.

'Yes, the army veteran,' he agreed. 'Zach. All his stuff got smashed up last night. I wonder how he managed.'

'Looks like he could do with something to eat,' said Lindie. She checked out the takeaway sandwiches in the glass display units. They were expensive, and the wages at the theatre weren't the highest in the city. As she hesitated, behind her, the manager sighed and moved.

He frowned as he made a coffee in a takeaway cup. Loading it with sugar and pulling a sausage roll from the display, he opened the café door. Ben and Lindie watched as the man wove through the morning shoppers and sat on the bench beside Zach. An exchange followed, and Zach's shoulders slumped as the manager handed over the food. He patted Zach on the shoulder as he left him, stomped back through the café and disappeared into the kitchen at the rear of the shop, leaving a puzzled-looking young woman in charge of the counter.

'You finished?' asked Ben. Lindie nodded. 'Come on, then.'

Lindie hung back as Ben approached the bench outside.

'How you doing, mate?' he asked.

Zach looked up, his mouth full of pastry, and shrugged. He looked tired but resigned.

'Where did you spend last night?'

'On the floor of a church hall,' said Zach wearily. 'It's a thing they do for us in the winter.'

Ben saw Lindie wince. The man certainly had an unsavoury odour. 'Your tent was broken up. Did you lose everything?'

'Most of it,' said Zach. He patted a pile of stuff at the end of the bench. 'Retrieved my sleeping bag and rucksack. Could have been worse. I thought I could borrow one of Kells's or Tam's tents, but when I went to look this morning, all their stuff was gone. I don't suppose you know how the fuzz are getting on finding Nafisa, do you?'

'You haven't heard?' Ben sat up in surprise. Well, how could he? 'They've found her. Alive, thankfully.'

Zach slumped against the back of the bench with a little thump. 'Thank God. How is she?'

'Not great,' admitted Ben. 'The bastard had kept her tied up in an undercroft. The city is full of these places, and he knew how to access this one without people seeing.'

'Poor woman,' said Zach sadly. 'She was trying to get me a temporary placement. Some charity or other. That won't happen now, I guess.' He glanced at Ben as he ate the rest of the sausage roll. 'I'm sorry. That was selfish of me.'

'You're bound to be worried.' Ben shrugged, wondering what could be done for the man. Lindie sat on the bench next to him, chewing her lip.

'Did they catch him?' asked Zach. 'The one who attacked you?'

'I'm afraid not.' Ben shook his head. 'His things were down there, unless I'm much mistaken. They're taking it away for evidence.'

'So, he's got nothing. Bit like me.' Zach drained his coffee and shuffled forward on the bench to stand up. 'Thank you for talking to me. You've been kind to all of us, while we've been an eyesore to you and your theatre.'

Zach wearily made the few steps to the rubbish bin and deposited the empty cup.

'What will you do now?' asked Ben. Zach shrugged. Lindie leaned in and whispered quickly to Ben, who looked past her as he searched his memory. 'I think I do. It would be at the back of the store.'

'Would anyone notice if it went missing?' she asked.

'Why should they? We were supposed to have got rid of it ages ago.'

When Zach returned to pick up his over-stuffed rucksack, Lindie stood up and walked rapidly away. Ben helped Zach hoist up the bag. 'Think we might be able to help a bit.'

Zach brightened. 'Really?'

'There might be a small tent you could have. We got it for a show about a camping trip three years ago.'

'That would be amazing,' said Zach gratefully.

'It was new at the time,' Ben explained. 'It should still be waterproof. Lindie's gone to have a look. Want to come back to the theatre with me?'

'Thanks, mate.' Zach held out his hand, and Ben shook it somewhat reluctantly.

As they wove their way through the crowds queuing at the fish and chip shop on the corner, Ben fervently hoped that his memory was right and the damn thing was still there.

CHAPTER 57

Sara drove back to the office via the hospital. She was grateful to see that Nafisa had a female officer sitting with her, as well as an older couple she assumed to be her parents. Nafisa was clearly too upset to be fully interviewed, so Sara introduced herself and left them with her assurances that the team were searching everywhere for the culprit.

Sara was the last to join them in the SCU office. Several detailed street maps were spread out on a spare desk, and the team was arguing over them, with DS Ellie James among them. Glaring up at her as she dumped her coat was DC Dante Adebayo, his antagonism showing. Sara felt uncomfortable despite knowing that this was what the man was trying to make her feel. She squared her shoulders and joined the group as far away from him as she could manage.

'We need to figure out where Kenyon may be hiding,' said DCI Hudson. 'What about another cellar somewhere?'

'There's a small website called Norwich Undercrofts,' Aggie was saying. 'Lots of pictures and details of undercroft systems in the city centre. Guess who runs it?' No one stole her thunder. 'Daryl Stone.'

'The ghost walk guy?' asked Bowen.

'I've already contacted him,' Aggie nodded. 'He's happy to come and advise.'

'Pity he didn't mention this earlier,' said Bowen bitterly. 'We might have found her sooner.'

'There was no reason for us to suspect Kenyon was hiding in an undercroft,' said DCI Hudson briskly. 'He could have been anywhere.'

'Even though he was absent when we found Nafisa,' said Sara, 'Kenyon must have seen the circus by now and realise he can't go back to that building.'

Ellie pointed to the maps. 'He might not be in the city at all. We should check on the Mile Cross and with his dealers. Adebayo, how did you get on with them?'

Dante pulled his gaze away from Sara and back to his sergeant. 'As you know, we dismantled the network Eddie Kenyon was involved with at the time of his arrest. Several people higher up the chain got away, as they usually do. It didn't take me long to find that two of them had returned some months ago.'

Ellie nodded. 'We've had some intelligence about this but hadn't connected it to Kenyon's case because we didn't know he was also back on the patch.'

'A low-level snitch told me that Kenyon had been buying baggies recently,' added Adebayo. 'One of the old crew recognised him. They cut off his supply.'

'Must have realised we would be looking for him as he'd jumped bail,' said Bowen. Adebayo agreed.

'Any chance someone on the Mile Cross might give him shelter?' asked Edwards. 'We know the family moved away, but what about old friends from school or the estate?'

'Noble, get an urgent request out for uniform to go door-to-door looking for him up there,' said Hudson. DC Noble nodded and returned to his desk to make the call. 'Adebayo, can you look up a list of interviewees from the old case? People who knew him. That would be a good place to start.'

He nodded and stalked out of the room with an angry glance at Sara. Aggie stole a look at her and pulled a sympathetic face, which made Sara feel better.

'Do we know if he has a mobile phone?' asked Edwards.

'Not officially,' replied Ellie. 'I checked with the bail hostel. They said they confiscated it before he skipped out. It's still in their possession.'

'No point in pinging it, then,' muttered Edwards crossly. 'If he has another one, it'll be a burner. What else?'

'What about other unoccupied buildings in the area?' Sara asked.

'He could just be loose in the city,' said Hudson, her frustration sounding clear. 'He thought he was safe enough down there until we worked out where Nafisa might be. Has he had a chance to find anywhere else?'

Sara patted the city centre map. 'I reckon he's obsessed with the theatre and the people he thinks betrayed him. He'll be somewhere close to hand.'

'There's the empty shop on the corner of Charing Cross,' offered Bowen. 'And if you go along Westwick Street, there are those old storage buildings underneath the shops on St Benedicts.'

'Find the landlords and ask for immediate access,' demanded Hudson. 'Check them all. Walk the area if necessary and call anyone with a *To Let* or *For Sale* board. Empty office spaces as well. Check with Shepherd from Bethel Street and get his team to help you.'

Bowen nodded and pulled Aggie away with him to help.

Hudson turned to the DI. 'Edwards, you and Hirst meet this ghost man. If Kenyon knew the city well enough to find one undercroft, he might find another.'

* * *

'Happy to help,' said Daryl Stone when Aggie had called him. He was waiting for Sara and Edwards on Pottergate at the top of the alley which led to the theatre. His knee-length, billowing coat and steampunk hat had been replaced with a dark hoodie and beanie. Long hair pulled up inside the hat, Stone looked less theatrical than usual.

'There are dozens and dozens of these undercrofts,' he told them. 'All date from the medieval period and are within the old city walls. Some are reputed to connect underneath the streets, although I've never seen that myself.'

'Starting from the theatre, can you work us outwards?' asked Edwards. 'You know why we're looking?'

'Norwich is small enough for the gossip to have reached me already,' nodded Stone. 'Why undercrofts, though? Most of them are difficult to get into. I needed special permission for access when I wanted to take pictures for my website.'

'Any secret or empty space around here would do,' said Sara. 'You know the city centre well from your walks. Show us the nooks and crannies.'

Stone nodded and pointed along Pottergate. 'Let's start up here, then.'

They followed him along the cobbles until they reached a set of iron gates between two shops. Beyond them was a courtyard of old houses, the communal outdoor space full of pots and raised flower beds.

'There's an undercroft here that you can reach from the yard,' said Stone, briefly stopping by a panel on the wall with a row of doorbell buttons and their numbers. 'Council housing, would you believe.'

Sara would believe it. The council held lots of old properties on their housing list, which were much prized by their occupants. Stone rang three buzzers before someone answered the intercom. A young mum with a toddler in her arms opened the gate for them. The entrance to the undercroft was up against the wall of the farthest house. A heavy wooden trap door was bolted and padlocked. There was no sign of a break-in, so they moved on.

The fish and chip shop had turned their undercroft into part of the restaurant. The pub on the corner used theirs for storing beer and wine. The shops on the green all accessed and used their cellars. They checked them all, as their warrant cards provided the magic open sesame. The shops ran out after the benefits office, and it became a residential street. They were close to the courtyard where the Morgans lived.

Stone pointed along the street. 'I've accessed undercrofts in seven of these houses. There are more which I haven't been in. All the ones I've seen along here have trap doors in the kitchen floors or other downstairs rooms. Your man would have to break into the house first to access those, so they seem unlikely.'

Sara walked carefully down the cut-through alleys, checking back gates for signs of recent forced entry. Nothing.

'It's the same on St Benedicts,' said Stone as they walked down a cobbled street to come out opposite the Arts Centre. 'Inside access to all the undercrofts along here.'

Kenyon had a predilection for theatre, so they called into the Arts Centre, where a friendly volunteer showed them around. Despite several good hiding places, none held much except dust, cobwebs or dead leaves.

Sara was getting frustrated. Edwards showed signs of an imminent temper explosion. They had been at it for over an hour, and the afternoon was wearing on. 'If we forget undercrofts as such and just look for any places our man could hide, where in all this jumble would you go?'

Stone considered this carefully. 'I don't think I'd use any place where the homeless tend to bed down. They could be there even during the day. He'd be seen.'

'Any abandoned or derelict places?' pushed Sara. 'Anywhere else the Rosegarden might have used as a store or be associated with?'

Stone's face brightened. 'That would be Ninhams Court.'

'Where?' snapped Edwards.

'It's across the city, near Chapelfield Gardens,' said Stone. He began striding off, and the two had to hurry to catch up. 'It was Nugent Monck's house. He lived there for decades. He left it to the City Council when he died. Now they don't know what to do with it.'

Edwards was puffing as they climbed the short but steep Cow Hill.

'And it's empty?'

'Has been for years,' said Stone. 'It's a real shame. Beautiful place.'

They had reached Upper St Giles, and Stone led them across the road to Bethel Street. Without warning, he turned sharply up a tiny brick-lined alley between two buildings. Sara hurried after him as Edwards leaned against the entrance wall to catch his breath. Old, high brick garden walls ran along either side of the alley. Stone reached an entrance gate. A wooden panel door filled the gap, so you couldn't look at what was behind the wall. Leaning back, Sara could see the jagged roof line of several very old-looking houses.

'It's normally locked,' he said. 'You can't blame the folks who live here. They'd get all sorts hiding in here otherwise.'

Stone rattled the handle on the gate, and to his surprise, it opened.

* * *

The evening was drawing in enough for the street lights to come on. Stone led Sara into the garden area. A terrace of three old houses faced them, each three storeys high. The one at the right-hand end turned at right angles and had a two-storey extension which almost reached the garden wall. The communal garden area was well kept, as were the houses, apart from the one on the right.

'These were all medieval merchants' houses,' explained Stone. 'Council houses now.'

He pointed to the end house. It was painted a pinky-cream, where all the others were painted white. The roof appeared to have had emergency repairs; some tiles looked newer than the rest. The ancient mullioned windows had dozens of broken diamond panes, and the black paint on the frames was peeling.

'That was Nugent Monck's house. The Norwich Players used to perform in the music room up there.' He pointed to the upper floor of the extension, where tall mullion windows were packed tightly in a row to provide the maximum interior light. 'They outgrew it by 1921 and bought the chapel, which became the Rosegarden Theatre.'

'1921?' asked Sara.

'Monck lived there until the 1950s. When the council inherited it, they put in a caretaker tenant. He lived there for decades. It's been empty since he died.'

'Really?' Sara didn't often think about history, but even she was shocked that the council could leave a medieval house like this empty for so long without doing anything with it. In a city that prided itself on its tourism, surely it should be an asset.

Stone nodded. 'It's big inside and in a bad state. The floors are rotting, the stairs are dangerous, and there's no power because the wiring hasn't been touched since the 1960s. The roof nearly went in a while back, and they repaired it. Nothing else, though. I got permission to go in a couple of years ago to record the undercroft for my site. It's a bit *Marie Celeste* in there. I'll see if I can get the key.'

'What?' Sara hurried after Stone, who went to the house at the far end of the row.

'The couple in the end house keep a spare set in case of emergencies,' he said as he rapped at the door. 'They might remember me.'

Sara's warrant card extracted the keys from the suspicious older man who spoke to them.

'I'd no idea this was here,' said Edwards as he joined them.

'Most people don't,' agreed Stone.

The door to Monck's house was solid old oak. A Victorian lion's head with a knocker in its mouth stood sentinel. Sara half expected to see Marley's ghost gurning at them before she smiled at herself. Stone grunted with the effort of turning the key, and both Stone and Edwards had to put their shoulders to the panels to push it open. It scraped over the pamment tiles inside as piles of dirt, old leaves and bits of ceiling plaster subsided behind it with a crash. If anyone was in here, they couldn't have missed the noise.

'He didn't get in that way,' said Edwards, pushing the dirt away with his foot. 'Hasn't been opened in years.'

Sara was shining the beam from her mobile torch around the kitchen. The place was caught in a time warp. The cabinets must have been fitted in the early sixties. There was a rusted Rayburn cooker in a chimney fireplace. Piles of crockery and detritus lay on every surface. Five doors led off the room.

'Small downstairs room that way,' said Stone, his arm pointing to each one in turn. 'Undercroft down there. Scullery through that one, big downstairs room through there and the stairs there.'

An ancient sink stood under a wide window by the scullery door. Its glass was overgrown with ivy, filtering what little light was left from the sky and turning it dark green. It was so gloomy that all three used their torch beams to see.

Sara crunched across the dirty floor, her feet crushing lath and plaster into the dust and broken pots. There was a strong draught coming through the scullery door. She pushed it open as far as it would go. Broken brickwork from what once would have been a wash copper littered the floor. The window here was also overgrown with ivy, cutting off any natural light apart from the back door. That had been broken open — and recently, if she was any judge.

'Boss,' she called. 'Look.'

Edward's torch preceded him. The door had been locked inside, but freshly splintered wood showed how someone had gained access. They had simply kicked at the lock on the outside, and the rotting wood had given way.

'I'm calling for help,' said Edwards. 'Outside in the fresh air.'

Sara nodded. The place smelled musty and damp. 'I'll go over the rest of the house. See where he's been.'

'Be careful,' instructed Edwards. He shook Daryl Stone's hand. 'Thank you for your help, Mr Stone. I think we need to clear the property now. Our suspect is dangerous.'

'No problem,' said Stone. Edwards gently guided him outside. 'Good luck, DS Hirst.'

Sara lifted her hand as a goodbye, heading for the other downstairs room. It was large and derelict. Old furniture stood where it had been abandoned. Piles of books balanced on shelves and were scattered on the floor. The wide stone fireplace still had ash and bits of log in it. She bent to hold her hand over it, but there was no heat in the dead fire. She checked the windows, which all seemed to be intact. A door opened into an old-style cupboard, its shelves largely empty. The dust in here hadn't been disturbed in years.

Returning to the kitchen, she followed Edwards out into the garden. Large drops of rain were starting to batter the plants. The sky was dark with clouds, and the wind was getting stronger. It seemed that after a short respite, the storm was returning.

'If that's the best you can do,' Edwards snapped into his phone. When Sara tapped his arm, he turned to her and rolled his eyes. He finished his call with a grunt at the poor person on the other end. 'Forensics say they can't come, the teams are all tied up. Probably tomorrow morning.'

'Do you think he'll come back here?'

'He might if we don't make a big show of being here. Hudson wants me to go back into the office.'

'I'll hang around for a while,' offered Sara. 'I might see something.'

'I don't like you being here on your own.' Edwards sounded concerned. 'I've given Noble a call. He's just parking up and will be with you in ten minutes or less.'

'Great,' she nodded. 'Meanwhile, I'm going to have a look upstairs.'

'Be careful,' said Edwards. 'I wouldn't trust those floors if I were you.'

He stalked off through the increasing rain. Sara hurried back inside, pushing the front door closed behind her. Wind was pulling at the ivy on the windows, making it scratch and shiver. Rain began to drum on the tiny glass panes and on the roof. The place would have been entirely silent if it weren't for that. She couldn't even hear any city traffic.

The stairs were behind a small wooden door. The dust on them might have been disturbed, but she couldn't be certain. Minimal light crept down from the first floor. Sara shone her torch at the rotting treads. One or two had holes, making her step cautiously to the side, where she hoped the wood might be firmer.

There was a small landing on the first floor. The door to her right led to a bedroom. A dusty old divan stood near the window. It was covered in men's old suits, which had been laid there on their hangers at some point. Now, they only hosted moths and dust mites. The curtains were hanging in threads where sunlight had destroyed the fabric.

A second door led to an ancient bathroom. The bath and toilet were so stained that they looked like some modern artwork gone wrong. Sara wrinkled her nose at the smell of rot and blocked drains.

Turning around, she tried another door. This one swung freely. Beyond was a long, empty room. To her right, the wall contained that long row of mullioned windows she had seen from the garden. It was dark outside now, the storm cutting off the daylight early, and the street lighting was ineffectual in the sheeting rain.

On the far wall were more mullioned windows. These were clogged with ivy, just like the one in the kitchen. In the corner, there was a door, which seemed odd. Why would a door open out into the garden on the first floor? Surely, to step out would be to fall to your death.

The wall to her left was solid. It contained a large stone fireplace, identical to the one in the room below. Two heavy wooden armchairs with carved legs and arms and mouldering fabric stood before it, mimicking a homely scene around a roaring log fire. The only roaring now was the gusting wind in the chimney.

Sara stepped into the room, her breath rasping in the silence, and the dust she was kicking up itching at her nose. The hackles on the back of her neck shot up. She wasn't alone. She didn't believe in ghosts. She did believe in the large hand that clamped itself over her mouth and pulled her head backwards.

'Too clever for your own good,' snarled a man's voice. 'Shouldn't have risked being here on your own.'

A vicious punch landed in her kidneys before she could jab backwards with her elbows. Retching with the pain, she tried to grab at the man from behind her. His hand released her mouth, allowing her to spin as she raised her hands to cover her head. She was too late. Scything out of the darkness came something even darker, and as solid as a lump of concrete.

CHAPTER 58

Sara's eyelids flickered. They were too heavy to open fully. She let them rest half shut and focused elsewhere. There was a throbbing pain in her head and left shoulder. Rain drummed on the roof and windows. The wind howled around the chimney pots and whistled in the old fireplace. It was a wild night outside. She was inside. The place smelled of damp and dust and decay. Presumably, she was still in Ninhams Court, but she had no idea what time it was or how long she'd been there.

Someone was moving around in front of her in a regular rhythm. Two confident footsteps, a pause, the tick of a cigarette lighter and repeat. A warm glow of light built up before her. She was sitting on something with an off-square frame, her body uncomfortably twisted sideways and her left thigh pushed against a bar. Her arms lay along rests which felt wooden under the palms of her hands. Her wrists and ankles were bound with plastic cable ties. Sara tried to shift.

'Awake already?' said the man's voice she recognised from just before the attack. 'I should have hit you harder.'

Sara tried to answer, but some kind of tape was holding her mouth closed.

The voice laughed. 'You can't move. I've made sure of that. Wondering why?'

Sara nodded and forced her eyes open. She was in the room where she had been attacked. The two ancient, dilapidated chairs that had stood in front of the fire had been moved, and now she faced the wall with the door where she had come in. She was strapped up in one. The other stood to her right.

'I'm going to give you a performance,' he said. 'The last one you'll ever see. Then I'm going to kill you. Because I can.'

There seemed little point in struggling at this juncture. Sara concentrated on looking around. A row of candles in various containers had been placed in a line on the floor between the chairs and the wall, forming a temporary stage. Two small tables had been dragged by the far wall, one to each side of the stage. More candles stood on them, the wax dribbling down and securing them to the tabletops.

The figure was lighting the last candle in the front row. He stretched up. Tall and well-built, he was dressed all in black. A balaclava with a skull design was pulled over his face. Moving to the centre, he leaned out so the candles would light his face from below.

'Think help is coming? Think again.' He held up her mobile. It was smashed.

Sara frowned. Of course it was. DI Edwards had been going to contact DC Noble, hadn't he? The memory made her shudder with fear. Her eyes strained to look at the chair to her right. Ian Noble sat in a position similar to her, bound tightly. His head lolled forward on his chest, and even in this poor light, Sara could see that there was a gaping wound on the back of his head. Blood had matted in his hair. More blood had run down his neck into his clothes. It'd had time to dry.

Her heart sank. Sara cursed herself for being lax. They knew that someone had broken into the house. Why had she assumed they'd already left again? It was stupid. Noble would have come to join her and been ambushed as surely as she'd been. Life was too easy in the Norfolk Constabulary. She'd lost the edge she'd maintained in the Met.

'Do you know who I am? Worked it out yet?' Kenyon interrupted her angry thoughts.

Sara nodded again, ignoring the pain that shot around her skull and jaw. She tried to form the word 'Scooter', but it came out as two grunts. The skull mask grinned at her.

'Scooter? Yeah, that's what they used to call me. Childish, isn't it? It was because I had a moped. They don't call me that now. Meet Eddie Kenyon, the Don of Deerbolt.'

Kenyon pulled at the base of the balaclava. The skull design wrinkled as he slowly lifted the black fabric up his face. With a flourish, he pulled it off his head and laughed. Sara recognised him from his prison photo. Six weeks on the road hadn't treated Eddie Kenyon well; he looked almost cadaverous. There were dark shadows under his eyes. His cheekbones stood proud of sunken cheeks. Ragged stubble darkened his chin and neck. His skin was sallow, and his lips looked sore. Kenyon's tongue flicked over the flaking skin as if responding to her look.

Stepping through the line of candles, he brought his face close to hers as if he intended to kiss her. His eyes glinted, and his breath was sour. Suddenly, his hand came into her peripheral vision, and he yanked the tape off her mouth. Sara grunted in shock. Kenyon laughed as he stepped away, the black tape dangling from his fingers.

'Gaffer tape,' he said. 'The band-aid that keeps theatre running. I'm proud to say I've found even more uses for it.'

'Eddie. Please let me go. I'm Sara. Sara Hirst.' It was what that lecture on hostage negotiations had said. Keep talking to them. Encourage them to see you as a person. 'If you want me to watch your performance, then I will. But I'm really uncomfortable like this.'

'You'll watch it all right,' sneered Kenyon. 'And you'll keep quiet if you have any sense. I know what you're trying to do. It won't work.'

'No problem,' she said quietly. She couldn't afford to screw this up. Her eyes scanned around, flitting fearfully from window to door and back again.

'Did you know that the Norwich Players did their first performances in this very room?' Kenyon looked admiringly around the space.

'The company Nugent Monck founded?' Sara nodded.

'The audience used to come up the outside stairs and in that door at the back. Wouldn't do it now; the fire escape is in pieces.' Kenyon pointed to the door behind Sara. So that was what it was for.

'I've been learning a lot about the players and the theatre.'

'Good,' said Kenyon approvingly. 'It's only fitting that I should get to perform in the founding space. Ready? This is from my favourite play. It's the part I was born to do.'

Kenyon moved to centre stage, pulling himself tall. Then, his face crumpled with anger as he began to intone something from Shakespeare.

'Thou, nature, art my goddess; to thy law
My services are bound. Wherefore should I
Stand in the plague of custom . . .'

He was transformed. Sara watched his body flow slowly into the stance of a villain plotting his revenge. She searched her memory anxiously. Was it *Richard III*? They'd done that at school. He was a murderer.

'Why bastard? Wherefore base?' Kenyon continued.

No, not that one. Her mind raced. She'd taken little interest in Shakespeare, finding the language almost incomprehensible, even when Chris had still been her boyfriend, and she'd been going to see his shows. It was too much like hard work. Now, she had to try and use it to her advantage somehow.

'Well, my legitimate, if this letter speed,
And my intention thrive, Edmund the base
Shall top the legitimate.'

Kenyon was looking at the ceiling now, his hands clenched before his face. His pitch was rising along with the volume of his voice.

'I grow; I prosper.
Now, gods, stand up for bastards!'

Panting with emotion, Kenyon held himself still. Sara knew this was her moment.

'Bravo,' she said quietly. 'Bravo. I'd applaud you if I could. That was excellent.'

Kenyon's body relaxed. He gave her a superior look. 'It was going to be my audition piece for drama school. I'm sure I'd have got into one of the best ones.' Anger returned. 'Until that bitch of a policewoman stitched me up, and the twats at that theatre helped them.'

'I'm sure you would have been snapped up,' said Sara, her words sounding insincere even to herself. How would she know? 'Where's it from?'

'Fancy you not knowing. *King Lear*, of course.'

'The play the theatre was going to put on before you turned up.'

Kenyon laughed so hard he bent over at the waist. 'How much of a fucking coincidence was that?' he gasped. 'Could have been doing any old shit, yet there it was. I couldn't believe my eyes when I walked down the alley.'

'Why did you come back, Eddie?' Sara asked carefully. She needed to keep him talking as long as she could. Make him feel that he was her friend. 'How did you get here?'

'It was my home,' replied Kenyon. 'I needed to come home.'

'We all feel that need sometimes,' nodded Sara.

'Do you? I mean, where the hell are you from?'

'Tower Hamlets,' said Sara with a smile. In her desperation, she would say anything to keep his mind occupied. 'I know I don't look it. My mother was from Jamaica.'

Kenyon nodded. 'Met a lot like you up in Deerbolt. Half-castes. Hard bastards, most of them.'

Sara nodded in return. 'You were Norwich born and bred, weren't you? Still got friends here?'

'No friends,' scowled Kenyon. 'Only enemies. When I walked down that alley and saw the rehearsal photos, they all were there. The cunt who got me put away. The little bastard who shopped me to the police. Nothing had changed for them while I was being raped daily in that hellhole.'

'That was when you decided to get your revenge?'

Kenyon looked up sharply. 'This isn't an interview. I don't have to tell you anything at all.'

Sara threw caution out into the storm-filled night. 'Let's make it one, then. Eddie Kenyon, I am arresting you . . .'

Kenyon laughed hard, then began to join in with the words used to arrest him like it was a party game. He inched towards her. Sara pushed on, despite his help, until she reached, 'Anything you do say may be given in evidence.'

'Did you think I wouldn't know those lines?' he sneered. He put a hand on each chair arm and leaned towards Sara until his face was inches away. Her head pressed back into the filthy fabric, the old wooden frame dragging at her hair. 'Good luck arresting me. Stupid bitch.'

He spat at her. The spittle landed on her cheek and ran down. Sara shook with disgust. It took all her nerve to keep her voice level. 'Look, Eddie, I'm enjoying your story. If it's the last thing I'll hear, I'd like to get to the end.'

Kenyon considered this. 'All right. No one knows you're here, so why not? By the time they find both your bodies, I'll be long gone.'

'Thank you.'

'It was easy, really,' said Kenyon. He sat on the floor, crossed his legs and went into storyteller mode. 'I liked Ben. He was always kind to me. Taught me lots of things. But I knew he was untidy and always left the backstage area open during the day while doing stuff. I stashed my bag in the graveyard and waited until he went off on a mission for something or other. Then I let myself in backstage and took the keys from his secret box.'

'That gave you access to the theatre whenever you wanted it? Eddie, how did you know the code for the alarm system?'

Kenyon laughed again. 'It's the same as the year the place was bought. 1921. I thought they might have at least changed that by now. But no.'

'So you could come and go as you pleased?'

Kenyon nodded. 'And I could use the Birketts building. I'd had a wander around looking for a corner to stay in and realised that Birketts was flats now. I got lucky because once I was through the old doors, there was a spare key for the new inside door hanging in the hallway. I've been living in the undercroft ever since.'

'How long?'

'Weeks.' Kenyon hunched a little. 'Weeks of living out of dumpsters and using public bogs. Even Deerbolt was cleaner than that. Then I got lucky. Those homeless fuckwits settled in the graveyard, and I knew I'd be able to make a bit of dosh off them.'

'You went back to selling drugs?'

'Until they cut off my supply. It didn't matter by then, as I knew I was getting close. I'd got into the wardrobe and taken the monk's costumes. They're wonderfully warm, did you know that?' Sara conceded she didn't. 'Then, I waited for my chance. Checked the rehearsal schedule in the office and hid backstage until the bitch made her mistake.'

'Carole Morgan?'

Kenyon's eyes were staring far away now. 'She got what she deserved. Took me out of the gutter only to throw me back again.'

Sara didn't argue with this version of events, even though most didn't fit with her knowledge. He was heading down the road of self-pity, making him talkative.

'Why did you put her under the stage like that?'

'Not many people know about that grave pit. I thought she might lie there for days before the stink raised the alarm. Like the rats do after they've eaten the poisoned bait. When Ben found her the next day, I was disappointed.'

'You went back for Chris Webster?'

'He was the one who told that fucking DC Hart he'd seen me selling baggies. He never did. He framed me. Morgan and Webster framed me, and DC Mollie Hart took me down. I bet it did her career a lot of good. I was just collateral damage.'

'Why did you attack Ben Marsden?'

'I wanted to frighten him off, that's all. He nearly caught me dumping Webster's body.'

'And Nafisa? She can't have done anything to you back then.'

'She saw me. Persuaded that smelly homeless fucker to identify me. That made things a whole lot more difficult. More collateral damage.'

'Why did you trash the costumes?'

Kenyon shrugged and stood up. 'I just got angry after I'd dumped Morgan. Call it Gestalt therapy.'

If he hadn't been a lying, thieving, drug-dealing little bastard, Sara reflected, he could have been a well-educated and talented actor. As the tall man walked slowly towards her again, his hands held out to grab her throat, she just hoped that she'd read the situation correctly.

Sara knew she had when the door to the garden burst open, letting in the storm and three firearms officers, and the door to the landing was flung back by DI Edwards.

With the storm came chaos. The armed officers who had risked the crumbling fire escape were fully kitted up, looking distinctly like Halloween monsters. Head torches and body cams suddenly lit up the scene. Kenyon's mouth dropped open as he staggered backwards, kicking over several candles as he went. They began to splutter and flame around Sara's feet, where she was bound to the chair. With an incoherent cry, she tried to shuffle it backwards without success. It creaked its resistance loudly.

Yelling fiercely at Kenyon, the firearms guys, with their stab-proof vests, dark clothing and black neckbands pulled up around their faces, stamped across the wooden floor, raising dust devils as they ran. Even Sara felt she was descending into hell. In seconds they had Kenyon, shrieking and cursing, pinned against the wall.

'I'll get you all,' he cursed as they spun him around to handcuff him. His voice was muffled against the wall. 'Vengeance comes to those who wait.'

'And is a dish best served cold,' muttered Bowen as he reached Sara. Stamping on the flames that licked at the ancient floorboards, he snatched at the chair arms as Sara felt herself begin to topple backwards. 'Let's not be going anywhere.'

'Oh Bowen, thank God,' breathed Sara. He flashed her a cheeky grin.

DI Edwards rushed to join them, passing the struggling group that was trying to turn Kenyon round. He had locked his legs and now threw himself backwards, felling the officer behind him as he headed for the floor. The pair crashed into the dust and broke a floorboard beneath. Sara wasn't sure what the officer caught below said, but it sounded rude enough. The other two pulled Kenyon up none too carefully and forced him to his knees.

'How you doing?' asked DI Edwards as he began to cut the cable ties that held Sara.

'Not bad. Noble's in a worse state. See to him.'

'We've got ambulances standing by,' said Edwards gruffly. He clipped the last tie and moved across to help DC Noble, who was still unconscious. 'You did well to get that confession out of him.'

'Did you record it?'

'Most of it. We were—'

'Behind the door,' said Sara with a sigh. 'You could have been more careful. I saw the light from your mobile flicker around the gap when Kenyon was pontificating. Luckily, it was behind him, and he didn't notice.'

'So, the gods didn't stand up for bastards,' said Bowen to Kenyon as the firearms officers dragged him upright. 'Did they, Edmund?'

'Edmund?' Sara was confused.

Bowen grinned at her. 'Famous speech from *King Lear*.'

As he led the struggling Kenyon away, Sara wondered how Bowen the dinosaur had come to know so much culture since he'd taken up with Aggie.

CHAPTER 59

Nafisa had been kept in hospital for several days. One of the detectives had called in to ensure she was doing well, and then it all went quiet until she got home. After a couple of days, a woman rang and made an appointment to interview her the following morning. Her parents sat guarding her on the sofa, her father to her left anxiously fidgeting and her mother to her right looking grim. The two men sat on armchairs opposite.

'I'm DI Edwards,' said the smarter-looking one. 'This is DC Bowen.'

'I remember you from the theatre,' she said.

'You may have already been informed of this, but I wanted to assure you that the man who held you prisoner is now in police custody.'

The scruffier-looking DC Bowen smiled. 'In a secure unit at HMP Norwich for now.'

'We have gathered what evidence we can from the undercroft,' said DI Edwards. He put a small recording unit on the coffee table. 'Unfortunately, we need your testimony to move the charges forward.'

'I was expecting to have to give a witness statement,' agreed Nafisa.

'Unless the felon pleads guilty —' DC Bowen looked apologetic — 'I'm afraid you will also have to appear in court.'

Nafisa felt her heart flutter at the prospect of standing up in front of strangers to talk about what Skull-man had done and said to her. She felt her mother taking her hand in hers to hide the trembling. Nothing escaped the observant DC Bowen.

'There are people to help you,' he said quietly. 'Counsellors and such like.'

'I know. We use them at work sometimes. Let's get this over with.'

DI Edwards turned on the recorder, and they began.

* * *

Nafisa forced herself to return to work after two weeks of sick leave. Samantha, her boss, was dubious that she was fit enough and confined her to her desk to begin with.

'I want you to finish at three each day,' Samantha insisted. 'I've also set up an appointment with Victim Support. We don't want you suffering from PTSD, do we?'

Like Zach did, Nafisa thought as she looked through the huge pile of files on her desk. Russell Goddard approached her hesitantly, bearing a cup of tea. For once, it was made just as she liked it.

'Welcome back,' he whispered. 'If you need to talk, I'm here for you.'

It was sweet, but there was no way Nafisa would tell Russell what had happened in the undercroft. The odds were that it would all come out in court anyway. She shrank into her chair at the idea. It would hang over her like a curse until it was over, and Nafisa wasn't sure if counselling would help with that.

'If I can do anything else for you.' Russell pointed to the pile of work.

'Actually, there is,' replied Nafisa. Russell perked up. 'I'd love to know what happened to Zach. Would you take me into the city at lunchtime to see if we can find him?'

'Of course,' agreed Russell happily.

* * *

A man with a toolbox was fixing the gate at the entrance stairs of the graveyard. He nodded at them as they went up to look around. There was no sign of the tent people in the burial ground. Someone had cleaned the area of residual rubbish and trimmed the bushes. A few days of late autumn sun and warmth had begun to repair the damage from the bonfire and the dead grass under the tents. Nafisa shivered as she passed the box tomb.

'He had your number, didn't he?' asked Russell. Nafisa looked despondently around the headstones. 'Did he never try to contact you?'

'No. I was too ill to look at my phone in the hospital. I checked when I felt better, and there were no calls except yours. I appreciated your kind messages, by the way.'

Russell ducked his head in embarrassment. 'We were all worried for you.'

Nafisa nodded absently. 'I wonder where he went or what he'll do. He'd reached the point where he wanted to get off the road. I let him down.'

'It was hardly your fault.'

They headed down the alley past the theatre courtyard. Ben Marsden was walking towards them, heading in to start his day's work. He smiled at Nafisa and stopped to talk.

'How are you doing?' he asked. 'Surely you aren't back at work yet?'

'Part-time,' she said. 'I think I owe you a big thank you. DC Bowen told me that it was you who thought that I might be in . . .'

When she faltered, Marsden spoke hurriedly. 'I'm sorry you went through all that. And I'm glad we were able to help.'

Nafisa looked at the Rosegarden building. 'This has been an awful time for you too. What will happen to the theatre?'

'Oh, it'll survive,' said Marsden. 'It somehow always does. One of our directors claims that the place is self-healing, and he's right in a way, although that sounds a bit too mystical to me. Things always seem to come about if the place goes off course. Tickets for the Christmas show are racing out the door. It's an ill wind and all that.'

Nafisa nodded. There wasn't much else she could do in the face of such pragmatism. 'I don't suppose you know where the people in the tents went? I wondered what happened to Zach.'

'The army veteran?' Marsden nodded. 'I know a little. He lost his tent in the storm while you were missing. He was at a pretty low ebb. Lindie and I saw him near the café on St Gregorys.'

'The Wizard's Lounge,' said Nafisa hopefully. 'He knew the manager there. They'd served together. Did he help him? I hoped he would.'

Marsden shook his head. 'I don't know about that. I gave him a new tent, and Rachel gave him some spare clothes from the wardrobe. We suggested that he get in touch with Help for Heroes.'

'Do you know if he did?'

'I don't,' admitted Marsden. 'He did say that he had a friend down in Suffolk who sometimes helped him out. I guess he headed there.'

Nafisa thanked the stage manager again and went with Russell to his car. 'I guess that'll have to do. The man's a survivor.'

'You should focus on your own recovery,' said Russell. 'There are plenty more people who need our help in this city. You can't do that if you aren't well.'

And with that, Nafisa had to be satisfied.

CHAPTER 60

They were worried about brain damage. At least, that was what Sara assumed. Her head throbbed even lying down in the hospital bed. When she tried to move it, shafts of pain zig-zagged across her skull. She was given Oramorph and wheeled on her bed down to the MRI scanner. Despite the racket that the machine made circling her head, Sara dozed off lying there. A nurse waggled her toes to wake her up.

She wasn't sure if it was a hallucination or reality when she was wheeled back to her space on the ward. Adie Dickinson was sitting on the visitor's chair, looking extremely anxious. Sara knew it was reality when he took her hand in his and squeezed it.

'What's all this, then?' he asked with a watery smile. 'You being a heroine again?'

Sara couldn't raise a smile in return. She tugged her hand away. 'What are you doing here? I thought you were somewhere in India.'

Adie frowned. 'Nepal. We'd got back to Kathmandu airport when a woman called my mobile. Told me you had been attacked and were in hospital. Mum drove to Heathrow to pick me up, and I came straight here.'

He looked travel-weary, Sara realised as she looked more carefully. He needed a shower and probably some sleep. He had come to find her instead.

'What woman?'

'I think she called herself Aggie,' said Adie. He picked up her hand again, holding it gently. 'Said she worked with you and that I ought to know. I've been to the Far East several times before, but I've never had a flight as long as this one. I thought I was going to be too late.'

Sara didn't have the energy to be excited at his words, although a warm glow spread through her. 'Not this time.'

Adie bent over and kissed her. 'I know this is going too fast, but I must tell you I love you.'

When he sat down again, Sara sank back into her pillows. Confused, she said the first thing that came to her mind. 'My mother is here, I think. She came up the day after it happened.'

'I look forward to meeting her. Where is she staying?'

'Cottage,' was all Sara could manage. Sleep was taking over again. 'You should go home.'

'Only if you promise to wait for me here while I get rid of my travel vibe,' said Adie. Sara smiled.

'Okay.'

* * *

They kept her in hospital for nearly a week, fussing and fretting over her head. After days of tests and examinations, the doctors agreed she could go home with supervision. Tegan, Sara's mother, was installed in the spare bedroom of Sara's cottage, which had been tidied and cleaned within an inch of its life. Tilly the cat followed Tegan around like a ghostly shadow, as Sara's mother constantly slipped the creature little titbits of food.

Adie had borrowed his mother's car to bring Sara home. He lit the open fire, quietly explaining to Tegan how to do it next time. Sara knew her mother had never dealt with logs and firelighters in her life. However, Tegan was at home in charge of the kitchen.

'Doing your favourite,' she said before vanishing to chop vegetables.

Adie plonked himself on the sofa next to Sara and put his arm around her shoulders. 'I need to go back to uni tomorrow.'

'I thought you might have to.'

'I've got to submit my report about the trip and plans for the show garden. I don't suppose you've had time?'

'They're in the top drawer.' Sara waved at the desk. 'I thought you'd changed your mind.'

'About what?' Adie retrieved the crumpled garden designs.

'About the garden.' Sara spoke hesitantly. 'About me.'

'I'm never going to do that,' said Adie firmly. 'You should know that I'm hard to get rid of. A horribly loyal type.'

'It won't change. My job, I mean. It's my life and I love it. There will always be danger and crap shifts and long hours.'

'I figured.' Adie spread out the plans. 'And I'll always be digging up someone's dirt and probably working away or abroad. I still think we could make it work if we both wanted it to.'

He looked at her, waiting for her reply.

'We could try,' said Sara.

'Good enough for me,' he said. 'Let's start with making you a dream garden. Oh, and you're joining Mum and me at the hall for Christmas lunch.'

'Don't mind me,' called Tegan from the kitchen. 'Javed and me are going on holiday this year.'

Sara looked at Adie, and they both began to laugh.

* * *

Sara was pleased when, just a few minutes after Adie had left, a knock at the door revealed Aggie and Mike Bowen bearing cakes and cards.

'Bring me up to speed,' she demanded as Tegan and Aggie brought plates and cups of tea.

'We got the bastard.' Bowen grinned. 'He tried the old "no comment" routine to make us do all the work. Until he realised that we'd been recording him in that old house. Then, he clammed up entirely. CPS is still deciding if your rights reading was good enough for it to be used in court. But we've got lots of other evidence. Weird place, isn't it?'

'It is,' agreed Sara. 'His performance was weirder. The sheer arrogance of setting that up and standing there quoting Shakespeare with two kidnapped coppers in front of him. How's Ian?'

'Out of the woods,' said Bowen. 'Likely to be off longer than you, I suspect.'

'What else?'

'Kenyon is in the high-security unit in Norwich Prison.' Bowen sucked his lips. 'We're cracking on with the paperwork, and we'll need a formal statement from you when you've recovered. CPS is deciding the full set of charges based on the forensics.'

'Two murders and an abduction?'

'Three abductions,' said Bowen. 'You and Noble both count. Assaulting a police officer will be the least of his worries.'

'It could be a long trial if he doesn't cooperate,' said Sara sadly. 'That's all right for us, but what about the families? How is James Morgan, do you know?'

'Doing okay, I believe. He seems to have settled with his daughter; she's looking after him. I don't think they'll want him as a witness; his dementia is sufficiently advanced for him to not be considered reliable.'

'The homeless people?'

'Zach has vanished again,' said Bowen. 'Marsden gave him a new tent, and he wandered off. Tam is recovering in Addenbrooks. Kells has turned up there with all their stuff. God only knows how she managed it. Waiting for him to be discharged. Hudson has done a good thing too.'

'What's that?'

'Put in an official thank you and request for a commendation for Officer Fraser Shepherd. He really got invested in helping us. Let's hope it does him some good in the long run.'

'Our friend Kenyon ran a vicious ring around all these people,' said Sara angrily. 'I can't help wondering why he got back into selling drugs at the theatre, when he'd escaped the dealers on the estate. But did you hear his claims about prison? That he was raped and beaten up, when he was the one doing it to other people? Using it as an excuse for his behaviour. Bastard.'

'He may have been the victim at first,' said Bowen. 'Young, pretty boy and all that. I've been talking to Deerbolt. He soon turned himself into a hard man. Honestly, I wouldn't be surprised if he isn't advised to go for a sanity plea. Either way, I doubt he'll ever come out of the system alive.'

Sara nodded as Aggie held out plates of brownies and Victoria sponge. 'Your cat looks to be putting on weight.'

And so will I, thought Sara as she helped herself to Aggie's homemade goodies.

CHAPTER 61

Ben had been putting together the props for the Rosegarden Christmas show. It was an adaptation of a classic children's novel. A deliberate choice to do something different to the traditional pantomimes found at multiple venues at this time of year. It usually worked well for them and was selling fantastically. He'd given his statement to the detectives some weeks ago, pleased to hear that the injured were getting better and feeling that he was done with the whole situation until the trial. There was no escaping that this time. His evidence could be crucial, and he was dreading it. He put it to the back of his mind and carried on as usual, allowing Doctor Theatre to heal him as it always had done.

One morning in early December, he was surprised to receive an official-looking envelope from Norwich Prison addressed to him at the theatre. It was a visitor request form from Eddie Kenyon. He thought about it for three days before calling the SCU team for advice.

It was cold and rainy as he waited outside the prison visitors' entrance. Standing here made him feel nervous, and he was grateful to see tall, elegant DS Sara Hirst striding across the car park to join him.

'I'm glad they decided to send you,' he said as they waited to be let in.

'I didn't give them the choice,' she muttered. 'Wasn't going to pass up the chance to look the bugger that attacked me in the eye.'

There were several procedures to be followed before they were led into a cream-painted room. In the centre was a long table with three chairs, two on one side and one on the other. The table and chairs were fastened to the floor, Ben couldn't help but notice. They waited several minutes before Eddie Kenyon was escorted in from a different door. He was wearing a tracksuit, pale-coloured trainers and handcuffs. His hair was cut short. His skin looked sallow, and his expression was grim.

'Couldn't you come alone?' he asked Ben when he sat down.

'Not allowed,' stated DS Hirst. Kenyon nodded. He turned his gaze to Ben. The eyes were full of anger, and the lids never seemed to blink. It was like being hypnotised by a snake.

'How are you doing, Scooter?' Ben asked. He had never felt more uncomfortable in his life. Or more determined.

'Scooter!' Kenyon snorted. 'That's old school, mate. No one calls me that these days.'

'Okay. How are you, Eddie?' Ben rephrased it.

'It's shit,' said Kenyon. His lip curled in a sneer. 'I'm the victim here.'

'If that's all you wanted to say . . .' began Hirst.

'It's all right,' Ben said to her. He nodded to Kenyon. 'I'm not sure why you asked me to come. Is there something you want?'

'To talk about old times,' said Kenyon after a lengthy pause. His voice cracked as he continued. 'You were the only one who treated me like a human being. Who was kind.'

'That's not how I remember it.' Ben shook his head. 'What about Lindie? She's nice to everyone. Or Rachel in wardrobe? We all supported you. Wanted you to be a success.'

Kenyon stared at Ben. His body began to sway back and forth. 'I could have been someone.'

'Yes, you could,' agreed Ben. 'You were good on and off stage. You could have made a good living in the business. Maybe even been famous if that one moment of luck had come your way.'

Kenyon nodded vigorously. 'I knew that you saw it. And you didn't betray me. Not like that bitch Carole Morgan or that piece of work Chris Webster.'

Ben paused to choose his next words carefully. 'They didn't make you sell drugs, Eddie, did they? Why did you do that?'

'I needed the money,' snapped Kenyon. 'It was always about the money. I wanted to make those auditions and the cost was horrific, what with the fees and the train fares.'

'Why didn't you ask us?' said Ben sadly. 'We could have found some support for you. All the same, they didn't deserve what you did to them. Whatever you might think.'

Kenyon began to speak, then stopped again. He turned his head to one side, wiping his nose on his sleeve.

'At least you got to perform at Ninhams Court,' Ben continued. 'No one has done that for over a hundred years. What a privilege. Edmund's speech, wasn't it? I'm told you were rather good.'

'Yeah, my last performance,' said Kenyon, still glaring at the wall.

'Not necessarily.'

'What do you mean?' Kenyon jerked his head back to face Ben.

'Have you ever seen a movie called *Angels with Dirty Faces*?'

Kenyon frowned at the non sequitur.

'Made in the 1930s. About a gangster. It's American, of course.'

'I don't watch that old shit,' said Kenyon.

'You did with me sometimes,' said Ben. 'Anyway, this gangster is going to be executed, and at the last minute, he starts to beg and scream for mercy.'

'Huh! Fucking coward!' Kenyon grinned.

'No, the point is that the priest had asked him to do it. To set an example to the kids who worshipped him, so they won't take up a criminal life.'

'So?'

Ben heard DS Hirst shuffling in her chair impatiently. 'The point is, Eddie, that this man did a brave thing. He gave a wonderful performance. So that some good might come out of his life. You could give a great performance too.'

'What?'

'I know you're a bright man,' said Ben. 'If you plead not guilty or something like that, then those people, their families, even that poor social worker you kidnapped, even me — we're all going to have to go to court.'

'Yeah! That's the point. Make their lives hell, just like mine's been.'

'I don't know about your life in prison. It must be awful. Do you have to punish them too? Or can you be brave like James Cagney in that movie?'

Kenyon shrugged and turned to the prison officers. 'I want to leave now.'

They all stood up. As Kenyon reached the door, Ben asked, 'Does he get any privileges? Could I send him a copy of the film?'

'I'll ask the governor,' agreed one of the officers. 'He might allow it. Not sure where they'd watch it, but I'll ask.'

'Let me know, Eddie. James Cagney was a wonderful actor. Just like you could have been.'

'James Cagney,' said Kenyon. 'I'll look him up.'

Then he had gone, back into the prison.

* * *

'I wondered where you were going with that,' said DS Hirst as they reached the car park.

'I couldn't think of any other way to access his ego,' admitted Ben. 'Except to appeal to the actor in him. We used to talk about old movies and long-dead actors when he was working at the theatre. He used to lap it up. It probably won't work this time. I just felt I had to try.'

'Can I ask you something personal?'

'Sure,' Ben shrugged. 'I may not answer.'

'Why do you dislike the police so much?'

'DC Mollie Hart,' replied Ben.

'The detective on the original investigation?'

'I think Scooter should have got away with a fine or a community work order. He was hardly a major drug dealer. Just a kid making mistakes. She was trying to get a promotion and saw this as her big chance. Asked several of us to make false statements to ensure Eddie got a long sentence.'

'You refused?'

'Damn right I did.'

'I've been looking Ms Hart up recently,' said DS Hirst. They were walking to their cars, carefully avoiding each other's gazes. 'Pulled a few strings, got some classified information, just for my own satisfaction. She got a promotion after that case. Moved to Manchester and made DI two years later. Went to London to get the next leg up. Then, for some unspecified reason, she left policing three years ago. Under a cloud.'

'After that?'

'I've no idea. She must have changed her name because I can't find her anywhere. No social media footprint, nothing on the internet.'

Ben nodded slowly but didn't comment.

'Will you see him again if he asks?'

'No. I don't think so.'

DS Hirst nodded and climbed into her car. Ben watched her drive away towards the city. He took his car around via Britannia Road, pulling up for a few minutes to look at Norwich from the vantage point on Mousehold Heath. The city looked newly washed after the rain despite the grey clouds. He could see the cathedral beyond the bend in the river and Pull's Ferry on Riverside, the old mill at St James's

Yard with its ivy-covered red walls and the street layout that had survived for centuries.

With a smile, he drove on towards the Rosegarden Theatre. He had lots to do if he was to follow Alice into Wonderland this Christmas.

THE END

ACKNOWLEDGEMENTS

I would like to thank Antony Dunford and Wendy Turbin for their beta readings and notes. I am so grateful for their time and energy on my manuscripts. I am also thankful to Clive Forbes, a former DI for the NCA, for his police procedural advice and thoughts on whodunnit. Any incorrect procedures remain because I made an executive author's decision (or mistake!).

My gratitude goes to Jasper Joffe for welcoming me to Joffe Books. It means more than I can say to belong to this fantastic publishing house. I am grateful to all the other authors and the staff, who are so supportive and generous with their time. My special thanks to editors Laura Coulman, Tara Loder, Matthew Grundy-Haigh, Julia Williams and Kate Ballard for their help, suggestions, edits and weeding out random punctuation. My grateful thanks to the rest of the Joffe Books team for all their work, from organising blog tours to spending time on reviews. I am proud to be a member of this wonderful band.

Last but not least, my love and thanks go to my husband, Rhett, now struck down by the demon dementia. These days, I write while being his full-time carer. If you know anyone struggling with this condition and their carers, why not pop round for a coffee and a chat? It would mean more than you might realise.

You can find advice and information about dementia in the UK from:

The Alzheimer's Society (www.alzheimers.org.uk)
Dementia UK (www.dementiauk.org)
and Age UK (www.ageuk.org.uk).

THE JOFFE BOOKS STORY

We began in 2014 when Jasper agreed to publish his mum's much-rejected romance novel and it became a bestseller.

Since then we've grown into the largest independent publisher in the UK. We're extremely proud to publish some of the very best writers in the world, including Joy Ellis, Faith Martin, Caro Ramsay, Helen Forrester, Simon Brett and Robert Goddard. Everyone at Joffe Books loves reading and we never forget that it all begins with the magic of an author telling a story.

We are proud to publish talented first-time authors, as well as established writers whose books we love introducing to a new generation of readers.

We won Trade Publisher of the Year at the Independent Publishing Awards in 2023 and Best Publisher Award in 2024 at the People's Book Prize. We have been shortlisted for Independent Publisher of the Year at the British Book Awards for the last five years, and were shortlisted for the Diversity and Inclusivity Award at the 2022 Independent Publishing Awards. In 2023 we were shortlisted for Publisher of the Year at the RNA Industry Awards, and in 2024 we were shortlisted at the CWA Daggers for the Best Crime and Mystery Publisher.

We built this company with your help, and we love to hear from you, so please email us about absolutely anything bookish at feedback@joffebooks.com.

If you want to receive free books every Friday and hear about all our new releases, join our mailing list here: www.joffebooks.com/freebooks.

And when you tell your friends about us, just remember: it's pronounced Joffe as in coffee or toffee!

www.ingramcontent.com/pod-product-compliance
Lightning Source LLC
LaVergne TN
LVHW040101010525
810110LV00033B/618